"*I just happen to be
a clairvoyant, a medium.*"

Her gaze flitted over him. "I would have thought an extra large."

"I stopped laughing at that one after the first ten thousand times I heard it . . . wait, what's that?" He lifted his head as if to listen to voices from upstairs . . . or the spiritual ether.

He watched as Andie crossed her arms over her waist, her brow arched in impatient expectation.

With a theatrical flair, Logan put his fingertips to his temples. "Aye, I have it. I'm picking something up."

"What a surprise."

"There is a man," he said slowly. "He has you in his sights. He means to take you . . . " He stopped, looked meaningfully into her eyes.

Leaning closer, he whispered, "For everything you're worth."

By Marianne Stillings

KILLER CHARMS
SATISFACTION
AROUSING SUSPICIONS
SIGHS MATTER
MIDNIGHT IN THE GARDEN OF GOOD AND EVIE
THE DAMSEL IN THIS DRESS

KILLER CHARMS

MARIANNE STILLINGS

AVON

An Imprint of HarperCollinsPublishers

This is a work of fiction. Names, characters, places, and incidents are products of the author's imagination or are used fictitiously and are not to be construed as real. Any resemblance to actual events, locales, organizations, or persons, living or dead, is entirely coincidental.

AVON BOOKS
An Imprint of HarperCollins*Publishers*
10 East 53rd Street
New York, New York 10022-5299

Copyright © 2008 by Marianne Stillings
ISBN 978-0-06-085074-6
www.avonromance.com

First Avon Books paperback printing: September 2008

Avon Trademark Reg. U.S. Pat. Off. and in Other Countries, Marca Registrada, Hecho en U.S.A.
HarperCollins® is a registered trademark of HarperCollins Publishers.

Printed in the U.S.A.

10 9 8 7 6 5 4 3 2 1

Chapter 1

Everyone lives by selling something.

Robert Louis Stevenson

San Francisco, California

Logan Sinclair was surprised when Drew Mochrie herself opened the front door. He'd expected to see some harried maid and not the woman he'd set up as his mark. The fact she was so anxious to meet him that she'd ignored one of the maxims of wealth and performed an underling's chore, mitigated any lingering doubt as to the course he was hell-bent to take.

Aye, and wasn't the hungry shine of her eyes more revealing than anything he'd find in even the most comprehensive personnel file?

"Miss Mochrie, is it?" he said, as though he didn't know damn well who she was. He considered a bow, then discarded the idea as being a bit much. "I am Logan Sinclair, and this is my assistant, Oliver Kerr." He gestured to the man standing behind him on the bottom step of the porch.

Ignoring Ollie, she said, "I've been expecting you." Her gaze raked him head to toe. "And a distinct pleasure it is to see a fellow Scot after these two years in America." She offered her hand.

He clasped it between his own, giving it a squeeze. Immediately, her lips bowed in a demure smile. She lowered her lashes, and her cheeks flushed.

"The photo on the back of your books don't do you justice, Mr. Sinclair," she purred. "It's a fact, you're younger and more handsome in the flesh."

Her none-too-subtle innuendo aside, it was clear she didn't realize who he was; more's the better since his plan would go straight to hell if she did, and all would be for naught.

She might even figure out what he'd come for.

As he held her hand and waited—lest recognition dawn belatedly—Drew Mochrie's blue eyes did not narrow in recollection. There was no suspicious "Have we met?" No tilt of the head and thoughtful finger tap to the jaw. No "You seem so familiar." Instead, she appeared to accept who he said he was without question.

Aye, then. The con is on.

The knots in his gut that had plagued him for these last many weeks began to loosen. His shoulders relaxed, and he allowed himself a genuine smile of relief.

He released her hand, and she said, "Agreeing to come all the way from Scotland, and so quickly, too, is most gracious of you, Mr. Sinclair. I'm forever in your debt."

Then, as though she couldn't restrain herself one second longer, she sucked in enough breath to douse five thousand birthday candles. Clutching at his sleeve, she gushed, "I must add, Mr. Sinclair, 'tis God's own truth that I'm a great admirer and have read both your books, and I've been so looking forward to meeting you, and you so . . . well, you standing here, handsome as a Hollywood film star, and won't all my friends be jealous, and well, impressed, too, that the renowned Mr. Sinclair himself was willing to come and help me urge my brother to move from where he lingers just beyond the veil to a place of peace and tranquility, and since I did promise Bartholomew when I first arrived here from Edinburgh that he would *nae* be sorry for taking me in after my divorce from that bastard who treated me like so much baggage, and penniless as I was since my first husband had done much the same thing, leaving poor, helpless me with nothing . . ."

When the woman seemed in no danger of deflating for several seconds yet, Logan simply nodded absently, his attention caught and held by a photograph on the far wall of the grand foyer.

As Miss Mochrie jabbered on, he stared at the

picture of the girl and young man, realizing at once who they were.

Grief and guilt turned to anger, surging through his blood, washing away any hesitancy that might have remained.

For once in his life, he was doing the right thing. Aye, it was a rare event, given his proclivities, but this debt was an old one, and he intended to repay it the only way he knew how.

At last, Miss Mochrie seemed to run out of breath and words at the same time, ending her fawning, self-indulgent tirade on a tittering snort.

When she finally fell silent and just blinked worshipfully up at him, he said, "Thank you for your warm welcome, lass. Now, please be so good as to show me where the tragedy happened."

Her expression went instantly from open admiration to closed apprehension. Her fingertips covered her lips. "Hmm. Of course. Aye. It's this way and through the kitchen."

Glancing over his shoulder, he nodded to Ollie, who shot a sardonic look at the retreating Miss Mochrie, then picked up his enormous camera bag and joined Logan in the foyer.

Whether from inclination or nerves, as she escorted them through the mansion and down the cellar steps to the scene of the "unfortunate incident," she chirped away like an overcaffeinated parrot.

Drew Mochrie had been much younger when

Logan had last seen her in Edinburgh. In the intervening years, she had gone from a pretty, self-indulgent, silly teenager, to an attractive, self-indulgent, silly woman.

As for himself, he'd morphed from a young man with too much money and too little humility, to the *curiosité du jour* of the rich and famous, a tabloid "clairvoyant" . . . among other things.

No wonder Drew didn't recognize him; he barely recognized himself.

When they reached the bottom of the cellar stairs, she made as if to speak, but he stopped her.

"Say nothing," he instructed. "And leave off the light, if you will. I want no influences. The information I receive must be pure."

In the near dark, he saw her nod. "I understand," she whispered, then closed her mouth and pressed her lips together.

Silence at last. Logan wanted to shake his head and cast off the woman's babbling the way a retriever shakes off water.

Instead, he inhaled a calming breath and let it out slowly, then moved to the center of the room. His stance solid, his jaw tight, a serene expression planted on his face, he waited for, eh, contact.

Whenever he performed, he hoped he portrayed the vision of a dauntless champion, stalwart yet humble in the face of a force far greater than he. Mere Logan Sinclair he was, reluctant cog in the vast wheel of the churning and mysterious Universe; a simple servant to the Powers That Be, and though he hadn't asked to be burdened with this unique gift, oh, no, he soldiered on—for the good of mankind, of course.

He bowed his head in reverence to those very Powers that had designated *him*—of all mortals—as their liaison, their ethereal middleman, as it were.

Furrowing his brow, he sought to display that wee touch of modesty that convinced clients he was sincere in his duty, humbled by his task.

True believers just loved that crap.

Even so, once he could seduce them into trusting him, he closed the deal; done and done, and they never knew what hit them.

Pressing his fingertips to his temples, he cocked his head as though listening heavenward for his name to be read.

In the dim light, he could just make out Drew's face. Was that anticipation contorting her features? Or apprehension? In any event, the lass was primed and . . .

"Ready?" he said.

She licked her lips and gazed up at him, an odd look in her eyes. "Might I share a . . . ehm, a confidence with you?"

He grinned, pouring on the charm. "Now, if you can't trust the likes of Logan Sinclair, dear lady, who can you trust?"

She lowered her lashes and shrugged. Sticking

out her lower lip like a child about to confess stealing oatcakes, she murmured, "Well, you see, it's just that you never know who in this world you can truly rely upon to keep one's secrets, do you, Mr. Sinclair? I mean, people so often are not at all what they appear to be, and it's left to us to discern the heroes from the villains in our lives."

If he'd've let himself, he would've felt her remark pierce his chest like a Highland dirk. But he'd hardened his heart years ago, and the blow slid harmlessly off and away.

"Indeed, lass." He smiled. "Indeed." Taking her hand, he patted it. "Now what is this secret you wish to share?"

Hesitating for a moment, she cleared her throat, and said coyly, "I . . . well, it's possible I *may* not have done right by my brother. I suppose I just want to make certain *you* can convince him to, you know, go on his way. His . . . his spirit haunts me, blames me, I think for . . . for . . ." She shook her head. On a soft, high breath, she said, "*Och*, never mind."

His first thought was that any haunting she was feeling was her own guilty conscience, but when she looked up at him and batted her lashes, he realized she was simply trying to seduce him into her game.

"Aye," he coaxed. "Your trust in me is not misplaced, I promise. I will do exactly what I have come to do."

While it wasn't a lie, it wasn't the truth she would be expecting.

He grinned again. "Let's get on with it now, shall we, lass?"

Her eyes widened, and she nodded, then licked her lips in a quick, nervous gesture.

"The energy here is strong," he began. "I'm already picking up . . . I'm getting something . . . something . . . someth—. . . ah, I understand now. This is where your brother's body was found. Here. On the floor twixt these first twae wine racks."

As predicted, Drew gasped in amazement. "Indeed it is!" More tentatively, almost as an afterthought, she inquired, "Are you getting anything . . . else, Mr. Sinclair? Have you made contact—"

"*Wheesht*," he gently admonished. "'Tis complete silence I need, or he who has passed beyond the veil will not venture back."

"Aye, of course," she mouthed.

"Anything showing up through your lens, Ollie?"

Ollie held a camcorder rigged with night vision and a microphone to capture a manifestation, should one occur.

Right.

"*Nocht*," Ollie muttered, then snapped his gum.

"Perhaps we need to try another . . . hello, what's this?"

Logan lifted his voice to just the right pitch between awe and curiosity. Straightening, he nodded several times as though someone had spoken to him.

He turned to Drew. "Your late brother's given name was Bartholomew. You called him Tolley."

"I did!" she squeaked, her voice pitched high as though she'd just been taken aback by a beady-eyed rodent. "Everyone dear to him called him that. But he has *nae* been known by it since our *hairnskip* in Edinburgh. Certainly nobody in America called him that for these last many years." She blinked in awe, like a child attending her first *hogmanay*. "So you've reached him, then? You truly have? Can you tell him he's dead and needs to move on—"

"Your brother has a message for you," Logan interrupted. "He wants you to know . . . what's that? My spirit guide, Allister, informs me your brother is most concerned for your finances. He fears you may succumb to the lure of some nefarious scoundrel."

"*Och*, tell him to have no fear then," she scoffed. "I'm not so foolish as that. His . . . that is to say, *my* millions are quite safe. Assure him of the fact, if you would be so kind."

Logan sent her an approving look, adding a dash of tenderness to his next words. "Just so. Aye. He's heard you and glad for your caution. But there's something else, something . . . what was that?"

He raised his head again, squinting his eyes as though it was an effort to hear. "The what, necklace? Thank you, Allister. Tolley wants to know about a necklace of some sort. A large diamond offset by rubies. A gift to your family from the last tsar of Russia, perhaps?"

"The Star of Avril? My, but you are so clever, Mr. Sinclair!"

He grinned shyly to hide his satisfaction at confirming the gems were still within reach. "Oh, I am not the clever one, lass. It is Allister who speaks to the departed. I am merely his obsequious transmitter. This, eh, Star of Avril which concerns your brother so much. Is it . . . tucked away where greedy hands *nae* can reach it?"

"Of course!" she snapped. "'Tis in a safe-deposit box at the bank. I would never keep such a treasure about the place."

"Indeed not." Logan continued smiling, though not so brightly as before. "We must move quickly now," he warned. "Tolley grows tired. His energy begins to wane. Have you any questions for your brother before he withdraws once more?"

Her hand fluttered in front of her mouth for a moment, and her thinly plucked brows edged toward each other in a worried frown. "Aren't you going to tell him to move along now?"

"First, I must assure he's prepared for such a shock."

Lifting his voice, Logan said, "Allister, kindly ask Tolley if he is happy and free of worldly ills, if you will." He waited a heartbeat, then, "Your brother is at peace, Miss Mochrie, but seems a bit bothered by something to do with how he met his *daith*. Something . . . unresolved. Something that keeps him from accepting his fate."

She looked up at him, then clasped her hands in front of her waist. "This is most distressing, Logan," she said, her voice choked with tears. "May I call you Logan?" She laid a trembling hand on his arm.

"Of course," he said warmly.

She sniffled. "Something unresolved? Oh, dear."

Tugging a tissue from a pocket in her dress, she touched it to her nose. "Can you not simply instruct him to let go and go into the light, or something?"

Heaving a sigh of deep, *deep* regret, Logan said, "I no longer feel his presence. It seems we've lost Tolley, lass. For now." He took the woman's hand, patting it gently. "I'm so sorry. 'Twas too much for him. But we can try again another day if you like, when he's more up to it."

He felt her body shift as she reached toward the wall to snap on the light switch. Overhead, a single low-wattage bulb flicked to life, but was only marginally better than the dark. Logan glanced around at the racks and rows of dusty bottles and the intricate cobwebs anchoring the corners of the room.

"Tolley always was a fragile sort." She sighed absently, then smiled up at him. Her blue eyes were glassy with either unshed tears or dust allergies. Hard to say, given the nature of the woman.

Shifting her gaze to the cement floor where her

brother's dead body had lain, she explained, "'Twas just over a year ago. He'd come down for a bottle of after-dinner port, you see. Tripped on the steps and bit the biscuit."

Logan said nothing.

She sniffed, straightened. "Well. This has been a most satisfying start, Logan, though I'm disappointed Tolley lingers about so."

Logan turned to Ollie. "Anything, lad?"

There wouldn't be. There never was.

Oliver shut off the camera. "*Nae*, sir. Time to be packing up." He crouched in front of his case on the floor and began preparing his equipment to be shut away.

"Perhaps we'll have better luck on the next go-round, lass," Logan said. "Shall we set another appointment, Drew? May I call you Drew?"

Her lashes fluttered as she pressed her glossy lips together and smiled. She made a singsong hum at the back of her throat that Logan took to mean she was considering her options. A moment later, she said, "Come with me up to my office. I'll write you a check."

"You are most gracious, lass."

As she turned toward the wooden stairs, she held her head high, her trepidation and fear seemingly vanished. "It was five thousand, wasn't it? An acceptable figure, don't you think?"

He watched the back of her head as she began the climb, the sway of her hips, the curve of her calves, and he wondered to which figure she was referring.

His voice a mixture of solemnity and hesitation, he said, "I don't feel right taking your money, Drew. I barely scratched the surface and didn't relieve poor Tolley of his pains. Perhaps a mere four thousand would be more appropriate."

"Nonsense," she countered as she opened the door. Light from the scullery, er, kitchen, he reminded himself, spilled out, casting her body in dark silhouette in the open doorway. "Since my dear brother has gone on to his reward, I'm a very wealthy woman. So it'll be five thousand for you, and not a pound less."

Logan followed her across the threshold and into the vast and gleaming kitchen. "If you insist, I'll simply have to accept."

She stopped abruptly and whirled to face him. A seductive grin tilted her lips. He seized the opportunity to press the issue.

"You're very kind, Drew," he said, looking deeply into her eyes. "Very kind, indeed."

With a slight toss of her golden head, she inched a bit closer. He felt her fingers curl around his in a more-than-friendly squeeze. "And you, my dear Mr. Sinclair . . . Logan . . . are far too handsome for your own good I'd say."

"When might I return to finish our . . . business?"

She nibbled coyly on her bottom lip as her cheeks flushed. Then she grinned.

And the hook is set.

"What do you say to Thursday next?" she purred, squeezing his hands again. "Eight o'clock?"

He winked and bestowed on her a promising smile. "Thursday next it is then. Most definitely."

Standing in the curved drive outside what had once been Tolley Mochrie's exclusive Sea Cliff estate, Logan watched Ollie carefully place the recording equipment in the back of the van and secure the door.

"So she went for it." Ollie chuckled, turning the key in the lock. "Made *anither* date, and five thousand to sweeten the deal. By-the-by, is that dollars American, or English pounds?"

"Money isn't everything," Logan said solemnly, loosening his tie and his foul temper. It would be a blessing to get out of his charcoal Hugo Boss suit and slip into something more casual, like a warm and willing woman. He thought of Drew Mochrie. Obviously willing, but hardly warm. "Thursday next at eight. I won't be needing the services of my cameraman."

"Aye," Ollie said. "I'd only be in the way." At thirty, Ollie Kerr had short-cropped brown hair, a long, crooked nose, and a chipped front tooth. He'd never bothered to get it repaired, for he claimed it made him more charming to the ladies. "The minute you're in the door, she'll be all over you like flies on *shite*."

"Eloquently put, as usual." Logan arched a brow and pursed his lips. "But no matter. One more conversation with her late brother will seal the deal, and I'll have the Star of Avril in my hands before you know it."

"What if she won't show it to you?"

Logan grinned. "She will."

Ollie snorted a laugh.

Shoving his hands into his pockets, Logan took a deep breath of the salty ocean air.

It felt good to be in San Francisco once more. He hadn't been back to the city by the bay in nearly twenty years, not since he'd visited with his family when he'd been fourteen. Today, in typical northern California style, the October sky was brilliant blue over the land, yet gray and dense and damp where the heavens bent to the sea out on the far horizon.

"I've been a long time gone," he said, more to himself than Ollie. "I rather fancy the States this time of year, the seasons changing and all."

Ollie leaned against the van and crossed his arms over his chest. "I keep forgettin' yer half-Yank. Yer *mither*, right?"

Not in the mood to discuss his parents, his dual citizenship, or anything else of a personal nature at the moment, he said only, "Aye."

Pulling his keys from his pocket, he pressed the auto-unlock. Next to Ollie's van, the leased silver Lexus chirped to life. "I'll contact you after I've acquired the Star."

"Make sure you don't stuff it into your pocket and take off for some tropical island, partner. I'd hate to have to track you down and put a bullet behind your ear."

Ollie grinned at Logan.

Logan grinned at Ollie.

Then, placing his hand on his forehead as though tipping a hat, Ollie walked to the front of the van, slid behind the wheel, and drove on up the street and out of sight.

Logan paused before getting into the Lexus, instead letting his gaze wander down the hill and out to the bay. The sun had just dipped its toes into the sea, turning the Pacific the color of pale champagne. He blew out a breath. Soon now, it would be dark; he had no plans for the evening.

The niggling notion he'd stuffed away at the back of his brain since he arrived in San Francisco, edged its way to the front . . . again.

He could call her. She wouldn't have to know he was in town; she'd assume he was in Scotland or maybe London, and just out of the blue had decided to ring her up—for old times' sake. It wouldn't occur to her he could be at her front door in a mere minute.

He blew out a hard breath. How long had it been since he'd spoken to her? Rubbing the bridge of his nose between his fingers, he tried to remember.

Years. Aye, it had been years.

Letting his hand slowly slide into his pocket, he curled his fingers around the cell phone. When he pulled it out, he stared down at it in the palm of his hand. Tiny portable instrument of mental torture. Omnipresent. Obliterating the excuses of a time not long past.

No excuses not to call these days. No excuses . . .

Though he'd never used the cell to call her, he'd programmed in the number in the event that someday . . . some distant day, he'd use it. In the meantime, the number sat there quietly in the background, waiting for the day he was too sick or lonely or desperate to put it off any longer.

And if he called her today, what would it say of him . . .

Before he could change his mind, he pressed the button and put the phone to his ear. His gut tightened, his jaw clenched. The number began ringing. He steeled himself.

She was a busy woman; maybe she wouldn't be home. If he got her voice mail, he'd leave a quick message, no more than that. No need to explain why, after all these years, he'd decided to—

"Hello?"

He was silent for a moment, too startled to speak. When finally he opened his mouth, no sound came out. His throat closed, and his eyes.

"Hello?" she said again, a wee bit louder now. "I know someone's there."

He licked his lips, swallowed. This was ridiculous; he never should have called. After all these years, he'd finally found the desire, the courage, only to discover he had lost the words.

"Look," she growled. "If this is another damn telemarketer, I'm on the Do Frickin' Not Call List, and I've half a mind to report . . ."

Her words trailed off as though all the air had gone out of her lungs, and she didn't know how to draw in any more.

His eyes still shut tight, he put his head down and drew in the breath it seemed she could not. A moment later, she whispered, "*Logan.* Logan? It's you, isn't it? Don't hang up! Logan? Oh, please, sweetheart, please say something."

He cleared his throat, lifted his head, opened his burning eyes. "Hello, Gran."

She made an odd noise that sounded like grief mixed with joy. On barely a breath, she said, "Oh my God, has anything happened? Are you all right?"

He swallowed again before answering. "Aye."

By his calculations, she had to be in her late seventies, but her voice didn't seem to have changed much. The last time he'd seen her was at the funeral. Her hair had been gray, her eyes red-rimmed and swollen. Her back had been bent from the weight of her grief. Though she'd barely spoken to him, he'd read the condemnation clear enough in those eyes.

He wondered if she still looked the same . . . if she still looked like his mother . . .

"Are . . . are you well?" he managed.

"Yes, quite well. Where are you, Logan?"

"I . . . actually, I'm calling from London," he lied. "I've been doing fine, and, uh, I was wondering if you needed anything."

There was silence for a moment, then she said, "It's you, isn't it."

"Is what me?" he said, as though he hadn't a clue as to what she was talking about.

"For the last ten years or so," she said quietly, "my bank balance increases as if by magic. The bank assures me it's no mistake, and that there's nothing illegal about the transactions."

"I . . . I just figured you could use a wee bit of help now and again, being alone and all."

"I don't have to be alone, Logan. I'm not alone. I have you."

He shook his head. "No, Gran. 'Tis not possible, and you know why."

Judging from the sniffling he heard, she was crying, or trying hard not to. His heart cracked at the sound, but he could not relent. For her own good, he could not relent.

"I thank you for the money, Logan," she said, as her voice broke. "Are you really in London?"

Instead of lying again, he said, "I have to go now, Gran. I . . . I just wanted to see if, you know, if you needed anything."

"You, sweetheart," she sobbed quietly. "I need you."

"After what happened—"

"I forgave you, Logan," she whispered. "A long, long time ago."

"Aye, well, maybe so, Gran. But I've not forgiven myself. I never will."

Ending the call, he shoved the cell phone back into his pocket, cranked the ignition, and put the car in gear.

He should not have called her. Doing so had only hurt her, and he'd already brought her enough grief.

As he guided the Lexus out of the driveway onto Franklin, he made his way over to Van Ness, glancing at the dashboard clock as he turned the corner. While four thirty was too early for supper, a sandwich and a pint might sit pretty well just about now. Glancing about for a neon sign that announced an eatery, up ahead, flashing red lights off to the side of the road snared his attention. Wary of an accident on the busy avenue, he slowed.

The gleaming white Mercedes was sleek and expensive-looking. The driver's side door stood open, and the bonnet was up.

Make that its *hood*. Why didn't the bloody Americans name their auto parts properly?

The car was basically unremarkable—except for the exquisite pair of legs extending through the open door. As he rolled to a stop behind the sedan, she crossed those legs, dangling one shiny black heel from her toes.

He flipped on his own emergency lights to warn drivers to go around both cars, then, shoving his hands into his pockets, he approached the sedan, a congenial smile on his face.

Elbow on knee, chin in hand, her face was turned away from him. Her tight black dress was scooped just low enough to reveal the curve of a very fine set o' *chebs*, while a thin diamond necklace winked at her elegant throat. Her short blond hair ruffled in the breeze.

He stopped, waited. Traffic was noisy. Maybe she hadn't heard him approach.

"Do you need some help, lass?" he said to the back of her head, adding a bit more brogue than necessary. American women were damned hard to impress, but his accent always gave him an edge. "Engine trouble, is it?"

Without turning toward him, she said in a bored tone, "I'm not helpless. I have a cell phone, which I have already used to call my mechanic. Buh-bye and thanks for stopping."

She flicked her foot, and her shoe dropped to the pavement.

Before she could retrieve it, he bent, picked it up, and held it out to her. She turned her face toward him then, looked him quickly in the eye, then averted her gaze the way women do when they first meet a man. Even so, he'd caught the unusual green of her irises in that flash—and wanted to see more.

Taking the shoe from him, she slipped it onto her foot. "Thanks. I don't know what's keeping him. I called twenty minutes ago. If I'm not home by six, it'll put me way behind schedule . . ."

She glanced up at him again, and this time, her gaze held.

As they looked into each other's eyes, a strange sensation began pulsing inside his chest. An awareness of sorts, expanding outward through his muscles and bones, down his legs and out his arms until his fingers tingled. His blood stirred, his brain sharpened. The intensity gathered strength, catching him off guard—unpleasant sensations for a man continually on the alert, and he wanted to shake it off.

She blinked, averted her gaze; the spell was broken.

Hell, she was an unusually beautiful woman. With a mental shrug, he attributed his reaction to extreme attraction. A massive dose of testosterone must have flooded his system, distorting his brain functions for a moment. Aye, that was it.

"What's at six?" he ventured, "if you don't mind my being nosy. Big party?"

She gave a wiggly little shrug of her shoulders, as though whatever it was she might miss either wasn't *that* important—or none of his business.

Behind him, cars roared by on the busy avenue, stirring up the air, bits of dust, exhaust fumes.

"Well then," he said, "if you needn't any help."

"I needn't." With her left hand, she stifled a yawn.

No ring on her finger. Something about the absence of a ring encouraged him to give it another go.

"Perhaps I should stay until your mechanic arrives," he offered. "I'm not entirely sure it's safe for a lass such as yourself to be sitting here by the side of the road with night coming down."

At last, she swiveled to face him full on, and his heart nearly flew away. A stunner she was, and no mistake. Though she didn't smile, her lips were full and ripe. Her darkly lashed green eyes shone bright with intelligence—and was that bewilderment?— as she looked him up and down.

"Uh, um, no," she stumbled. She licked her lips, straightened a bit. In a stronger tone, she said, "No need for you to stay. I'm fine."

With that, she turned away again, and the message was loud and clear: He was dismissed.

A tiny spear of irritation lanced his gut at the rebuff. Sure, he'd been rejected by women before, but rarely by one he'd decided he wanted.

"A good evening to you then," he said as he began backing away toward his own car. She never so much as glanced in his direction.

Well, to hell with that one, he thought as he cranked the ignition on the Lexus. Women usually fell all over him, not that he necessarily wanted them to, but it made getting the ones he did want that much easier. He seldom had to work to get any woman's attention, and as he glared at the back of this obstinate lass's car, he decided he didn't like the feeling.

As he pulled out into traffic, he kept his eye on his side view mirror.

She was looking down. From her purse, she pulled out a cell phone and put it to her ear, never once following his car with her eyes.

His irritation increased.

A block later, his palms damp, his jaw tight, he swerved into a grocery store lot and parked where he could see the flash of her emergency lights in the distance, but she couldn't see him.

She was obviously one of those women who didn't trust men and thought she could handle any situation with a can of Mace and a solid kick to the nuts. But he was willing to wager he knew one hell of a lot more about determined men than she did.

So he'd relax a bit, think about where he'd like to have supper, calculate the odds of the Tartans taking the World Cup this year—and if her mechanic didn't show up in fifteen minutes, he'd go back.

Chapter 2

I regard you with an indifference closely bordering on aversion.

Robert Louis Stevenson

SFPD detective Andrea Darling waited for the call to ring through, pretending not to watch the suspect's car disappear into the early-evening traffic. Just as she lost sight of the silver Lexus, her partner answered.

"Jericho."

She raised her head, searching the distance for any sign of Sinclair. "Arrogant bastard. He just left."

"Well, I may have a strong sense of self, but I wouldn't exactly say I was arrogant—"

"Not *you*, Jericho," she chuckled. "Okay, on second thought—"

"Let's not go there," Dylan said dryly. "What happened?"

She worked to keep the frustration from her voice. "I blew him off. He didn't like it."

"If you blew me off, I'd like it a lot—"

"Goddammit, Detective," she snapped. "Be serious for once and keep your mind on task!"

"What happened to your sense of humor, partner?" Dylan said. "This guy must really have gotten to you."

"Yeah, well, I've been sitting by the side of the roadway for frickin' ever, I'm starved, and I have to pee."

He paused a moment, as if assessing whether she was telling the truth. Finally, he said, "So you blew him off. That screws Plan A."

"We're still good with Plan A. I give him fifteen, maybe twenty minutes. He'll be back."

Jericho snorted a laugh. "I don't know. A man like Sinclair gets dumped by a babe, he never blinks twice. One woman gives him the brush-off, there's a hundred more ready to soothe his hurt."

"And you know this because?"

"I'll just keep that to myself," he said lightly. "I wouldn't want you to think less of me—"

"Than I already do? Yeah, well, he's not you, Jericho." Under her breath, she muttered, "He'll be back."

Her eyes searched the street for any sign the Lexus was returning. The streetlamps had winked on, illuminating Van Ness as far as she could see. Headlights reached toward her, taillights flashed, stoplights went from green to amber to red, neon business signs glowed in pinks, yellows, blues. A honk, a shout, the rev of engines, mixed with chatter from passersby on the sidewalks, but so far, no silver Lexus.

Still, she'd been reading guys for years, and Sinclair had given off all the signals of a man who followed the hunt until he bagged the prey—especially when it involved getting a woman into the sack.

"Okay, Inspector I'm-So-Sure-Of-Myself," Dylan chided in her ear. "Twenty bucks says he keeps right on driving."

Nibbling on her bottom lip, she tried to remember the look in Sinclair's glittering aquamarine eyes when she'd dismissed him. There was no mistaking the interest she'd seen in them when he'd first walked up—or the snap of irritation that replaced it when she snubbed him.

It worried her for a moment that if she really were a woman whose car had broken down, he might have gotten to her. He was a powerful force, tall, muscular, handsome, and much more charming than she'd anticipated. The photo in his file hadn't done him justice, hadn't captured the steely glint in his eye, the smoothness of his deep voice, his cajoling manner. And that brogue . . .

He'd spoken to her as if they were acquaintances, old friends, even lovers. It was distracting, alluring, and she forced herself to remember she was only pretending to find him attractive.

She released a nervous breath. Well, whatever. She'd rebuffed him, and his ego had taken a direct hit. Poor baby. A man like that might have a string of women a mile long, but he didn't take rejection lightly; he probably didn't take it at all.

"Twenty bucks, Jericho?" she mused, then tilted her head in defiance. "Yeah, all right, partner. You're on."

Twenty-two minutes later, Andie huffed out an irritated breath and smacked the steering wheel with her open palm.

Boy, had she ever called that one wrong.

Logan Sinclair had exhibited all the signs of a man who wouldn't take no for an answer unless he chose to. When he'd looked her up and down, that spark in his eyes had assured her he liked what he saw; the dull gleam that replaced it spoke volumes over his pique at her rejection. He was the kind of man who'd convince himself a woman needed rescuing—in spite of her protests or assurances she was fine—and would circle back around for another shot at playing the hero. She'd counted on him doing just that.

But he hadn't come back.

Well, dammit, this was going to make "accidentally" meeting him a second time much more difficult. What if her superiors saw this as a blunder and replaced her with another detective?

No, they wouldn't. Not yet, anyway. She'd have

to get very creative, though, if she wanted to cross paths with the subject again without raising his suspicions.

Before Sinclair's arrival, in the seventy-three minutes she'd sat "helpless" by the side of the road waiting for him to "happen" along, five men, two women, a Girl Scout troop, and one Emo kid whose gender was anyone's guess had stopped to offer assistance. Since the plan would only work if she appeared stranded, she thanked them all and sent them quickly on their way. The local police had been instructed to ignore her as well, yet when she saw the Lexus pull up behind her, she was both relieved and nervous.

This little ploy had to work; it just had to. Her entire world, her past, her future was riding on it. It was a make-or-break scenario and could catapult her to the next level, shoot her out of Vice and into Homicide, where she belonged, where her heart was, where her grandfather and father and brothers had all made their names . . .

She checked her watch again. In the twenty-four minutes since Sinclair had driven off, night had draped the world, leaving only streetlamps and taillights to illuminate her surroundings. Traffic thinned, pedestrians evaporated, gone to their homes to be with their loved ones—

Well, screw this, she thought. Either she'd underestimated her charms or overestimated Sinclair's ego.

Tucking her legs inside, she slammed the door and reached for her cell phone. Headlights flashed in her rearview mirror, then went dark. She froze.

Could be the Lexus, could be some other helpful citizen. If it was Sinclair, if he had come back, it was showtime.

Keeping her eyes on the rearview mirror, she watched as lights from a passing truck illuminated the man as he stepped from behind the wheel and into the street.

Yes. Her heart leaped up into her throat, and the butterflies in her stomach began an energetic hip-hop. Score one for women's intuition.

Not to mention, that chauvinistic brat Dylan Jericho now owed her twenty bucks.

Crossing her arms under her breasts, she waited, staring straight ahead as though she hadn't a care in the world.

Tap-tap-tap on the window. She made sure her bored frown was in place before turning her head.

Oh. It's you, she told him with her eyes.

Aye, it's me, his half-smiling expression said in return.

She made a show of her indifference by blowing out a long breath before opening the door. Scooting out of the seat, she stepped onto the pavement. Though Sinclair moved back to make space for her, he didn't make much.

At five-seven, she was not a short woman, but even so, he towered over her, all heat and testosterone and male aggression. Her brothers were tall, but she had nothing to fear from them; Logan Sinclair could be a completely different story.

His eyes drifted over her. The gleam returned.

"I'd fire that mechanic," he said softly. "If I were you."

Ef ahh-warr yue . . .

It was more a sigh than a sentence.

The skin on her arms prickled. He sounded like James Bond, the first one, the real one. That subtle Scottish burr was sleepy, like he'd just tumbled out of bed. Of course, he meant to do it. According to his file, he played women like fine instruments, and for one quick flash of insanity, she wanted to know what that would feel like to be the fiddle to his bow.

"He called," she lied. "His truck had a flat or something. He's sending a minion."

"But it's nearing six. You'll miss your party."

"It's not a party, and it's not your concern."

"Look, the name's Logan Sinclair, and I'd be happy to give you a lift."

That was what his mouth said. His eyes indicated he'd be willing to substitute "lift" for any number of other action verbs.

She glanced down for a moment, as though she were preparing a response. In truth, she was forcing aside her emotions so her inner undercover operative could take center stage.

This was the jumping-off point. Her next words

would open a door through which there would be no retreat until this man was in prison.

A loss to womankind, but those were the breaks.

When she raised her face to him, she capitulated blandly, "I'll need to see some ID first."

His eyes widened in amusement, then he pulled a billfold from his inside coat pocket. He had both a Scottish driving permit and an International Driver's License.

She glanced up at him—coyly, she hoped. "So you're from Edinburgh?"

He cringed. "Aye, but 'tis *nae* how you say it, lass. 'Tis pronounced *ED-in-bur-ruh*."

"Fascinating. Vacationing in *San-Fran-SIS-KO*, are you?"

His lips tilted on one end, but he made no reply.

So that's how it was going to be, hmm?

Narrowing one eye as though she were assessing him, she ventured, "You must have been to the U.S. before, Mr. Sinclair. Your accent doesn't seem extremely pronounced."

"I'm half-American."

It was her turn to look him up and down. "Oh? Which half?" She arched a brow, then blinked innocently up at him.

He laughed, startling her. Laughter shifted his masculine charm into a boyish joy so attractive, she had to work to keep her composure. His eyes crinkled at the corners, long dimples curved around his mouth. And the deep sound of his laughter . . .

"I have dual citizenship," he ended with a chuckle. "Now, do you trust the likes of me enough to drive you wherever you need to go, with the promise I'll be a proper gentleman?"

Shifting her stance, she met his gaze. "Your name sounds . . . familiar. *Logan Sinclair* . . ." She pretended to search her memory. "Are you an actor or something?"

The dimples in his cheeks deepened. "Not in the way you're meaning."

Not wishing to push too far, too fast, she said, "Well, whatever. I really need to get home."

"I assure you, lass, I'm no serial killer. Just an ordinary citizen trying to help a beautiful woman out of a pickle."

Since that was exactly what she wanted him to do, she made no protest as he reached past her into the car. Removing the keys from the ignition, he locked the door, then took her hand, turning it palm up. Dropping the keys there, he curled her fingers over the key ring, all the while, gazing warmly into her eyes.

Under hers, his hand was strong, steady. Yeah, boy, whew. He was hot all right. He could easily seduce a woman, make her want things she'd never even heard of, let alone done with a man. With looks like his, a few well-chosen words, and that charming glint in his eye, he undoubtedly got what he wanted.

Except for this time, of course. Little did he know he'd targeted a woman who'd been fending off sexual predators—more commonly known as teenage boys—since she'd turned fourteen. Thanks to her insanely overprotective brother Ethan, she'd learned early on how boys thought, what they were after, and how they had no qualms about saying or doing whatever it took to score. As a result, knowledge being power and all that, the male population never got anywhere with Andie Darling she didn't want them to get.

Opening her purse, she dropped the keys inside —right next to her cell phone and her backup .38. With a snap of the latch, she slipped the strap over her shoulder.

"Let's go," she said lightly. "I haven't got all night."

She walked beside him to his car, and when he opened the door for her, she slid into the buttery leather seat, her mind racing.

He didn't suspect anything, or if he did, he certainly hid it well. He was interested, must be. He wouldn't have come back if he wasn't interested. Would he?

"You're perfect for this assignment, Inspector Darling," Detective Lieutenant Eagan had told her three weeks ago. "You're just the type of woman he's known to associate with."

"I'm a *type*, sir?"

Eagan had swallowed, fiddled with the file in his hand. He shrugged, tilting his head at what appeared to be an uncomfortable angle. "Uh, well, yes, you have what many would call, uh, beauty, and uh, the body thing you've got going is, well, I mean you have, uh, you, uh . . ." He cleared his throat. "You must *know* . . . I mean, people, well, *men* in particular, I suppose, must have told you . . . see, it's the *department's* official assessment, not mine, personally, you know, as a man . . . as your superior that you, uh—"

"I'm not going to file sexual harassment charges because the SFPD thinks I'm nice-looking, Lieutenant." She lowered her lashes. Quietly, she said, "But thank you." She met his gaze once more. "Now, about this case?"

He ran his fingers through his thinning gray hair. "You're beautiful. There. I've said it. And you're smart, can think on your feet, and you're tough. In fact, you're well, it's the department's view that you're just a bit on the uh, well, on the, uh . . ."

"Bitchy side?" she finished for him dryly. Blowing out a breath, she said, "If a man's tough and aggressive, he's tough and aggressive. But if a woman is, she's bitchy."

"I never said that. *You* said that. *I* never said that." He adjusted his tie. "Besides, sometimes bitchy is good. Sometimes, it's just what we need—"

"Since I don't have any problem with who I am, sir," she said, then smiled, "I'm not offended in the least."

His short laugh sounded relieved. Adjusting his half-moon glasses on the bulb of his blunt nose, he said, "At least you're aware of it, Inspector. We want you to use it. Keep him on his toes, off-balance. He's known to be extremely charming, very smart, quick. He seems to take up with women who challenge him."

She nodded, flattered that her superiors were putting such confidence in her.

"We want you to try and get him to impress you," Eagan continued. "More importantly, confide in you. We need to find out how he pulls off his tricks. Nobody yet has caught him in the act."

"How do you know for sure it's an act?"

Eagan scoffed. "Well, he can't really be a clairvoyant, Inspector, now can he? It's all bullshit. What we want to know is, how he gets the intel he uses to convince people—wealthy gullible lovestruck women, mostly—that he's on the level."

"How many women have filed charges?"

Shifting in his chair, Eagan picked up his coffee mug, took a swallow, then set it heavily back on his desk. He stuck out his lower lip and shrugged. "To date, none. But he scammed a widow in New York a few weeks back, then showed up in San Francisco, targeting a wealthy heiress."

Andie let the information roll around in her head for a moment. "If he's a known con artist, why hasn't he been apprehended?"

"No evidence, and none of his victims seem inclined to press charges. He arrived on the West Coast about a week ago, ostensibly to do an interview for KALM-TV. But he seemed to home in right away on a woman he met at a party, one Drew Mochrie. She inherited a bundle when her brother was killed about a year ago. Ms. Mochrie is single, attractive, rich, and believes all that mumbo jumbo spiritualist crap . . . just the kind of mark Sinclair's known for going after."

She scowled. "What about jurisdiction? If he's involved in international fraud or theft, why is the SFPD—"

Eagan cleared his throat, leaned forward across his desk, lowered his voice. "Eh, you see, Inspector, it's like this. Ms. Mochrie is the, uh, special friend of a friend of the commissioner's. You understand what I'm saying?"

Ah. So this whole thing was really about sex— who would have it with Drew Mochrie, and who wouldn't.

Andie met Eagan's gaze. "Understood." Clasping her hands in her lap, she said, "How did her brother die?"

"Fell down some stairs, broke his neck. Had all the earmarks of a homicide, but the investigation

never went very far. It was finally ruled an accident."

She took the file Eagan handed her across his
cluttered desk, opened it. A photograph of Logan
Blakewell Sinclair stared up at her. Dark hair; intelligent, clever eyes the color of tropical rainwater;
dark brows and lashes; a sensuous mouth. He was
smiling, and she nearly smiled back. *Age, thirty-
four; height, six-two; weight, one-eighty*. Whew.
Pound-for-pound, the studliest guy Andie had ever
seen.

"I appreciate your faith in me, Lieutenant," she
said as she glanced through the file. "I did a little
undercover work before I was promoted to detective four months ago, but it was nothing like
this."

"Well, if you're half as good as your brothers . . ."
He left the sentiment unfinished and grinned congenially.

Love and pride mixed with irritation as she continued reading Sinclair's file. Her brothers. Two
big-shot San Francisco detectives, and two big
pains in the ego. *Her* ego.

The line of legendary detectives leading to Andie
was long and distinguished. She had some very im-
pressive shoes to fill, and she intended to fill them
until nobody on the SFPD remembered she even
had brothers, let alone a father and grandfather
who'd both served with honor and distinction.
Throw in the occasional uncle and cousin—all

male—and Andie stood alone as the only female Darling to face the challenge of proving a woman could serve with honor and distinction just as well as any of her illustrious male counterparts.

This undercover assignment couldn't have come at a better time. It was her ticket to making a name for her*self*. The Logan Sinclair case was tailor-made to raise her above the ranks, and she was going to make damn sure it did. Excellent police work on her part would nail this charlatan and put him away, and get her the next open spot in the highly coveted Homicide Division.

"You haven't told me your name," Sinclair said, interrupting her thoughts as he cranked the ignition on the Lexus.

"Oh, it's Andrea," she said, forcing her attention to the matter at hand. "Andrea Devon."

He looked over at her, a hint of confusion in his eyes. "Andrea *Devon*?"

"You have a problem with that?" Why was he questioning her name?

"*Nae*. None at all." Sparks ignited his eyes like fireworks in a fading summer sky. "Suits you, it does. I'll wager they call you Andie." He signaled, then pulled out into traffic. "I think it's darlin'."

She blinked hard, trying to retain her composure. "What's so . . ." She swallowed. ". . . darling about it?"

He shrugged. "Don't know. Came to mind, is all."

Dismissing the coincidence, she instructed, "Uh, turn left at the next corner. In three blocks, there's a four-way stop. Take a right onto Manzanita."

Her gut felt like it had just been zapped with a Taser. He couldn't know her real name. It had to be a weird, cosmic joke meant to create even more anxiety than she already felt. "It's this one. Turn in here."

After entering the U-shaped drive, the Lexus came to a smooth halt in front of the three-story Gothic-revival-style mansion. Andie glanced up at the imposing façade, square turrets, and cathedral-style windows of the house she would be required to frequent during the investigation.

They'd told her it had been built in 1883 by a wealthy San Francisco gambler, and even though it had suffered some damage during the 1906 quake and fire, had managed to survive several changes of ownership over the last hundred-plus years as well.

And—of course—local legend claimed it to be haunted, which was why it had apparently stood empty for a good while after the quake. Since the current owners lived abroad, the property management firm in charge was more than willing to do their civic duty by allowing the police its use.

The SFPD secured the mansion in the hopes its notoriety would add credibility to her cover story, and as such act as the perfect lure for a con-man "clairvoyant."

She sure hoped it would work because the place was like a mausoleum, cavernous and drafty and creaky, and she was only thankful she didn't actually have to live there.

She glanced at the house again, and a chill inched up her spine. Something about the place . . . the stark emptiness . . . the browns and black of the clapboards and trim . . . the dark windows . . .

For one, brief, insane moment, she got the distinct feeling the house was waiting for her.

Nerves. That's all it was. Nerves.

Redirecting her stupid thoughts, she focused again on Sinclair.

Okay, she'd snared his interest, had him on the hook, and now she needed to reel him in.

Turning her head, she sent him a tepid smile. "I suppose I should invite you in, offer you a drink or . . . something. You know, to thank you for rescuing me."

The words seemed to hang in the air between them, drifting a little this way, a little that, uncertain which way the wind blew. When he finally spoke, his tone was cool, detached.

"I cannot imagine another woman less in need of rescuing, Miss Andie . . . Devon."

Before she could form a cool reply, he reached across her lap, pulled the handle, and pushed her door open. As he settled back into his seat, his arm brushed against her breasts, but he seemed not to care.

For a moment, confusion warred with surprise inside her head. *He* was dismissing *her*? *Yeah, right!*

Instead of stepping out of the car, she raised her chin and looked over at him, arching her brow. Then, placing her hand on the door, she opened it wide.

The interior light flashed to life, illuminating Sinclair's dark sable hair and handsome face. Under straight brows, his aquamarine eyes squared with hers, then he smiled. He was going to accept her invitation after all.

His lips curved, and his eyes held an ironic glint as he flatly spoke the last words she expected to hear.

"Tempting as your offer is, Miss Devon," he said, "I find I must decline. Good-bye."

Chapter 3

Everybody, soon or late, sits down to a banquet of consequences.

Robert Louis Stevenson

The lass covered her surprise well, Logan would grant her that. Twice, she had given him the boot, but him turning the tables so neatly now, the shock of it registered in her eyes for only a brief moment. Had he not known what to look for, he might have missed it.

Having been raised in a world populated by a doting mother, several aunties, two younger sisters, and a grandmother—and no man about the place but his father—though he loved his ladies dearly, as a matter of survival, Logan learned early on to read women or risk being driven to the brink of lunacy—what with their giggling one moment, weeping hysterically the next.

By the age of ten, he not only knew what PMS

was, he could teach a comprehensive course on the subject.

Over the years, he'd turned this intimate knowledge of the female of the species into an art form, for the most part, using it to charm his way into the most recalcitrant lass's bed. And more recently, of course, conning them for all they were worth.

But Andie Devon was a different kind of female than he'd encountered in times past. He sensed his usual tactics wouldn't work with her, and suddenly, he considered it a personal challenge to find out just what would.

As her fingers splayed on the open door, their gazes met, separated, then met again. A quick intelligence flashed in her eyes. She was clever, confident. He liked a woman who could meet and match his wits. And she had that bit of frost about her. He fancied that, too, inclining him toward devising interesting ways to warm her up.

There was another quality about her, more elusive and not easily defined, that pulled hard at him. His gut told him he should resist, yet for some reason, he was intrigued, curious to see where such a strong and confusing attraction would take him.

Besides, in their two brief encounters, he'd only peeled away a portion of her shield; given time, he might reveal all that lay beneath—especially the soft, lickable parts.

For a heartbeat, she simply sat there, her hand on the open door. Given her snooty-assed manner so far, he half expected she'd turn up her nose at him, toss off an insulted *harrumph*, and stalk away, her bonny little ego bent into hairpin turns.

But she didn't.

Instead, her mouth kicked up at one end, drawing his attention there. On the steering wheel, his hands stilled.

She grinned full out then, a beauty-queen smile. But behind her eyes, she held fast to her secrets. One blink, and as before, they were shut away.

The urge came upon him to make her lose that control, abandon herself to pleasure, go wild in his arms. As though she knew what he was thinking, her smile twitched just then, and she burst into a hearty laugh. Sincere, it was, sweet, feminine, reckless . . . like a woman in the throes of passion.

He swore under his breath. If she ended with a sigh, he wouldn't be able to walk for an hour.

When her laughter trickled off to a softly amused, "Hmm," she just watched him, a wee cat smile curving her lips, her green eyes sparkling with mischief. Her hair shone like liquid gold and fluffed around her face as though a man's fingers had mussed with it. Her beauty and energy stunned him, intrigued him, captivated him, and he felt his chest constrict.

"Suit yourself, Mr. Sinclair," she whispered as she thrust the door open and stepped out of the car. Turning, she leaned in and grabbed her purse, allowing him flash of cleavage. "Well, if you're ever in the neighborhood . . ."

She sent him a wink and a farewell salute, then slammed the door and sauntered up the flagstone walkway that led to the house.

Well, fock it and dammit all to hell. If he followed her now, she'd have bested him, and she'd know he'd caved to her charms.

If he did not pursue her, he'd be a bloody fool.

Though he sat where he was, his eyes followed as she slowly walked up the steps to the door. The nip of her waist in that tight black dress, the curve of her bum, the bare backs of her knees had him pressing his lips together in quiet frustration.

Furious at himself for letting her get to him, he jammed the car into gear. It'd be wise to let her walk away, to forget about her. After all, he hadn't returned to the U.S. to become involved with a woman. There was work to be done and much at stake, and he'd best keep his mind on it.

Her front door opened, and—as seemed her habit—without so much as a glance back over her shoulder, she went inside and shut the door.

Fine then, and that was that.

But as he began to pull away, a woman screamed. He slammed on the brakes, alarm bells clanging inside his head. As he flung the car door open, she screamed again.

Logan took the porch steps three at a time. Without hesitating, he grabbed the knob and thrust open the front door.

She stood next to a table in the center of the large circular foyer, her fingers to her mouth, staring into the shadows at the top of one of the twin, curved staircases. Her face had gone pale as milk, and genuine fright shone in her eyes.

Glancing quickly about, he saw no intruder, nothing amiss, so he went to her, cupping his palms around her trembling shoulders, forcing her to look up at him.

"Are you all right, lass?"

For a moment, she stared into his eyes, then her mouth flattened and her face took on a sheepish expression. "I'm fine. Just my imagination working overtime, I guess. Sorry."

Maybe she was telling the truth; maybe not; maybe . . .

Suspicion edged its way into his brain and began working at the controls. A moment later, he suppressed a satisfied grin. *What better way for you to continue the game, lass, without admitting defeat than to scream like bloody murder?*

"If you hadn't called out," he said slowly, gauging her response, "I'd have been long gone by now, and who knows when our paths might have crossed again."

She shrugged, averted her eyes. "Lucky me."

"Tell me what frightened you."

Licking her lips, she swallowed. "The, um, the

stories about this place must have gotten to me, that's all. I *thought* I saw something . . ."

"A *ghaist* was it?"

"Certainly not a ghost," she snapped. "There are no such things. I'm simply tired, hungry, and I have an overactive imagination, especially since tonight I'm conducting a . . ." Halting her wee tirade, she cocked her head and sent him that snooty-assed look again. "Never mind. Thanks for checking on me, Mr. Sinclair, but since you declined my earlier invitation for a drink, I won't insult you by extending the offer again."

He could go now, probably should, but with his hands around her shoulders, and her body so close . . .

"If it's all the same to you, I'd like to check around upstairs, just in case what you think you saw was *nae* shadows and imagination."

"I'd rather you didn't," she rushed. "If I feel I'm in any danger, I'll call the police . . ." Her brow wrinkled. "What are you staring at?"

"Yer *ferntickles*. Very appealing."

Her eyes flared, and her bottom lip jutted out. She looked for all the world like a warrior goddess ready to do battle. "Keep your damn eyes off my *ferntickles*, pal."

Releasing her shoulders, he laughed. "'Tis no what you think. *Ferntickles* are . . . I believe you Yanks call them freckles. You've got a fair splash of them across your nose. Right bonny they are."

She lifted her hand and gingerly touched the bridge of her nose. "*Ferntickles*." With a bit of a smile, she said, "That's cute. I've always hated them, but if anybody'd ever called them *ferntickles*, I'd've been inclined to appreciate them more."

Smiling like that lit up her face, put a sparkle of devilment in her eyes, bowed her plush lips in a way that made him want to taste them.

He took a step back, allowing himself some breathing room. "You mentioned tonight you were conducting something. A train, is it? You're a wee overdressed for that." He shoved his hands in his pockets and narrowed one eye in thought. "Of course, you could be conducting an orchestra, or an experiment, but you didn't say *an*, you said *a*, which leads me to assume your next word would have begun with a consonant. Let's see, now, what does one conduct? A survey? A trolley car? A tour—"

"I'll save you the trouble of listing every noun you know," she huffed. "A séance. Okay? As if it's any of your business. Some of my friends. For fun, you know? I've rented the place for a few weeks because I'd heard it was haunted. I thought it would be a kick to—"

"A séance, is it? Well now, I know a bit about those."

Your name sounds familiar. Logan Sinclair . . .
So that was it.

Blinking up at him, her clever eyes wide with innocence, she said, "You *do*?"

"I just happened to be a clairvoyant, a medium."

Her gaze flitted over him. "I would have thought an extra large."

"I stopped laughing at that one after the first ten thousand times I heard it," he said lightly. "*People* put out an article on me a while back. You may have seen—"

"I don't read *People*." She moved past him, her heels making a tap-click sound on the white-marble floor. "Unless you change your mind about staying, you'll have to excuse me. I have stuff to do."

"Then I'll just be . . . wait, what's that?" He lifted his head as if to listen to voices from upstairs . . . or the spiritual ether.

He watched as Andie crossed her arms over her waist, her brow arched in impatient expectation.

With a theatrical flair, Logan put his fingertips to his temples. "Aye, I have it." To her, he said, "I'm picking something up."

"What a surprise."

"Someone wishes to communicate with you. Someone . . . caught in the place that floats between the earthly plane and just beyond the veil . . ." He let his voice trail off dramatically.

Her mouth flattened. "Mm-hmm. Well everyone I know is on this side of the veil."

Closing his eyes, he lowered his head. "What's that, then? Danger? She's in *danger*? Yes, thank you."

He opened his eyes to see her frowning. With her hands on her hips, she said dryly, "Just because I'm holding a séance doesn't mean I believe in that crap. I don't. It's all just so much bullsh—uh, baloney."

Then why go to all this trouble to get me to stay? "Whether or not you believe, makes no difference. What is . . . *is*." He gifted her with his most charming smile. If it was within his power to make his eyes twinkle, he would have.

She tugged in a deep breath and shook her head. "Okay, I'll bite. Exactly what kind of danger do the ooo-ahh spirits think I'm in?"

The hook was dangling. She need only take a nibble for him to snare her. The question was, did he want to?

"There is a man," he said slowly, lacing his voice with worry. "A nefarious scoundrel . . ."

"Shocking," she murmured.

"He's very dangerous."

"The hallmark of nefarious scoundrels, I believe."

"He has you in his sights . . . a target. A mark, I think they call it." He cocked his head as though listening to words only he could hear, nodding several times. "The man means to take you . . ." He stopped, then gazed meaningfully into her eyes. Leaning closer, he whispered, "For everything you're worth."

A moment passed. Then, "I'm worth a lot."

"He's happy to hear it."

"Mm-hmm. Tell me more about this . . . man."

"You have something he wants. Something . . . you aren't aware you have, but won't want to give him when the time comes."

"Hmm. I *wonder* what it is?" Her lashes fluttered. "Something a *man* wants from me, a *woman*. Hmm. No, wait. Give me minute. I'm sure I can get it."

"But if you give it up," he said, his voice low, his tone coaxing, "you'll be satisfied beyond measure. The both of you . . . I . . . I mean to say, well, he's your . . ."

Logan clamped his jaw shut. Where had those words come from? He hadn't manufactured them, not this time, not for this woman . . .

Yet as he stood looking down at her, he knew there was more than a wee bit of truth in what he'd said, and it disturbed him.

Emotionally, he closed himself down.

"He's my what?" she drawled, obviously unaware of the battle roaring inside him. "My soul mate? The yang to my yin? Let's see, what are some others? He who completes me? My cosmic snickerdoodle?"

"A bit cynical, aren't you, lass?"

She shrugged. "Simply wise to the ways of the world."

"And so alliterative, too."

Crossing her arms over her waist, she took a few steps away from him. "I don't think I need a clairvoyant to warn me about nefarious scoundrels, Mr. Sinclair."

"But you do need a clairvoyant, don't you, Andie darling?"

Her arms dropped to her sides, and she glared at him. "Why do you keep calling me that?"

He assessed her: defensive stance, accusing glare. Very interesting.

Mildly, he said, "I'd have to wonder why it bothers you so."

"It doesn't."

And that was a lie, judging by the quick blink of her eyes. People's faces, their expressions, gave them away. In his line of work, reading faces might mean the difference between success and failure, life and death, so he'd become damn good at it. Andie Devon was hiding something from him, lying to him outright, and he had a good idea why.

Leaning against the wall by the front window, he let his gaze flit up her body and down again. A pleasant trip, all things considered. "You haven't been exactly on the up and up with me, have you, lass?"

"Sure I have—"

"*Nae*, ye have not. And now, see, I'm on to yer game."

Her chin came up, her eyes narrowed. "What exactly do you mean?"

He considered his next words while he prepared to watch for her reaction to them. Dilated pupils, either avoidance of eye contact or unbroken eye contact, an inward roll of the lips—all were signs of someone holding back the truth. People lied for various reasons, sometimes to protect, sometimes to harm. And in Miss Devon's case . . .

"You can drop the pretense, darlin' girl," he said. "It's like you Yanks are so fond of saying . . . the jig is up."

Chapter 4

Don't judge each day by the harvest you reap, but by the seeds that you plant.

Robert Louis Stevenson

At Sinclair's ominous decree, Andie's heart missed a beat. Then her brain kicked in and overrode her gut reaction. Before any more internal organs became involved, she decided Sinclair's indictment did not mean he'd made her as a cop. Perhaps it was her own stubborn refusal to accept defeat, or maybe she was just being naïve, but too much was at stake to leap to conclusions.

"We Yanks have lots of sayings." She kept her voice soft, stopping short of an actual purr. With her hands at her hips, she stepped back, circled around, eyeing him as though he were a used car she was considering buying. "Sayings like, *Don't count your chickens before they've hatched.* Or, *If you can't be good, be careful.* Or . . ." She halted, meeting his searing gaze. "*Guilty men see guilt on the faces of saints.*"

Silence stretched between them like a high-tension wire. The air in the foyer nearly crackled from the force of their unexpressed thoughts. She could almost see the gears inside his head whir and twist, turn and angle, as he considered her parry to his thrust.

"So it's a saint you are, eh?" His gaze dropped to her mouth, then flicked again to her eyes. In a low and husky voice, he murmured, "I'd wager not."

Andie's pulse quickened, but she kept her eyes locked with his. "So where does that leave us, Mr. Sinclair?"

He took a step toward her. "I would first ask, what is it you believe me guilty of?"

She took a step back. "Well, I would first wonder why you doubt my . . . virtue?"

He advanced once more. "Let us cut to the chase, shall we? You recognized the name Logan Sinclair, knew I was a professional clairvoyant, and set about contriving to get me to participate in your séance this evening."

She tilted her head and slid him a sideways glance. "Even if that were true, why wouldn't I just come right out and invite you, why trick you . . . if, as you say, I recognized who you are?"

"I'm expensive. Maybe you're . . . tight."

She waited a heartbeat, then hummed, "I'll never tell."

Unmistakable desire flashed in his eyes. His gaze dropped to her mouth. When he looked her in the eye again, he said, "The way I figure it, you thought to have me hang about, use my services in your parlor tricks without forfeiting the going rate." He cocked his head in an *Am I right?* sort of way.

"And what exactly is the going rate, Mr. Sinclair? Tight though I may be, I'm certain I could accommodate your inflated . . . fee."

With obvious deliberation, his gaze meandered down her body and back up again. "No doubt."

Andie sent him a wry smile. "We Yanks have another saying . . . *Nothing ventured, nothing gained.* So, I'm guilty as charged, Mr. Sinclair. I tricked you, and you've caught me."

One more step, and he stood only inches from her. The heat from his body wrapped around her like invisible chains, reminding her she was playing a dangerous game with a dangerous man.

"Aye, I've caught ye," he murmured. "Question now is, what do I do with ye?"

Judging from his body language and the gleam in his eyes, he'd already pretty much decided.

And the hook is set.

Reaching toward him, she placed her open palm on his chest. Solid muscle met her hand, and a shiver of excitement she didn't want to acknowledge skittered along her flesh.

"Well, Mr. Sinclair," she breathed. "I suppose I'm at your mercy then . . ."

Behind her on the small foyer table, inside her handbag, her cell phone buzzed.

With a blink of irritation, Sinclair looked over her shoulder toward the noise. Andie dropped her hand and swallowed, grateful for the interruption.

"I have to get that," she said, trying to sound casual, composed. She'd been at the end of her ploy, and short of faking a heart attack, couldn't think how she'd put the man off. He was obviously in the mood for sex and expected to get it. While it was necessary that she become involved with him, he was moving so fast, she wasn't sure she could control the situation much longer.

Sleeping with a suspect was not only outside accepted police procedure, it was absolutely forbidden. Not that toying with him hadn't been a little fun, but she hadn't expected him to put such heavy moves on her within hours of their meeting.

She needed to regain control of the situation. *She* was supposed to be keeping *him* off-balance, not the other way around. From now on, she was going to have to be very creative in her refusals or end up in real trouble.

Moving away from him, she went to the table, opened her purse, and took out the phone. "Yes?"

"You get down and dirty yet, Inspector?"

Dylan, right on cue.

"Oh, damn," she said, adding a touch of regret to her voice. Aware Sinclair could hear every word, she continued, "Are you *sure* you can't make it?"

"So, Inspector," Dylan whispered in her ear. "What are you wearing?"

"Well if you're sick, you're *sick*," she said, emphasizing the word while trying to curtail a sneer at her partner's typical jerk behavior.

Whatever clever parting shot Dylan intended was wasted as Andie slapped the cell phone shut and tossed it back into her purse. With a small frown, she turned to Sinclair.

"No séance tonight, swami. Looks like my underhanded tactics to obtain your services on the cheap have all been for nothing."

"Well now," he said quietly. "That is a shame. And you having already paid to let the place." A frown creased his brow. "Surely you're not planning to sleep here tonight in this great big place all by yourself?"

"Maybe," she said lightly, looking around. "Maybe not."

Though her tone had been flip, once more, she felt her stomach tighten as a sense of dread overtook her. It was as though someone had just walked over her grave.

Unconsciously, her gaze flashed for a second to the top of the stairs. Nothing there. Of course not. Her shoulders relaxed.

The house was big and old and spooky, and she had been nervous—that's all it was. There were no such things as spirits, so it could *not* have been a ghost she'd seen hovering on the landing, staring down at her. Like a nitwit, she'd screamed, and the mirage had instantly disappeared. When she realized screaming was as good an excuse as any to keep Sinclair from driving off, she'd screamed again—loud, long, and with an enthusiasm that would put a banshee to shame.

In the end, she supposed having an overactive imagination had paid off—the suspect had entered the residence, giving her the desired result. *She* was in control. With any luck, it wouldn't take long to worm her way into Sinclair's confidence and gather the evidence she needed, the end result being, justice would be served, and so would her career.

With a quick glance up the stairs, Sinclair said, "You keep looking up there. Are you sure you did *nae* see a *ghaist*?"

"Positive." Her cell phone rang again, and she answered it, making sure Sinclair missed not a word. When the call ended, she tossed the phone back into her purse. "My mechanic had the car towed. It's in the shop. Something to do with a fuel line, whatever that is."

He walked to the front window and looked out into the dark night. With his back to her, he said, "I get the feeling you've done with me for the night, now that I'm no longer of any entertainment value."

"It's not that, it's just that the evening I had planned fell through. I'm disappointed."

He turned. "Perhaps we can find a way to ease your grief."

"Perhaps. But not tonight. I suddenly have a severe headache and want nothing more than to close this place up, sink into a hot tub, then go to bed."

He swallowed, as though the images she painted with her words formed exactly the way she wanted them to on his primitive male brain. "You sure I can't give you a lift somewhere?"

"Thanks, but no. I'm going to hang here for a while, then just call a taxi back to my hotel—"

"Where are you staying? Where are you from? How long will you be in town?"

She pressed her lips into a flat smirk. "For an all-seeing, all-knowing swami, you sure have to ask a lot of questions."

His gaze was steady and came that close to being dangerous. "No matter, lass. I'll find it all *oot*."

Her brow arched. "Going to look into your crystal ball?"

Sending her a slow grin, he whispered her own words back at her. "I'll never tell."

In spite of herself, she laughed. "Okay, look. To thank you for rescuing me from the side of the road, why don't I take you to dinner tomorrow night? I'd like to learn more about your . . . gifts, and I can tell you my long sad life story."

He tilted his head, then smiled. "Right. Have it yer way, lass. Where shall I pick you up?"

"I'll meet you. Eight o'clock at the Cliff House. The reservations will be under my name."

"I guess it's good night to you then, darlin' Andie." Without further comment, he turned and walked toward the door.

She closed it behind him, waiting until she heard the sound of his car fade in the distance. After she was certain he wasn't coming back, she called Jericho and filled him in on the arrangements for the following night. When he started to make some stupid-ass remark, she ended the call.

Oh, Dylan Jericho was harmless enough, just persistent. When they'd both been in uniform, he'd tried to date her. Her constant refusals had been tough on his ego, so he retaliated now whenever he got the chance with suggestive remarks and innuendo. Aside from his juvenile behavior, she liked the guy. And if he ever got too irritating, she simply shut him down. He was a smart man, a solid partner, and a damn fine detective. She'd trust him with her life, just not her heart.

Her heart, she trusted to no man.

Slipping the cell into her purse once more, she glanced around the silent foyer and let out a long breath of relief. The whole ordeal—from sitting and waiting in her car for Sinclair to "happen" by, to locking the door behind him as he left—had been exhausting. But she had hooked him in, and tomorrow night, she'd set the prong so deep, he'd never get away.

As she was about to call for a cab, she noticed a light was on somewhere down the hall, just past the left staircase.

Wandering in that direction, she realized the light shone from an open doorway. She peeked around the threshold into what she realized was the library.

The mahogany-paneled room was enormous, rising two stories, and stacked, baseboards to ceiling, with thousands of volumes, many of which looked to be quite old. The place smelled of beeswax, leather soap, and musty wood. Old houses smelled old, and though the cool air wasn't stagnant, the atmosphere itself was thick.

Comfortable-looking leather chairs sat adjacent to fringed Victorian lamps, and a circular reading table with six chairs waited in front of the massive carved white-marble fireplace. In the middle of the table lay what appeared to be an antique wooden Ouija board, its two rows of letters and single line of numbers painted in old-fashioned black-and-gold script. In the left corner shone a full moon; on the right, a sun. The words YES and GOOD-BYE and NO were spaced evenly along the bottom border. The triangular planchette sat in the middle of the board, benignly pointing to the golden moon.

Andie smiled. She and her best friend, Kim, had played with a Ouija board when they'd been kids, but she had always suspected Kim of shoving the pointer exactly where she'd wanted it to go, making sure the answer to the question, "Am I going to marry Tony Gibson?" was invariably YES. Tony was best friends with Kim's older brother, and either ignored twelve-year-old Kim completely or teased her about her red hair until Andie wanted to punch the kid in the *cojones* like her brother had shown her to do when guys got out of line.

Andie meandered across the room, running the tip of her finger around the board. That stupid Ouija board had been her only foray into the "spirit" world, but she'd always considered it an interesting coincidence that Kim did eventually end up marrying Tony Gibson, who, as it turned out, absolutely adored her and had all along.

Feeling weary after such a long day, she moved away from the table to let her body sink into the cushions of the overstuffed leather chair closest to the fireplace. Taking in a deep breath, she let it out slowly, trying to loosen the tightness around her neck and shoulders. A back rub would sure feel good about now.

She thought of Logan Sinclair's strong fingers. Boy, howdy. He probably gave fantastic back rubs, and the front rubs undoubtedly made women scream with pleasure.

Damn jerk. *Why* did he have to be a criminal? He was just the kind of man she'd secretly longed for all her life. Smart, handsome, witty, charming, sexy, with that something, that elusive quality in his eyes that spoke directly to her soul.

Of course he'd turn out to be the worst possible kind of man for her—a con artist, a cheat, a liar. Hell, for all she knew, he was a murderer, too. Dammit.

Well, the bottom line was, her heart was still right where it should be, inside her chest and not in the hands of a man who'd abuse it. Her career came first, rising within the ranks, making a name for herself. Let other women fall in love and have families; she was cut out for a career, and that being the case, she wouldn't settle for less than becoming a legend.

Her grandfather had done it. Her father had done it. Her brothers, Ethan and Nate had done it. She'd always come in fifth best, but not anymore. Now the fire that drove her would burn brightly for the world to see, and she'd outshine them all. She lived in an age where a woman could have it all, and she wanted it . . . all of it, and she'd get it.

No more, Oh, isn't Andrea pretty? She should be a model. An actress. A beauty queen. A politician's wife. Nobody gave her any credit for her brains, even today, even with women accomplishing great things. If you were good-looking, it didn't follow that you could be smart. Men only saw your face and body, and in some cases, a woman's looks were a detriment because men were too stupid to see past her boobs or butt to the dynamic, energetic, competent woman beneath.

She was lucky, and it was nice to be nice-looking, and she was thankful for the genetic crapshoot that had blessed her with an attractive face and good body, but it was also frustrating in many ways. Unless you were a model or actress or beauty queen or politician's wife, good looks could be a liability. Even though it was the new millennium, she had to work twice as hard to be considered half as good as her male counterparts.

Fine. She could do that.

And collaring Logan Sinclair was just the first step in that journey.

Suddenly very weary, she let her head fall back, her lids drift closed.

The image of the blurred outline at the top of the stairs eased into her mind, but this time, didn't startle her. A ball of opaque light, perfectly round, hovered in midair inside the shapeless form, then expanded, until a woman stood there.

A soft hum that seemed to come from nowhere, yet everywhere, lulled Andie's tired mind. The melody was gentle, like a lullaby, and she drifted down a bit, and down, and down . . .

The morning is warm, and the front door stands wide open to let in a coolin' breeze from the bay. Not a bit of fog this day, which for springtime is a rare thing indeed.

As I'm gazin' out onto Van Ness Avenue, a pair of sweaty gray horses pulls against their harness, their heavy burden bound for the docks, no doubt.

The teamster cracks the whip above their heads, and they mind to, and pick up their pace, poor beasts. The wagon wheels groan, and shod hooves clatter against the brick pavement as they make their way down the street.

The dray passes, revealing three boys playing at jacks in the hardpan in front of Houghton's Feed and Grain. The lads are wearing knee pants and black suspenders, and laugh and punch at each other the way boys do.

Heavy tread pricks me ears, and through the open doorway, what do I see, but himself stroll by. He disappears from view. I hear one step, another, then silence. A shuffle and a scuffle, and he returns to the threshold, filling it with his height and wide shoulders. He's handsome in his policeman's uniform and hat. Brass buttons gleam like small suns marching in a line down the front of his dark blue coat.

He smiles at me, and I look into his eyes. An unusual shade they are. Not quite green, nor not brown, neither, but both. Such as the sea at morning time, glittering-like, as it splashes about your ankles, and you can see through the water to the golden sand beneath.

I can see m'self in his eyes. No, not me reflection, like in a pane of shop front glass down on Market Street. It's that he admires me; that's what I see. And why shouldn't he then? I'm pretty enough, I've been told by the baker's son, and the lad who delivers the ice, and by the likes of Tommy O'Neill who kissed me on graduation day.

"Hello, Miss," the policeman says to me, and I say hello back like I don't care one way or t'other. Under the curve of his thick brown handlebar moustache, his fine lips tilt into a smile, and I feel like me heart just flew out the window to the far-side of the moon, and only he can catch it and hand it back into its rightful place.

And that's how we meet, you see. Him, walking his beat up Van Ness Avenue, glancing in the dusty windows and open doors to see that all is a'right.

"Do you work here, Miss?" he says to me, those eyes of his betraying his reason for wishin' to know.

"Me da is Timothy Conner, the man what owns this emporium," says I, pointing to the noonday basket under me arm. "I'm just bringing his supper."

His grin broadens. "Then I'm wishing I was one Timothy Conner at the moment, to share a meal with such a pretty girl."

I can feel me cheeks warm at his remark. "And maybe it's a fortunate thing that I bring Da his supper every day about this time."

"Ain't it, though," he says with a twinkle in his eye.

"And maybe tomorrow, there might be an extra piece of apple cake wrapped in the oilcloth, in case your duties bring you this way again."

"Is that by way of a bribe, Miss?"

I tilts me head and gives him a sidelong glance. "Might be it is."

"Then I'll give Conner's Dry Goods my full attention while I make my rounds, in case thieves have a mind to crack a window and make off with a bit of pink calico."

I laugh at that, me head spinning, me mouth nearly too dry to speak, truth be told. I swallow, knowing me cheeks are no doubt shiny now with the very heat of his attention. Under me long skirt, me legs wobble and knees knock together like the Nervous Nellie I am. "Then, perhaps I'll see you again, Officer . . ."

"Harte," he says boldly as you please. "Officer Jacob Harte. Ever and always, at your service, Miss Conner."

With the tap of his cudgel against the shiny rim of his hat, he smiles at me, and I know . . .

Chapter 5

Quiet minds cannot be perplexed or frightened, but go on in fortune or misfortune at their own private pace, like a clock during a thunderstorm.

Robert Louis Stevenson

Someone was crying . . . who was crying?

Andie sat up with a start, eyes wide, heartbeat banging her eardrums. The shaking hands that flew to her face were met with her own tears.

Blinking, trying to focus, she stared at her dampened palms in confused wonder. Why was she crying?

But even as she stared all around her, the mournful sobs continued. Slowly, she lifted her head, seeking their source. Her gaze flitted to every corner of the room.

She was alone.

The crying softened into a faint mewling, then

faded into nothingness. Andie licked her lips, trying to regain her composure.

As though pulled from the very ether around her, quiet words formed inside her head . . . *Jacob . . . dearest love . . . forgive me . . . Jacob . . . forgive . . .*

Andie pressed her hands over her heart, afraid for a moment that it would break in two from the sorrow permeating the room.

Pushing herself out of the chair, she bolted out the door and down the hall to the foyer. She sucked in deep breaths as she made a grab for her purse, then yanked open the front door, all but stumbling through the threshold onto the porch.

She hurried down the steps and moved quickly away from the house. The yard was dark, the air damp. Slowing, she turned to face the mansion.

Wiping the tears from her cheeks, she pulled in deep breaths of cool night air, trying to settle her nerves, get a grip on her emotions.

What in the hell had just happened? She must have fallen asleep and had a dream, but it was the most vivid nightmare . . . so real . . . as though she were another woman in a different body living a hundred years ago . . .

She laughed and tried to ignore the shaky sound of her own voice in the lonely dark. It was simply her overactive imagination again. Thank God she never had to go back inside that house. It was just too spooky.

Reaching inside her purse for her cell phone, she punched Dylan's number. As she waited for him to answer, she fixed her eyes on the house, all hard lines and shadows against a deep amethyst sky. A dim light glowed through the foyer windows—the library lights were still on, but she'd be damned if she'd go back inside and turn them off.

"Jericho." His voice sounded sleepy, as though she'd just wakened him.

"I need a lift," she said, without preamble. "I'll be waiting at the end of the drive. No skanky remarks and don't give me any shit tonight. Understood?"

"Understood," he said. "On my way in five." One thing about Jericho; he knew when not to mess with her.

As she slid the phone back inside her purse, movement behind an upstairs window caught her eye, and she froze. Her brain worked to find a logical explanation.

Maybe the window was slightly open and a breeze had fluttered the curtain for an instant.

Maybe headlights from a passing car had shifted the shadows, making it appear someone was inside the house.

Maybe . . .

Jacob . . . dearest love . . . forgive me . . . Jacob . . . forgive . . .

A hundred explanations raced through her mind, but all she could think of was how much her chest hurt and how she wanted to curl in on herself and cry and cry . . . but had absolutely no idea why.

As Logan walked toward the entrance to the Cliff House, he let his mind conjure up an image of Andrea Devon. Though he was right on time, she'd have gotten there ahead of him; she wasn't the type to keep a man waiting, though he imagined many would be willing to hang about in eager anticipation.

She'd've taken pains to look fetching tonight, enticing. Despite her aloof manner, the sparkle in her eye when she spoke to him could *nae* be denied. Maybe it was the game that excited her—a new man, a new challenge—or maybe she found him in particular more interesting that she'd care to admit.

Her perfume would be light and applied with an even lighter hand. A little makeup and no more. Her dress would hug her body, cut low with just a tasteful hint of cleavage. Jewelry would be minimal; gobs of gems on her would be gilding the lily, and she knew it. Simplicity, taste, elegance. Class, all the way. Every inch the kind of woman he liked.

And completely off-limits.

In frustration, he blew out a long breath. If he did what was good for him, he'd slide back into the

Lexus and get the hell out of there right now. If he did what was good for *her*, he'd disappear from her life and never look back.

But anticipation of the evening ahead heated his blood, so he avoided examining too closely what was good for him. As for her, well, hell, one dinner could *nae* hurt. He'd enjoy her company, kiss her if he could, touch her if she'd let him—which he doubted—then he'd vanish.

It had been too long a time since he'd let a woman near enough that it bothered him knowing he had to shove her away. When it came time to show Andie Devon the door, he had a feeling it would hurt him more than it hurt her, and would, maybe forever.

Och, best not to think about that. He was a free man and intended to stay that way. And if the loneliness crept in sometimes in the dark of the night when all was silent except for the torturous murmurs inside his head, then he'd do what he always did and seek out a willing—and temporary—woman to ease his suffering and keep the whispers at bay.

It would have been best if he'd canceled tonight and stayed away from her from now on, but damn, he had to see her—*had* to. She'd done something to him, woven some kind of spell over him, awoken in him something long dormant that raged to be acknowledged. Aye, he'd known many women, but none like her. *Ever.*

But for her own protection, for her own good, it would be one dinner only, one brief evening, then done. Besides, by the time he was through with her tonight, she'd never *want* to see him again.

He let a sardonic grin curve his lips. Unless she had an iron stomach and the will to match, by the end of the evening, she'd pay to be rid of him.

Turning his thoughts to the mansion, he recalled the silhouette of the old house, its gabled roof, turrets, porches, ornate trim. The place was haunted; he knew that now. Felt it. The spirits who called it home waited for him, but he'd deny them just like he'd denied all the others.

That was a world he'd sworn he'd never inhabit again. And since he'd been nineteen, he'd kept that vow and would until he'd breathed his last.

His mind turned once more to his grandmother and the sound of her voice on the phone. Instead of the ire and reproach he'd expected, her words had been kind, her demeanor one of love and loss and loneliness.

Once more, he admonished himself for contacting her. What good could possibly come of it? Hell, how could he give her what she wanted, needed? In denying himself, he'd surely denied her, blameless as she was and in just as much pain as he. But where could he find the joy, the tenderness, the happiness he'd destroyed so utterly fifteen years ago? Resurrected from the ashes of a burnt-out wreck?

He could not. It was too much to ask. He would

go back to his solitary life and not call Gran again. *Nae,* he would not.

With a harsh laugh at his own idiocy, he ended his emotional postmortem and turned his attention back to Andie Devon.

Though she denied the existence of *ghaists,* she must have seen or sensed something in the house. Her scream had been real; the first one, anyway.

But no matter. After dinner tonight, she'd never want to sup with him again. She'd feel such revulsion, she'd probably run from the restaurant in horror and be gone from his life forever.

As much as it pained him to push her away, he had to do it. For the sake of his sanity, and her very life.

"It's for eight o'clock. Under Devon. Please check again."

Andie scowled at the maître d', who scowled back. "One moment, Madam," he said with a stiff, self-righteous politeness.

"I canceled it." The deep masculine—and unmistakably familiar—brogue came from behind her. She whirled to stare into sparkling rainwater eyes.

"You *what?*"

"I don't believe there's anythin' wrong with yer hearing, lass. I canceled the reservation."

She was that close to being speechless. "Do you know how *hard* it is to get a reservation—"

"Does *nae* matter. Truth of it is, I did *nae* want to eat here."

"Well I did!" Hell, on her salary, she could never afford to eat at this place, but with the SFPD footing the bill . . . well, damn!

He smiled down at her in obvious triumph. "The fact that this is a fine eating establishment aside, it has no sense of adventure. And I figured you for the type of woman who likes to live on the edge, try new things."

Behind her, the maître d' cleared his throat.

"Thank you for your efforts, my good man," Logan said, reaching around her to press a folded bill into the maître d's palm. Satisfied, the man turned away.

Easing his fingers around her arm, Logan turned her toward the door.

"Not that this isn't a nice enough place, but when I take a lady to supper, I prefer to choose the restaurant."

"Oh, really." She glared up at him as he trotted her down the steps and into the brightly lit parking lot. As he handed the valet his ticket, she shook Logan off—not because his grip was too tight but because she liked it too much.

Tilting her head, she gave her escort-slash-suspect the once-over. He was wearing a dark suit, perfectly tailored to his perfect physique.

"What's this?" she chided. "No kilt?"

Not that he needed one. He looked handsome

enough as it was without adding any Scottish Highland warrior accoutrement.

He grinned. "Sorry to disappoint. Left m'tartan at the caber toss."

She pursed her lips. "Just how far can you toss your caber?"

"Far as necessary, to get the job done." He winked.

Damn, she wished he'd stop doing that. "I've always wondered something. Just how long is your average caber?"

He leaned toward her ear. "Nothing average about it, lass," he whispered. "A good six meters, I'd say."

Rolling her eyes as though she were about to faint, she murmured, "You must be one popular fellow in Scotland."

"Aye," he said. "But tossing it's nothing. You ought to see the one-eighty it does in the air afore it hits the ground."

"Oh, now you're just bragging," she said dryly, earnestly suppressing a smile. "What colors are in the Sinclair plaid?"

His car arrived, and he opened her door for her. As she slid into the plush seat, he said, "Depends on whether yer talkin' modern or traditional, formal or hunting, summer or winter. Mostly, it's red with green and blue, and either brown or white weave running through it, sometimes both."

He closed her door, then walked around to the

driver's side and slid behind the wheel. Turning the key in the ignition, without looking at her, he said softly, "You look beautiful."

Hell, she'd better! She'd spent two hours getting ready for this dinner in the hopes of setting the hook so deep she could keep him on the line as long as she needed to. The dress was too tight, the neckline too low, the heels too high for her comfort, but her own sense of personal style or taste weren't allowed into the equation. She'd dressed to snare a con man who had a taste for leggy blondes, and judging from the appreciative look in his eyes, her calculated agony was paying off.

"Thank you," she murmured, snapping her restraints into place. "Where exactly is it you think my sense of adventure needs to go for dinner tonight?"

"'Tis a surprise. I was fortunate enough to locate an eatery that serves traditional Caledonian delicacies."

"Caledonian?"

He shot her a quick glance. "'Tis what the Romans used to call Scotland. Ever had Scottish food?"

"Not that I'm aware of. Can't say I know much about it."

His smile seemed a little mysterious as he guided the Lexus around a corner. "Well then, prepare to be amazed. You have no idea how you've been missin' *oot*."

Twenty minutes later, he parked near the water-front at a small restaurant called The Highland Inn. Only ten tables graced the place, all of which were covered with cloths in various red, black, blue, green, and purple plaids. On the walls hung gorgeous framed photographs of ruined castles, bagpipers in full regalia, and steers that looked like Texas longhorns wearing brown shag carpets.

As Andie took her seat, Sinclair pointed to one of the photographs. "That's Hamish, a rather famous *hell in coo*."

She blinked at Hamish, then at Sinclair, then back at Hamish. "What's a hell in coo?"

"Highland. Cow," he enunciated slowly, then gestured once more at the photo. "Hamish means James, but there's no J in the Gaelic alphabet. The *coos* used to be black and the meat quite tasty, but Queen Victoria, on a trip through the *Hielans,* decided she did *nae* like black *coos,* so she ordered them interbred with other types of cattle to lighten their color. Now they're brown, right enough, but the meat's been ruined."

"Well, it's good to be queen. So no steak for dinner tonight, I guess."

"Ah," he said, a bit of a twinkle in his eye. "Something much better."

She did *not* want to like this man. She was here to do a job. Her career was on the line, and she needed to get information out of him, but he was so charming and affable, she was having trouble remembering that.

Swallowing, Andie straightened her shoulders, and strengthened her resolve not to let his easy smile and even easier sexuality distract her.

Though the place was packed and noisy with diners laughing and chatting, and good smells emanated from the kitchen, she suddenly felt over-dressed for the simplicity and clientele of the place. No biggie, though. It's not like it was a real date. After all, it didn't matter how she was dressed when her only agenda was to get information out of the suspect.

He raised his hand, gesturing to someone behind her. "I can order wine if you like," he said, "but the traditional thing to drink with haggis is whisky." He seemed to study her for a moment, as though he expected some kind of reaction.

"Then whisky it is," she said, unfolding her blue-and-white-plaid napkin, placing it in her lap. *Go along to get along* was this evening's motto. No rocking the boat. Besides, she knew how to hold her liquor; maybe he didn't. Maybe she could get him blotto and worm a few secrets out of him. "Haggis," she mused. "Is that some variation on a *Heilan coo*?"

He raised a brow. "You've never heard of haggis, then?"

With a quick shrug, she said, "I've heard the

term. I always pictured some kind of fluffy goat or something. Exactly what kind of animal is a haggis?"

Just then, a dark-haired waitress deposited a bottle of Scotch whisky and two glasses on the table, then scurried away. As Sinclair poured several ounces of the golden liquid for her, their waitress appeared again with two plates, which she set in front of them.

"There ye be," she said with a smile, then wiped her hands on her yellow-and-green-plaid apron. "Haggis with *neeps* and *tatties*. Enjoy."

As the woman scurried away, Andie gazed down at her plate, feeling her expression morph from gosh-that-smells-good to Jesus-Christ-what-in-the-hell-is-*that*?

That looked like somebody had decided to play balloon animals with Paul Bunyan's lower GI tract. Brown and glossy, the gigantic U-shaped tube sat amid what appeared to be two mounds of mashed vegetable matter. A bit of parsley peeked from around the side of the thing like a weed decorating a decaying Yule log. A bone-handled knife protruded from the center of the bloated object as though the cook had tried to pinion it to the plate in case it tried to get up and bounce away.

Across the table, Sinclair said heartily, "We can *nae* eat without first giving the haggis its due."

She swallowed. "Its due?"

What, like a human sacrifice?

"Aye. A salute to the haggis, to thank it for nourishing our bodies." He raised his whisky glass. "Robbie Burns said it best: *Fair fa' your honest, sonsie face, Great chieftain o' the puddin'-race! Aboon them a' ye tak yer place, Painch, tripe, or thairm: Weel are ye wordy o' a grace As lang's my airm.*" He downed his whisky with one gulp. "There's more to the poem, but we don't want the haggis to get cold, now, do we?"

She shook her head, eyed her whisky—suddenly understanding without question its necessity—lifted her glass, and tossed back the contents. Gripping the knife, she sliced the haggis open, then stared down in horror. What appeared to be mud scrapple oozed out. "What's in haggis?" she whispered.

"Haggis is a traditional Scottish dish," he said. His eyes were serious, but there was something about his demeanor that alerted her that he'd intended to shock her. The question was, why? "It's made with sheep's pluck."

She swallowed again, certain her complexion had paled to the color of that wilted parsley. "Do I want to know what sheep's pluck is?"

"Heart, liver, and lungs," he announced, taking a large bite of his own haggis. "It's minced together with onion, oatmeal, suet, spices, and salt, then mixed with stock, and boiled in the sheep's stomach. Has a sort of nutty texture, really. Very savory. Try it."

"That's a sheep's stomach?"

He shook his head. "No. They're hard to get in the States. That's a pig's intestines, I'll wager. And I'll bet there's no sheep's lung in there. Americans seem to have some rule about that, so the lungs have most likely been substituted with a gizzard."

"Most likely," she breathed, not taking her eyes off the abomination in front of her. With one finger, she shoved her whisky glass toward him, and he refilled it. Knocking back another gulp, she set the empty glass down and stared at the enemy on her plate. "Nutty and savory, huh?"

"Aye. Just like me."

She would have laughed, but was too focused on getting that first bite to her mouth. "What are *neeps* and *tatties*? Sounds sexual somehow."

He grinned, shoved another forkful into his mouth. "Rutabagas and mashed potatoes."

She felt her shoulders relax. Ah. Normal food. Root vegetables.

Like a surgeon probing for a tumor, she dipped her fork into the sludge, took a deep breath, closed her eyes, and shoved the bite into her mouth.

"Oh!" Opening her eyes, she blinked, looked across the table at Sinclair, and blinked again. "It's not awful."

For the tiniest second, Sinclair's eyes flashed with something that looked like dismay. He lowered his gaze to his plate, and when he looked up again, he was smiling. "Glad you approve."

Actually, she had to admit that the haggis—for all its bizarre ingredients and basic ugliness—wasn't half-bad; it wasn't half-good, either, but that was beside the point. Haggis must either be an acquired taste or eaten out of sheer desperation. But with the delicious buttered *neeps* and *tatties*—not to mention the occasional dram of whisky—all in all, the meal was very . . . not bad.

"Tell me about your family," Andie said, taking another sip of whisky.

"Nothing to tell."

"Sure there is. Everybody—"

"They're dead," he said, his expression suddenly somber, distant. "Long time ago." The dull gleam in his eye, the flat line of his mouth shouted *Don't go there*.

For the first time since she'd met him, she got a glimpse under the veneer. And she knew without doubt that when crossed, Logan Sinclair could be a very dangerous man.

His posture shifted, shoulders relaxed, and the easy smile returned to his face. With his fork, he indicated the haggis that remained on her plate. "So you liked it well enough did ye?"

"Aye. Well enough," she mimicked. "So this clair-voyance thing you've got going." Lifting her gaze to meet his, she said, "How do you do it really?"

He returned her gaze, steadily, a hint of challenge in their depths. "You don't believe in my renowned psychic abilities?"

"I don't believe in psychic abilities period, yours or anyone else's." Settling back in her chair, she picked up her whisky glass, rolling it between her fingers, watching the amber liquid tilt this way and that. "How'd you get so famous?"

"Did a few séances with a few celebrities." He leaned forward, and whispered, "Actors are an insecure lot. They're always looking to see what their future holds." He picked up his own whisky and sipped at it. "I went on a few tours, wrote a couple of books. The tabloids splashed my name about a couple of times, and I was off and running."

"Must turn a tidy sum."

"It does."

Crossing her arms over her waist, she said, "So what do you do with your millions?"

He lifted one shoulder in a careless shrug, then gave her a toothy, used-car-salesman grin. "Why, don't you know, I send it all to my poor widowed grandmother."

Andie snorted. "Right."

A strange look crossed his face for a moment, and he swallowed. "Nevertheless . . ." Sticking out his lower lip, he studied his whisky glass. "Money is only . . . money. They say the best things in life are free."

"I'll take your word for it," she quipped.

His eyes flashed up at her, and for a moment, he seemed to grow somber. "Aye, you do just that."

Wiping her hands on her napkin, she said, "Okay, so tell me, how do you convince people you can talk to their dead relatives, when there's absolutely no way you can really do that?"

He studied her for a moment. "You'd be surprised."

"Okay. Surprise me."

"Perhaps we should talk about something else."

"Ah, come on," she teased. "Do a séance for me. Talk to, um, let's see. How about my father? He's dead. I've a few things I'd like to get off my chest—"

"Doesn't work that way," he growled, shoving his empty plate away.

"Just how does it work?" She sent him her most charming smile, the one she had used when she was seventeen to get out of a well-deserved speeding ticket. "You must have some cutting-edge information network you access that provides you with all kinds of data, personal and public, about a potential client before the so-called séance. Then you turn on the charm, do a little smoke-and-mirrors thing, tell them whatever they want to hear, then cash the check." Setting her whisky glass on the table, she circled the rim with a fingertip, then looked over at him. "C'mon. You can tell me."

He studied her for a moment, his expression unreadable except for the hard glint in his eyes. "Like the man says," he drawled, leaning across the table until they were nearly nose to nose. "I could tell ye, but then I'd have to kill ye."

Raising her chin, she met his gaze dead on. "But you wouldn't kill me," she whispered. "Would you."

Chapter 6

There is only one difference between a long life and a good dinner: that, in the dinner, the sweets comes last.

Robert Louis Stevenson

Had she won, or lost? Had she hooked him, or pushed him too far? Would he want to see her again, or had she blown the whole operation?

In confused silence, Andie walked beside Logan toward the underground parking garage where they'd left his car. She replayed their conversation in her head, trying to calculate her gains and losses and figure her next move.

But her next move depended on his.

Her superiors had chosen her for this assignment, confident she could pull it off, and she'd assured them—and herself—she could. After all, this was her big break, the first stamp on her ticket out of Vice and into the elite Homicide Division, where her brothers and father had distinguished themselves. Now it was her turn to prove she could measure up, do the job, bring down the bad guys. No more "little sister Andie," a small trembling leaf shadowed behind the big ones on the family tree.

Lieutenant Eagan had given her a remarkable chance to prove herself, her worth, and she would not let him down.

But Logan Sinclair was much more complex than she'd bargained for. He was smart, cagey, crafty. He used his charm and sexuality to manipulate, control, subtly persuade. He was nobody's fool.

But then, neither was she. The question was, which one of them played the game better? In the end, which one of them would back the other one into the corner?

When she'd taken this assignment, Andie had been sure it would be she who'd prevail; she still was. It was just going to take more planning, more focus, and tiptoeing very carefully to avoid falling into his trap before he fell into hers.

They reached the elevator, and he pressed the button for the garage level. A moment later, the dull steel doors rattled open, and she stepped inside the tiny compartment. Without a word, Logan followed her, then thumbed the button for the lower level.

As the doors slid together and the elevator began its descent, Andie considered her next words. But before she could say anything, he took a step toward her. In one smooth move, he tugged her into his arms and kissed her.

It was as though she were being consumed by a forest fire. Heat seeped into her skin through her palms, flat against his chest. His fingers left a searing trail as they traced her waist, then slid down her hips to grab her butt in a firm hold. His warm breath mingled with her own as he kissed her until she thought she would melt.

His lips were soft yet in total command. His tongue teased. He must have kissed a thousand women—hell, maybe a million—to get this good at it.

Pulling back, he nibbled and suckled her lower lip as he ended the kiss.

She wanted to moan from the loss.

The elevator halted at the garage level; the door opened, but neither of them moved.

His sleepy eyes gazed down into hers, searching. Then he lowered his head, kissing her again, more tenderly this time, thrusting his tongue into her mouth, sending a chill of desire through her body.

His big hands skimmed up and around until he cupped her breasts through the fabric of her dress. While his thumbs rubbed her nipples into peaks, his kiss coaxed, his tongue caressed. Against her stomach, she felt the hard length of him.

Andie fought like mad to avoid succumbing. Mentally, she detached herself from what her body was experiencing. She could not, would not under any circumstances, allow herself to respond.

He pulled away a fraction of an inch. Through labored breaths, he rasped, "Come back to my hotel with me, Andie. Let me make love to you."

Oh, God. Yes, yes, yes, and yes . . .

Well, so much for iron self-control.

"N-no," she managed.

"Come with me anyway," he coaxed softly. Another kiss. M-m-m. "For a drink," he whispered. "I promise I'll be good. We will *nae* do anythin' you don't want to do."

In a dreamlike state, she heard his promise; then the words registered.

Putting her hands to his shoulders, she shoved him away. "And how many teenage boys have said that, and how many teenage girls believed it?"

He smiled down at her, his tropical rain eyes filled with mischief, and desire. "But *you* didna believe it, I'll wager."

"Damn straight, *ah didna*," she mimicked.

"Yer crafty and overprotective brother again?"

"He made me wise beyond my years."

"So where does that leave the likes of me, who wants to make love to the likes of you?"

She tilted her head, giving him a coy grin. Time to go for broke, or the game was over.

"Frustrated?" she quipped. "And maybe hopeful enough to ask me out again?"

*   *   *

"I wish Daddy were still alive! If Daddy were here, you'd never get away—"

"Well 'Daddy' is *dead*, Gloria. Now shut up and do what I told you to do. If your mother's still there when I get home tonight, I'll kick her ass out into the street myself, then have her arrested for vagrancy!"

Brad Bostwick snapped his personal cell phone closed and threw it down on his trim and tidy desk.

That's what he got for marrying the police commissioner's daughter. Nag, nag, nag. *Daddy always this . . . Daddy never that . . . if Daddy were only here . . . Daddy, Daddy, Daddy* until Brad had wanted to shove his fist down his wife's throat.

Shit, the old fart had died four months ago, and his widow had been staying at Brad's house ever since. If it had been up to Gloria, she'd have had the old bat move in with them for good! Her constant presence put a crimp in his style. He always had to be on guard, on his best behavior when his wife's mother was around, and he was damn tired of being "on" all the time. If a man couldn't be himself in his own house, what did that leave him?

Enough was enough—it was time for his mother-in-law to go the hell home. What was the old bag now, eighty? Eighty-five? Why wasn't she in some senior home where they put the worn-out people nobody wanted?

As he tried to calm himself before anyone saw him in this unprofessional and agitated state, he let his angry gaze flit around his office.

Looking at his things, bowling trophies, the photograph of him with the mayor—a few mayors back, of course—his several distinguished service plaques, always made him feel better about himself. He was the best, and had earned his current position. He'd been told that his direct reports admired him for his tenacity and fairness, and sought to emulate him. The fact he'd married the police commissioner's daughter was simply his due and not related in any way to his steady rise within the ranks. Over the years, he'd made sure—damn sure—no scandal was ever attached to his name.

And he intended it to stay that way.

When he noticed that his cell phone had knocked the brass nameplate on his desk slightly askew, he reached to straighten it, but instead picked it up.

COMMANDER BRADLEY R. BOSTWICK. He smiled, using his thumb to wipe away bits of dust and a smudge of some kind. Stupid, unfit cleaning crew.

Carefully, he placed the nameplate on his desk so it aligned with the corner perfectly, and was the first thing anyone saw when entering his office.

Standing, he went to the narrow, but nearly full-length mirror on the wall next to his locked filing cabinet. He raised his head, squared his shoulders, sucked in his gut. Hell, not half bad for fifty-five. Yeah, there was that little bald spot at the crown of his head, but the comb-over pretty much took care of that. Women still came on to him, all the time, as a matter of fact. Gloria should be damn lucky she had him, and that he had remained relatively faithful over the course of their twenty-something-year marriage.

He looked himself in the eye. Now that her old man was dead, maybe it was time to move on, get himself one of those trophy wives. Gloria was okay, but really, didn't he deserve better?

If he left her, he knew what people would say, that he was shallow or unappreciative, but he was neither. He was deep, very deep, and he did appreciate Gloria. Hell, she'd been a good wife, he had no complaints. She'd given him a couple of daughters—who never seemed to be around anymore, the ingrates, but that wasn't Gloria's fault.

He knew the rumors, that he'd only married her to further his career, but that wasn't true. The first time he'd set eyes on her, he'd fallen in love. She'd been a stunner back then, so pretty, sexy even. He'd wanted to marry her, build a life with her.

It was just that she wasn't the beauty she had once been. Time had passed, and she'd grown a little soft around the edges. Makeup, good jewelry, and nice clothes could only take a woman so far. A tiara on a pig didn't change the fact it was a pig.

After all, he had his career, his ambition to think about. Gloria was dragging him down.

He turned sideways to check out his biceps. Flexing, he smiled at the bulge he saw rise beneath the fabric of his white-cotton shirtsleeve. The low-fat diet, working out, lifting weights, running, all kept him trim and in fighting form. And he knew from recent experience, if called upon to do so, he could best a man half his age.

Stretching, he straightened his tie, then returned to his desk. He checked his calendar, then his watch. Almost ten.

He settled back into his chair and let his mind drift a bit. She was beautiful, she was under his command, and she was on her way to his office. Life just didn't get any better than this.

Knowing what he did of her, if he suggested a liaison, she'd knee him in the groin despite the evidence he had in his locked cabinet that would make her toe the line. So he'd keep it businesslike, tell her what he wanted, and instruct her in how to provide it for him.

Very simple, really. He'd make her an offer she couldn't refuse.

He laughed. God, how he loved that line.

When he heard the knock on the door, he sat up straight, inhaled a deep breath, let it out.

"It's open," he said lightly, congenially. It was his way; it was expected. Brad Bostwick, always the courteous professional. He curved his mouth into a smile so she'd see it as soon as she walked in—after she saw his nameplate of course. Inside his chest, his heart beat a little faster.

"We have an appointment, Commander," she said. "At ten?"

He stood. "Come on in, Inspector Darling. Have a seat."

She smiled and took one of the two chairs that faced his desk.

Wow, what a knockout. Too bad he wanted other things from her—at the moment.

"You have a status update for me?"

"Yes, sir," she replied, obviously trying to hide her nervousness and pride at having been called into the great man's presence. "I'm seeing Sinclair again tonight."

"Where?"

"The mansion." She licked her lips, cleared her throat, raised her chin. "He's ostensibly going to perform a séance for me. It'll be my first chance to—"

"How long do you think it'll take to wrap this up?" he interrupted, tapping his tented fingers together. His gaze remained steady on her.

Andrea straightened in the standard-issue office chair. "Well, I really couldn't say, sir. I've only encountered the suspect on two occasions. Not quite enough time to gain his—"

"Did you know," he said, examining the tips of his fingers. "I was the one who recommended to

Lieutenant Eagan that you be assigned to this operation?"

She blinked. "No, sir. I mean, well, thank you sir. This is a great opportunity—"

"And . . . that I expect you to perform to my expectations? Your family has a reputation with this department that is going to be difficult to meet, or exceed."

"Yes, sir. Thank you, sir—"

"Even though you haven't as much undercover experience as many other officers, and even though you have only recently been promoted to detective, I *insisted* you be the one to infiltrate Sinclair's little operation."

The detective sat perfectly still. "Thank you again, sir. I'm flattered."

He smiled. "I appreciate your heartfelt thanks, Inspector, but I'd much prefer a practical demonstration."

She said nothing, but simply stared past his shoulder out the second-story window behind him.

Lifting a pair of reading glasses from the blotter on his desk, he unfolded them and slipped them on. A file lay under his hand. He opened it.

"I would think a police officer of your caliber," he drawled, "with your exemplary record, and certainly one with your ambitions, would have better sense than to have an affair with a fellow police officer."

She blinked like she'd just been smacked in the head with a brick. "I've never . . . what are you talking about?"

He slowly removed his black-rimmed glasses, tapping them against the pale manila folder. "Dylan Jericho. You and he were lovers."

He watched her green eyes go wide. She choked. "What? No sir, that's not true. I would never . . . I mean, we dated once, one date, that's all, back when we were rookies in uniform. Nothing ever . . . I mean, we never—"

"I really don't care if he fucked you or not, Inspector," he said blandly. "All I know is, I have a photograph of you and your coincidentally now-partner wrapped in a passionate embrace, and if you don't follow my instructions to the letter, I'm going to make it public. Any questions?"

Andie sat in shock, unable to speak, let alone ask a question, while Bostwick thumbed through the file, removed an eight-by-ten glossy, and held it up for her to see.

It was a photo of her and Dylan. Of course she remembered that night eight years ago—her one and only date with Dylan Jericho. But how in the hell had Bostwick gotten ahold of a photograph? Who had snapped it, and why?

Her cheeks heated, and her throat seemed too tight for words to form. "I . . . Commander Bostwick, I—"

"You know it's against department regs for officers to have personal relationships, and if you do decide to fly in the face of policy, you must notify the commanding officer."

Finally finding her voice, Andie said, "Well, there was no relationship, sir. We went to dinner one night. One dinner. Nothing came of it. We were just coworkers spending time together. If it somehow had developed into a relationship, I would have made the department aware of it." She cleared her throat. "As for the photograph, that's *not* an embrace. *Sir.* He was helping me into my coat."

Bostwick turned the photo toward himself and gave it a casual perusal, then smirked. "Doesn't look that way to me. And I doubt Internal Affairs—if you'll pardon the pun—would view it any differently . . . if they were to see this."

Andie's stomach had turned sour five minutes ago. Now it curdled. "Why are you showing me this?"

He smiled. "Ah. Now we're getting somewhere. I need your . . . assistance."

"What kind of assistance?"

He set the photo into the file and closed it. "I want Sinclair's balls on a platter, and you're going to give them to me."

"I don't understand. I'm already working the—"

"Whether you find any evidence to support an arrest . . . or not."

Her brows lowered. "Or *not?*"

He snorted. "You disappoint me, Inspector. Here I thought you were supposed to be so smart, but you're just another bimbo looking to get ahead using her tits and ass instead of brains. Well, I'm not really surprised." He pinned her with a direct stare. "What I'm saying is, if you can't *find* any evidence on Sinclair, *manufacture* it. Now, have I made myself clear?"

"You're blackmailing me into framing a suspect?"

"I didn't say that. I never said that. *You* said that."

"But what you're implying—"

"I need a quiet, subtle helper in this, Inspector Darling." He shrugged, sat back in his chair. "And, tag, you're it. Now, what do you say?"

Gathering herself, her wits, what little there was left of her composure, she said, "I'll go myself to Internal Affairs and file a complaint against you."

"No. You won't."

There was something in the way he said it, the confidence, the certainty, that kept her from leaping out of her chair and making a break for the door. She watched as he pulled a second file from underneath the first. Resting his folded hands on it, he said, "Your brother, former SFPD detective Ethan Darling. He raised you, didn't he?"

Ethan? What did her brother have to do with any of this? Unsure where Bostwick was headed, she said, "Obviously you already know the answer to that question."

"Indeed I do. And you pretty much worship the ground he walks on. Maybe would even do anything it took to save his reputation?"

"His reputation doesn't need saving. He was an exemplary police officer, both in uniform and as a detective. And his security firm, Paladin Private Investigations, is well respected. His clients—"

"Would be astonished to learn he's a murderer."

The air between them grew heavy and thick. Inside Andie's head, her brain stalled. Inside her body, her lungs refused to take in air. She stared at Bostwick across his desk, at the glimmer in his eyes, the look of triumph on his face.

"That's why he left the department so abruptly," he said lightly. "That's why his files have been sealed. All very hush-hush. But I found out anyway. Knowledge is power, and I do so love getting my way."

Andie jumped to her feet, her hands clenched tightly at her sides. "What in the hell are you talking about! Ethan never . . . he would *never*—"

"Sit. Down. Inspector," he bit out. "Or the whole deal is off."

Her knees trembling, Andie glared down at Bostwick, then silently eased back into her chair.

"Obviously, he's never shared this tidbit with his baby sister. And why would he? Should this become public knowledge, your beloved brother's stellar reputation both in the department and in the private sector would be shot to shit. He'd lose face, his business would go belly-up, he'd go broke. The shame and disgrace would damage him forever, not to mention the departmental superiors who aided him in his little cover-up. But you have the power to keep that from happening."

Raising her head, she glared at him. "I don't believe it. Where's your evidence?"

He patted the file. "Didn't you ever wonder why your brother left the department at the height of his career? Didn't you ever wonder why the death of a police officer during a hostage negotiation he was in charge of made barely a wrinkle in the press? In the last six years, has he ever given you a plausible explanation for leaving the SFPD so abruptly?" Another lift of the shoulder. "He murdered a fellow cop. Shot her . . . yes, *her* . . . in cold blood to keep their affair quiet. I have the ballistics report right here if you'd like to see it."

Reaching into the file, he pulled out a piece of paper and flapped it in front of Andie's face. Through blurred eyes, she read as much of the report as she could.

It was true; everything Bostwick said was true.

He laid the report back inside the file and closed it. "Just be thankful I don't want sex from you, Andie. That would be way overstepping my bounds, and there are just too many ways you could entrap me. Making you my factotum is quite good enough for me. For now. You *are* very beautiful . . ."

Her fingers gripped the armrests on the chair as she sat motionless, stunned at this turn of events. She needed time to think, to process what was happening, and to figure a way out of it. She needed to talk to Dylan, warn him. She needed to see Ethan, to find out what had really happened . . .

"I can see those wheels turning, Inspector," Bostwick chided. "So let me add that, what we're having today is a onetime conversation. We will never speak of it again, so don't bother wearing a wire in the future. I do have eyes and ears everywhere, so trying to find an ally will prove fruitless and possibly fatal to your career—not to mention Jericho's, as well. And I understand your brother Ethan recently married a rather high-profile woman. Can you imagine what that kind of scandal would do to *her* reputation, not to mention your brother's future happiness?"

She wanted to vomit.

She wanted to crawl to the door and go off into a corner like a wounded animal and hide, heal, process all this shocking information.

She wanted to pull out her .38 and blow Bostwick's dick off.

Apparently sensing victory, the commander tented his fingers and tapped his chin.

"Tell anyone about this, and I'll take you down with me. But hey, try to look at the bright side. With my help, you can rise very quickly indeed, get promoted into Homicide in record time. Cross me, and you'll not only ruin your own life but the lives of everyone you care about. Trust me. I can do it."

Past her fury and helplessness, Andie found her voice. "What if I leave this office and go straight to Internal Affairs—"

"I'll deny everything." He tapped her file with a thick index finger. "A picture is worth a thousand words. That shot of you and your partner, innocent though you claim it to be, will put doubt in some minds. There will be a chink in your armor, and I'll make sure there are others. Your highly anticipated career as an SFPD detective will never manifest." He took in a deep breath. "Now. Get me what I want on Sinclair."

She pushed herself to her feet and walked to the door. Over her shoulder, she said, "What if he's innocent? What if there is no evidence—"

"I. Don't. Care." Bostwick's tone was measured, soft, and unmistakably lethal. "Do as I ask, or suffer the consequences."

Her numb fingers curled around the knob. She

opened the door, stepped into the threshold. As she tried to remember which way it was to the women's room, behind her, Bostwick said cheerily, "Oh, and you be sure and have a nice day, Inspector. Please close the door on your way out."

Chapter 7

Keep your fears to yourself but share your courage with others.

Robert Louis Stevenson

Andie went through the rest of the morning in stunned silence. If Bostwick had taken out a revolver and put a bullet between her eyes, she could not have felt more brain-dead. She spoke only when spoken to, and then only in grunts and nods. She shuffled the papers on her cluttered desk, stacked them, restacked them. The words and numbers on the forms in front of her made no sense, refused to come into focus. Finally, in total frustration, she lifted her head to gaze around the precinct floor, cluttered with desks and people, computers, phones, filing cabinets, and chatter. The scent of stale coffee and burnt microwave popcorn assaulted her nose.

Even though her fellow officers seemed to be engrossed in working at their desks or standing in groups bullshitting, one of them *could* be watching her, victimized, as she had been, into doing Bost-wick's bidding.

How many police officers had he coerced? How many cops did he have in his pocket?

She licked her lips. What would be the price for defying him—and who would pay it?

Though she tried to remain calm, she was certain everyone in the room would view everything she did as suspicious. She felt like a sane person who'd been locked in a mental institution—no matter what she did, it would be perceived as the actions of a lunatic.

When Inspector Wright moseyed by her desk and asked to borrow a pen, her body jerked in response, and she nearly shot out of her chair. Though he arched a bushy brow and smiled, Wright made no comment but must have wondered at her nervous behavior.

She swallowed, trying to moisten her dead, dry throat.

Damn, this was no good. She had to get out of there, find a place where there would be no hidden cameras or wires. The safe haven of her precinct had become a terrorists' landscape where everyone and everything suddenly had the power to strike a fatal blow. The casual camaraderie of her fellow officers became suspect. Bostwick had warned her there were others. Had it been a ploy to keep her under his thumb? Or was it the awful truth?

As she considered her next move, a slow, cold fury started to edge up her spine. She felt her heart rate elevate, her stomach tighten. Her jaw clamped down so hard, her teeth hurt.

How dare Bostwick do this to her? How dare the son of a bitch reach into her life and twist it so painfully, make her doubt her fellow officers, jeopardize her partner's career, threaten to ruin her brother?

He had no right . . . *none*. She had to find a way to out the bastard . . .

But what if nailing him meant he'd use that stupid photo against her? Though she knew it was innocent, it was definitely open to interpretation. And if he went public with the findings of Ethan's ballistics report? There was no way Ethan had murdered someone in cold blood, but she needed to talk to him, find out what happened, and make sure he was safe before she made a move against Bostwick.

And if she did find a way to expose the SOB, how many other officers besides her would he try to take with him on the way down? Would she be destroying innocent lives if she exposed his treachery?

She stared at her computer screen but might just as well have been staring into outer space.

So, okay, she takes Bostwick down. Where was

her guarantee he'd be held accountable? He'd been a cop a hell of a lot longer than she had. He was well-known, powerful. By all accounts, he had a spotless record. What if nobody believed her, and she trashed her career, and Dylan's and Ethan's and God only knew who else's . . . for *nothing*?

A string of curses rolled through her head, but instead of giving them voice, she rose from her chair, shrugged into her suede jacket, and headed for the door. If anyone followed her, fine. Let 'em. She needed to walk, think, get organized, make a plan.

As she pushed through the double doors leading to the parking lot, she glanced at her watch. Damn. She had to meet Sinclair at the "haunted" house in less than two hours.

And wasn't that a whole other kettle of fish. Why was Bostwick so bent on collaring Sinclair, even to the point she was supposed to manufacture evidence in order to make the charges stick? She'd already figured that the Scotsman was guilty of something, or they wouldn't be investigating him, but the idea of fabricating lies didn't set well at all. If he *was* guilty, she'd find the supporting evidence and make her case to the DA and that would be that.

A couple of uniforms nodded and said something to her as she passed them, but she only mumbled a greeting and kept walking. She needed to talk this over with someone she could trust, with no prying eyes around.

She looked at her watch again. Not enough time to do anything right now. She had to go home and get all gussied up to meet Sinclair, then get over to the mansion by four. He had her cell phone number, but didn't know where she was staying or what she did with herself during the day. He probably figured she spent her leisure hours shopping, which was fine. Tonight, she'd get as close to him as she could without getting burned. Maybe he'd share a secret or two. Maybe he'd ask her for money, or make an outrageous claim he had no way of backing up. She'd be wearing a wire . . .

Pulling her cell phone from her pocket, she punched in Dylan's number.

"Jericho."

One date. She'd had one lousy date with him, and look where it had led.

"Yeah," she said, trying to hide her anxieties. "I'm supposed to be at the house at four. You gonna be ready?"

Pause. Then, "What's the matter?"

Damn the man. Not only did he have cop's eyes, he apparently had cop's ears as well. "Nothing. We can talk about it later. You going to be ready to go, or do I have to do all the work myself?"

He snorted a laugh. "Don't get your knickers in a knot. I'll be there." Silence for a moment. "You sure you're okay?"

"Absolutely." As she was about to disconnect, she stopped herself. "Hey, Jericho?"

"Yeah?"

"Remember that so-called date thing we had a few years back?"

"Like I could forget it." He sighed. "It was the highlight of my misspent youth, babe."

"Right, hotshot," she drawled, trying to sound normal, as though her emotions weren't as brittle as shards of glass. "Listen, I have a question. I was reading over some regs, you know, for fun, and I got to wondering . . . do you think we should have reported it? The date thing? I mean, it was only one dinner, and nothing happened . . ."

"You were reading regs for *fun*?" he interrupted. "Shit, your life's even more boring than mine."

"Yeah. Right. Anyway, do you think it matters now, eight years later? I mean, the fact we ended up partners? You don't think anyone would misinterpret that, do you?"

An uncomfortable quiet ensued for a moment, and Andie sensed a shift in Dylan's attitude. "Misinterpreted? Uh, as what exactly?"

"As . . . well, as fraternizing."

He cleared his throat. Casually, he said, "Well, I don't see how. Everybody knows what a ruthless, ambitious, coldhearted, sexless, calculating bitch you are. You'd never do anything to ruin your shot at Homicide."

"Ah, you're just saying that to make me feel better." She lowered her head and smiled.

"Hey, you sure you're okay?"

"I'm good," she lied. "See you at four."

When Logan arrived at the mansion, he parked next to Andie's car. He felt the bonnet; still warm. She had arrived only a few moments ago.

Where was she staying? he wondered. At dinner the other night, she'd been evasive, not speaking of her family, her origins, or what she did during the day to keep herself busy. She was obviously well-heeled, but even wealthy women often held jobs. Perhaps she spent her days devoted to various charities. No, that didn't fit. She'd want to *do* something, make her mark.

The lights were on in the foyer, and the front door stood slightly ajar. A cold mist swirled around the house, lending it a bleak, atmospheric mood. Perfect for the night's events. She wanted a séance; he'd give her one. Since he didn't know a thing about her, and hadn't had time to do a background, he'd be vague. He'd cast out some prattle, and she'd put a personal spin on it. They all did, that's what made his job so easy.

Years ago, when he'd established that Logan Sinclair was a clairvoyant-for-hire, he'd learned quickly how he could use it to get what he wanted, how eager his clients were to believe, how willing they were to fill in the blanks.

"A man who once broke your heart wishes you

to know he's sorry," he'd say, and his client would respond, "Oh, it must be Ricardo! Yes, he broke my heart, the cad!" Or, "A female relative stays close by, watching over you," and his client would affirm, "It's got to be my great-aunt Tildy. I was always her favorite. Oh Mr. Sinclair, you are so good at this. You've eased my troubled mind. Come, I will tell you where I keep all my valuables, then we can have sex!"

Though the offer of a tumble was always enticing, he never indulged himself; it was learning the whereabouts of those valuables that put the spring in his step and offered the biggest reward.

As he reached the porch, he shoved hands into the pockets of his brown-leather bomber jacket. Peeking inside the house, he saw the foyer was empty except for her handbag sitting on the little table in the center. With a quick motion, he rapped his knuckles on the door. "Anybody here call for an extra large haggis pizza?"

A choking sound came from down the hall, followed by footfalls on the marble floor.

She appeared from around the right side of the staircase, and his heart both eased and constricted at the sight of her. As she walked toward him, he took in her long legs encased in faded blue denims. Her silk blouse was blue, too, but more the color of a clear spring sky. Around her hips, she wore a narrow black belt that matched her high-heeled boots.

But it was her face that captured his attention and would not let go. Was it possible she'd gotten more beautiful since the last time he'd seen her, or were his eyes simply starved for another look at her?

The smile she gave him didn't reach her eyes. "If it's a haggis pizza yer bringing me, laddie, you can turn back around and head fer the *Hielans*."

He closed the door behind him, his gaze never leaving her face. Something was wrong. While her lips curved, the lines around her mouth were thin and tight. Her normally rosy complexion was pale, and her lovely eyes held a stark look to them, reminding him of a hunted animal.

"That's a mighty fine brogue you've got there, lass," he said slowly, "if ah do say so m'self."

She shrugged. "Let's just get on with it, okay? This place gives me the creeps." Rubbing her arms, she whirled on her heel and headed back down the hall. Over her shoulder, she said, "Walk this way."

I wouldn't, even if I could, he thought, his gaze glued to the sway of her hips.

He followed her to what obviously was the library, a cavernous place where volumes stood in parallel rows, tightly pressed together like dominoes in a box. The scent of wood polish, old paper, and faded roses met his nose in a familiar and not-altogether-unpleasant way. Red, brown, and black bindings covered books both large and small, thick and thin, their gilt-embossed titles timeworn to a dull chrome. On an oak pedestal next to the fireplace sat a globe of the world in relief as it had been perceived to be a hundred years ago, its mountain peaks now eroded to mere bumps, its continents and oceans dulled to contrasting shades of parchment. Heavy floral drapes had been pulled across the three tall windows at the far end of the room.

Andie stood in front of the library table, her hands folded, waiting. He stepped across the threshold into the room . . . and he knew.

Feeling the breath go out of his lungs, his step faltered, and he made a grab for the nearest chair.

It was still here, that thing that had happened in this room, absorbed into the walls, reflected in the mirror over the fireplace, echoing like a heartbeat . . .

A soft humming began inside his head. And as he had since that fateful summer he'd turned nineteen, he clenched his jaw and blocked it.

Andie stepped toward him, said something to him. He could see her lips move, but the humming in his ears drowned out her words. He shook his head, hoping to rid himself of the noise. Pulling in a breath, he willed the assault be gone.

Dammit, not now.

She said something else, placed her palm on his arm, laughing. Then her expression changed to concern, and she spoke again. But her words came from too far away for him to comprehend.

He tried to keep the room in focus, but it was growing difficult. Objects around him lost their hard edges, hues and tones bled into each other like a child's watercolor. His heartbeat pounded against his eardrums. The hums turned to whispers . . .

He was losing control . . . needed to get out . . . get the hell out . . .

Logan? He searched her eyes. Had Andie spoken his name, or had it come from the ether? Staring at her, he didn't know how to answer.

Her lips moved. *Are you all right? Would you like some water? Logan? Can you hear me?*

Logan . . . hear me . . . tell her . . . tell her to help . . . 'tis only she can help . . . tell her . . .

His dry throat constricted painfully around the words he had to speak.

"I . . . so sorry," he choked, "to *cowp yer hurlie, lass* . . ."

Then the darkness closed in. Blind to the room and the woman standing before him, he lost his balance and tumbled forward. Someone called his name. Andie? Or the other?

The chair he'd been gripping crashed against the hardwood floor. A glass spilled, and he heard liquid splash onto the table behind her. Arms came around him, easing him to the floor. Behind his closed lids, the faces came. Their mouths made shapes, opened and closed, and he heard their words. The humming in his brain turned to buzzing, like a hornet's nest he'd disturbed. Clamping his hands over his ears, he tried to shut out the cacophony, but it only grew louder, more insistent.

Logan . . . tell her . . . tell her . . . 'tis none but she can help . . . tell her . . .

"*Nae*," he rasped. "*Nae.* I willna . . ."

A chasm opened, light spilled through. Disembodied fingers beckoned, tugged . . . pulled at him . . . and he fell . . .

Chapter 8

There is but one art, to omit.

Robert Louis Stevenson

On the phone, Ross's voice sounded skeptical.

"Are you sure of it, Logan? You say they spoke to you, did they? And you're positive?"

"Do you doubt it, Father! Take the Glasgow Road, I tell you. You'll be safe. You'll all be just fine—"

"They insisted, you say?" he interrupted, his deep voice, generally so confident, surprisingly hesitant. "The Glasgow Road, Logan. They told you by name, aye?"

Logan blew out an exasperated breath. "Look, Father. Even if they hadn't assured me, I saw it just now on the TV, the storm's moving off to the west, intensifying. You can avoid the worst of it by heading east on the Glasgow Road. It'll get you down the mountains and into Edinburgh in under an hour. I'll meet you at the Witchery on the Royal Mile, as planned. C'mon," he urged. "'Tis my birthday, and I'm in a mood to celebrate! You're not going to let some blashie storm keep you from dinner with yer only mac?"

His father sighed, and Logan knew he'd won. "Ah, but y'er spoilt, Logan, my boy," he grumbled. But he chuckled when he said, "Yer mither don't think so, but it's a fact nonetheless."

"Sad but true, Father." He'd laughed. "So you'll come on then?"

"Aye. We're on our way."

"I promise you, they said 'twas safe and no doubt of it. When will you learn to trust me? Has my wondrous gift ever sent you wrong . . ."

But Ross had paused a moment, obviously still uncertain. The storm of the century raged across the UK, washing out roads, downing power lines, flooding both narrow village lanes and vast fields of yellow rapeseed, making many thoroughfares inaccessible. Only fools ventured forth in such a tumult—unless they'd been promised safe passage by the powers that be.

Logan's studies at university had been a bore of late, the early-spring weather had been dreary, and his girlfriend had recently bolted—accusing him of being too good-looking, too rich, and too self-involved to love any woman more than he loved himself. He'd liked her well enough, and her words had stung more than he was prepared to admit, so he'd viewed his upcoming birthday as an excuse to break out of his brooding. His ever-doting family had promised to meet him in Edinburgh for their annual celebration of the birth of the family's only son, and Logan could see no excuse for a bit of bad weather to spoil the festivities.

"Meet up with you in an hour then, lad," Ross Sinclair promised, then hung up the phone . . .

Inside his head, Logan heard that final click of the receiver. It echoed across time, leaving a turbulent silence that beat against his eardrums like the fists of an angry mob; the violent quiet of the years rolling by like they do, not caring that a grief-stricken boy stood alone against them as they passed. They came and went, the years, adding one to another, until a mountain of time lay behind him, and the callous boy grew into a man so devoid of emotion as to be hollow—to be simply the container where the echoes lived.

As the memories began to fade, Logan felt the familiar sting behind his closed lids. The stabbing agony of unshed tears—tears he'd doggedly refused to shed. For fifteen years, he'd held them at bay. He'd hold them off forever, if need be. The pain reminded him of what he'd done—and who it was paid the price for his youthful arrogance and conceit.

So damn full of himself he'd been. So careless, cocky . . .

And wrong. Dead wrong.

After that day, he'd shut his humanity behind a wall of angry grief, self-doubt, numbing pain. After that day, he'd shunned the voices, the *knowing,* and began struggling against his powers, shutting them down, boxing them in, fearful of hurting anyone else, of ever forgetting what he'd done— and terrified he'd discover a way to absolve himself of his crimes, and forgive . . .

No man deserved absolution less.

While his pride had indeed been a cardinal sin, instead of destroying *him,* as it should have done, it had punished those he loved by taking them— leaving him in the world to ponder his transgressions, and pay for his hubris with vile loneliness and ever-abiding guilt.

"Logan?"

Andie, it was. Her voice soft, gentle, filled with concern. He imagined he lay in her bed, her arms around him, his tired head on her breast as she offered him sanctuary, a brief respite from his torments.

"Logan?" she repeated. "Are you with me?"

Keeping his eyes closed, he breathed wearily, "Aye, lass."

Warmth surrounded him like a velvet blanket . . .

He eased his eyes open, glanced about, got his bearings.

The two of them were on the floor, his head cradled in her lap as she looked down at him, stroking his hair. Against his will, he smiled at her. She blinked in surprise, then curved her mouth in a half grin. It was as though she glowed from a misty light that emanated from behind her body, making her appear like a golden-headed angel who'd swooped down to catch him, protect him as he'd fallen hard to earth; an angel he'd known all his life, and longer . . .

"So beautiful," he mumbled.

Her smile changed, tilted wryly on one end. "Must have cracked that skull of yours, *laddie*. You're imagining things."

"*Nae*," he whispered. "I am no'."

She averted her eyes for a moment; her cheeks pinked up a wee. Then, "You okay now?"

Instead of answering, he slowly rose into a sitting position, rubbing the back of his neck. With a shrug, he teased, "I'm grateful you caught me, lass. Might have smashed this gorgeous face into an unforgiving piece of furniture. You've done all of womankind a great favor."

She lifted a brow. "I'm not surprised you think so."

Silence lay between them as they looked into each other's eyes. Finally, she straightened her shoulders, took in a breath. "Why'd you faint? Low blood sugar or something?"

"Men don't faint. *Women* faint. Men . . ."

"Swoon?"

"*Och!* A man would rather drop dead altogether than *swoon*."

"How about . . . languish?"

He snorted. "I doubt even Mr. Darcy *languished*. No, lass. Men just black out."

"Because . . ."

He glanced around the room once more, letting his attention settle on the antique globe. Lying through his teeth, he said, "Because maybe they had a wee dram too much the night before and not enough to sleep or eat."

"That what happened to you?"

"Close enough."

She pursed her lips. "Well, if you need sustenance, there's some *Hielan Helper* in the pantry."

Reaching for her, he slipped a lock of her silky hair behind her ear. She stiffened and seemed to hold her breath, but didn't back away.

"You'd whip up a meal for the likes of me? You can cook, can you?"

"If a kitchen has a microwave, then yeah, I can cook." Her brows lowered, and concern showed in her eyes. "This place gives me the jitters, so if you're okay, I'd like to get the hell out of here."

Rising to his feet, he helped her stand. "Gives you the jitters, eh? And well it ought, haunted as it is."

"Right." She brushed dust from her skirt. "Is that your professional opinion?"

Though he shut them out—or tried to—the

voices reached him. Rather, *the* voice. *Her* voice. The one who lived here because she did not know how to move on. She'd spoken to him, desperation sharpening the edges of her words.

He looked down into Andie's eyes and wondered just what to tell her. A story? A myth? Conjecture? Truth?

"There's a woman here," he murmured. "From a long time past. She . . . she seems frantic to reach you, talk to you, tell you something."

Andie's face paled, and she took a small step back from him. "That's ridiculous."

"I might have agreed," he said slowly. "Except, you've seen her, haven't you?"

When she said nothing, he pressed the issue.

"'Tis why you screamed that first night. You saw her, aye?"

She shook her head, turned, and walked away from him. With her back to him, she said, "No. I, uh, I only thought I saw something. A shadow, nothing more. I don't believe in ghosts."

"Yet you're here, wanting to do a séance, wanting me to participate. If you don't believe, then why rent this house, why invite guests, why coerce me to come?"

"I told you," she huffed. "For fun. For kicks. For the hell of it. But I don't believe any of it. Do *you*? Do you *really*?"

"It's my stock-in-trade, lass. I have to."

Her eyes ablaze, she accused, "But you don't believe, not really." Taking a few steps away from him, she crossed her arms over her breasts. "Tell me, Mr. Sinclair, how do you pull off your tricks, exactly? How do you target your clients? What kind of research network do you have that enables you to convince them you're on the level, when it's clear you're not?"

"What makes you think I'm not on the level?"

"Oh, come on! I didn't just fall off the turnip truck. It's all smoke and mirrors, isn't it? What do you get out of it? Money? Inside information? Sex? Come on, Logan, spill it."

She was suddenly furious, and he had no idea why. Her green eyes snapped with irritation, and something else. Something that, if he didn't know better, he'd think was fear. But why would she be afraid of him?

"All right, lass," he said softly. "Since there's obviously no pulling the wool over your eyes, here it is. The truth."

Andie's heart beat so hard, she worried her boobs bounced in time with each pulse.

Sinclair was going to tell her? Just like that? He was going to confess?

Her thoughts went to the wire she wore. Was Dylan receiving the transmission okay? Would whatever Sinclair said be enough to indict? And Bostwick . . . would it assuage his demands, buy her some time while she figured out the best way to bring the SOB down?

"The truth?" she said, tilting her head. "This'll be interesting. Go on."

Sliding his arm through hers, he walked with her toward the library door. As they passed through the threshold, he said, "I could use a good stiff drink. What say we find some cozy spot?"

The Foghorn Tavern, a second-story hideaway on the waterfront, was as intimate a place as they got. A hole-in-the-wall decorated in rich oak and rusty red brick, the place boasted no more than five tiny tables banked against a long window that allowed a view of the Golden Gate Bridge glowing under the light of a full moon.

A soft-spoken barmaid placed their drinks in front of them, lit the candle in the hurricane lamp, then quietly departed. As soon as she'd gone, Logan raised his scotch and tapped the edge of Andie's glass of white zinfandel.

"To the truth," he said. Taking a sip of the whisky, he winked at her. "The whole truth."

She lifted her glass of wine, studied the blushing liquid, but did not drink. "And nothing but the truth?"

"Aye." He took another sip, then set his glass on the table. "You start."

"*Me* start? This was about you, *boyo*."

"But your truth would be far more interesting. Where were you born? What's your family like? What'd you like best about school? Who'd you vote for in the last election? Would you ever like to visit another planet? Have you ever been in love?"

She set her glass on the table. "Well, you certainly have a way of cutting right to the bone, don't you? I guess I could ask you the same questions, but I'm more interested in your so-called work. Why don't we begin with that? How'd you get your start in the séance business?"

Leaning back in his chair, he said, "Came with the soul, I guess you'd say. Born with it, the *knowing*, as I call it. I heard voices. Didn't think much of it; thought all kids heard voices until I said something about it one day and discovered it was a rare thing—and considered suspicious by most. Apparently there are those who believe anything paranormal is the work of the devil, yet those same people who believe God created *every*thing, exclude from *every*thing the things they don't like or understand, including the ability to hear voices. Needless to say, I've always been confused by the paradox, or dichotomy, if you will."

"What did these voices say to you?"

"Mostly told me they wanted to help."

Andie eyed him thoughtfully. "Help? Help who? Help what?"

"Help me to help people. Sad people, mostly. Confused people. They told me most people were in a world of hurt, and my gift would be a comfort."

With a slight tilt of her head, she said, "And has it been a comfort?"

"No. When I was nineteen, I shut it off. Don't hear the voices anymore, at least, I try not to. But I still sense things, whether I choose to or not."

"You're not making this up, are you." Furrowing her brow, she said, "You really are telling me the truth."

He sent her a smile filled with charm and promise. "Aye. So far as it goes."

"What does that mean?"

"What that means is, by the time I'm done telling you my long, sad tale, you'll be so distressed, you'll want to comfort me."

"And that comfort would take the shape of . . ."

"Coming to bed with me. It's what I've wanted since I met you. You've wanted it, too, so don't deny it."

Typical male. They were getting off her track and onto his. She needed to redirect the conversation.

"What exactly do the voices tell you?"

He assessed her for a moment, took a sip of his drink. "I have a spirit guide," he said. "The voices, the information, is focused through him mostly. Say you lose a memento, something important to you. You call me, I come to your house, contact Allister and ask him where it is. He tells me, you recover said object, then pay me a lot of money for helping you."

"But if you shut off the voices at nineteen, as you say, how is it you can hear Allister?"

He paused for a moment, cleared his throat. With downcast eyes, he murmured, "I want to."

"I'm not sure I believe you."

A shrug. "Your choice."

"I can't reconcile what I know to be true with what you've just said. You claim you actually talk to dead people—"

"Only Allister. And he's not dead."

"But you said—"

"Spirits never die. Souls never die. Our bodies die, but that elusive something that makes us who we are, lives on. So, in essence, Allister is very much alive. I just can't see or touch him."

Lifting the wineglass to her lips, she took a long swallow, then set the glass down on the table. "This is all very creepy, Logan, and a little unsettling. You seem so normal, but this . . ."

"Believe what you will, Miss Devon. You saw a *ghaist* in that house, and it's no use denying it. You saw her, but can't hear her. I can hear her, but I can't see her. I wonder why that is?"

"There's no ghost! That's *ridiculous*." In one long gulp, Andie downed the remainder of her wine. "You can claim to see or hear anything you want, but I don't have to buy it. That was a nice story you just told me, about you and Allister, but there's more to it, isn't there? Some . . . angle you've got going. C'mon, out with it, Logan. I'm not buying your BS, so you may as well tell me."

Across the table, he grinned at her. Softly, he said, "And what if there was more to it, and what if I was to share that with you? What would you do with that information, Miss *Devon*? You haven't exactly been on the up-and-up with me now, have you?"

Warning bells. Time to shift the conversation. "What's it mean to *cowp yer hurlie*?"

"What?"

"You said it to me, just before you fainted."

"I repeat—blacked out. It means to spoil somebody's good time."

"Yeah, well, I don't want to *cowp yer hurlie*, either, pal, but if you're not going to level with me, I'm calling it a night. Thanks for the drink—"

As she began to rise from the table, Logan said, "Her name is Emma."

Andie froze in place, her purse strap halfway up her arm. "Whose name is Emma?"

"The woman trying to contact you. Emma Harte."

"I've . . . I've never heard of such a person. My ancestors were all named . . . uh, I mean, there are no Hartes in my background."

"All the same. Her name was Emma Harte, and she died on April 18, 1906."

Andie slid back down into her chair. "That's the date of the earthquake and fire," she whispered. "Are you saying . . . just what in the hell *are* you saying?"

Logan raised his tumbler to finish off the whisky. Over the rim of the glass, he eyed her. Then, "I don't know exactly. Only that she died, but her spirit lives on in that house and she has something to tell you. You specifically. Something very important. Something she's been waiting a hundred years to tell. Question is, are you brave enough to listen?"

Chapter 9

Each has his own tree of ancestors.

Robert Louis Stevenson

Andie doubled her fists and punched her pillow, trying to knock Logan's words out of her head.

Smack!

He lied. He *had* to have lied. He made it all up, suckered her in, the smug son of a bitch. The con man. The carpetbagger. Criminal. Felon. Wicked-sexy malefactor . . .

Smack!

She let out an angry grunt, then pinched her eyes tightly shut.

Go away, her mind commanded. *Get out of my head. Don't make me doubt everything I've ever believed. Don't make me challenge what I know and pit it against what I feel, don't want to feel, what you're making me feel. Don't force me to examine my carefully ordered world. I might have to change it, and* that I will not do.

Slam . . . punch . . . smack!

On her stomach, she rested her weight on her elbows, bowing her weary head, letting Logan's words play through her brain once more.

. . . Emma Harte . . . spirit lives on in that house, and she has something to tell . . . you specifically . . . very important . . . waiting a hundred years to tell . . . brave enough to listen . . .

. . . listen . . .

. . . listen . . .

No damn way. Oh, he was good, all right. He "blacks out," then awakens with some cock-and-bull story about a hundred-year-old ghost that she could only "see" and he could only "hear." Uh-huh. Right.

He'd "go under" again and give her the full story on Emma Harte—for a price. True, he hadn't hit her up for sex or money yet, but it was only a matter of time. She knew he wanted the first and suspected his real goal was the second, but if he could take her for both, why the hell not?

Rolling onto her back, she let her head sink deeply into the pillow. Maybe Bostwick had been right; maybe if she couldn't get the goods on this seductive con man, she should manufacture them. After all, he *was* conning her, wasn't he?

On her way home, she'd contacted Jericho; he'd gotten the whole episode on tape. Problem was, Sinclair hadn't asked for anything, hadn't done anything illegal.

Well, he would. It was just a matter of time.

She took in several deep breaths and blew them out slowly, trying to recover her composure. Sleep. She needed a good night's sleep so she could attack this whole situation with a clear head tomorrow.

Sleep. Yeah, that was the ticket . . .

Sleep . . .

Perchance to dream . . .

Andie felt her world melt away. Her muscles relaxed, her lids closed. It was coming on her again, and she let it, opening her mind as she drifted into another time, another place . . .

And so I'm Mrs. Jacob Harte now, and damn pleased for it—despite the rude behavior my new husband forced upon me on our wedding night.

And wouldn't it have been a kindness afore-hand, had some knowing female shared with me the perils of the marriage bed!

After the deed was done, and my shame had started to thin as anger took its place, I had my say at last.

"Well you might have taken a bit more care with me, Jacob!" I cried, shoving his sweaty self off me and gathering the bedclothes up to cover me diddies.

He looked a bit sheepish but had smooth words at the ready. "I'm sorry," says he. "I knew it would hurt you, but I thought you understood what was to happen—"

"And how would I be knowin' that!" I snapped. "I've seen cows and horses in the fields, dogs in the streets, but all seemed willin' and none in pain, so far as I could tell!"

I sat up, glaring down at him, his eyes gone all sleepy now after he'd taken his pleasure and left me sore and suffering.

"Was it all bad?" *His beautiful eyes looked worried.*

"Not all. What led up to the thing was very nice indeed," *I admitted.* "The touchin' and kissin' and that. Why'd you have to spoil it by jammin' yer pole into me like you was tryin' to reach tomorrow?"

He scratched his jaw with his knuckles. "Because that's how it's done, Em. Didn't your mother ever tell you—"

"Ain't got no ma, and haven't had these long years. All the womenfolk in me family are sittin' back on the Old Sod, and none here to be tellin' me the ways of men and women."

Jacob nodded, then eased himself up next to me and slid his arm around my shoulders, gentle-like and cozy. "I'm sorry, Em. It'll be better next time—"

"Ain't gonna be no next time, and that's a fact!

I don't care if it is how you get babbies, I ain't gonna let no man prod and jab at me like a side of prime beef for sale down on Market Street!"

He scooted closer, nibbling my neck. Them little chills come back, the chills that felt so good when he'd been playing with me before. The little chills that made me think lying with my husband wouldn't be such a bad thing, like them women I'd heard snickering and gossiping behind the dry goods down at the mercantile.

He kept on with his kissing and them little chills kept on skittering down my spine, and all the way down, warming me secret place that had so recently been burnt by his own rough thrusting.

He tugged the bedclothes from my fists, exposing my diddies again. Gently, he cupped one in his large hand.

"C'mon, Emma," he coaxed. "I promise it won't hurt so much after a while." He kissed all along one shoulder and across to t'other, and my anger and resentment began to work its way from my heart. "C'mon. Here, you lie down, and I'll take care of everything. I won't go into you this time, but I'll make you feel good. Maybe make you change your mind about . . . things." His head moved lower, his mouth teasing and biting my tittie, and I swear, them chills numbed my body, so I did have to lie down and let him have at it.

He'd promised not to hurt me again, and I knew

it was a lie, had to be. Nothing that could feel so awful one time could feel good the next.

Still, I loved him, wanted to please him, and if lying stock-still and stiff as a sidewalk plank while he did the dirty deed would make him happy, then I'd clench my teeth, curl my fists, and submit.

"I was too anxious," Jacob confessed as he cradled himself between my lazy thighs. "Should have taken more time. It was selfish of me. I was eager to have you. I'll take care and won't make that mistake again."

I close my eyes. "No matter." I sigh in resignation. "I'm ready. Shove it in and be done with it then."

He chuckles, and I remember how much I love the sound of his laughter. "Not this time. Here, do you like this?"

"Oh!" Well now, that wasn't half-bad.

"And this?"

I suck in a breath and hold it. "I do. Yes. Can you do that bit again, please."

He does, and I let loose with a shaky kind of moan. Then I squirm, unable to stop m'self.

"And what about this?"

"Aye," I breathe, nearly incapable of speaking. "That's especially nice, Jacob, and . . . oh! Oh my! Oh dear God . . . so is that what that little nubbin is for?"

"It is," he murmurs. "Want me to stop?"

"No!" Why, I'd kill him if he did, God's honest

truth! First he tears me up with pain, then he gives me a pleasuring to the point of daftness, and he threatens to stop? I swallow, trying to catch my breath. "I mean, please, carry . . . oh, my . . . yes, like that . . . just like . . . oh, Jacob! Oh!"

Spasms of pleasure the likes of which I've never known overcome me, and my hips writhe and twist against my husband's hand. While I'm still panting and sighing, I feel him push a bit inside me, but only a little, not like before to where it hurt. Truth be told, it feels more acceptable than before, maybe even a little exciting, but he holds himself away, making a choking sound as though he's carrying a load of bricks on his back too heavy for a man to bear.

When I open my eyes again, Jacob stares down at me, a smug, pleased look about him.

"Better?" he asks, though I suspect he knows the answer, or he wouldn't have asked the question.

I cannot help but smile. "Indeed," says I. "Is that more the way of it then?"

"It is," he says, mimicking my brogue. "I love you, Emma Harte."

I throw me arms about him and hug him as tears burn my eyes, and I think my poor heart will break. "And I love you, Jacob. Tell me, promise me, will you, that we can stay this way forever. Promise me we can keep the bad times away, keep the sorrows of the world at an arm's reach. Tell me we'll have this, have each other, forever and always."

"Forever and always, Emma. I promise."
"Forever and always?"
He smiles into my eyes. "And always . . . and always . . ."

Andie awoke, tears streaming down her face and into her ears. Damn, she hated when that happened.

Bolting upright, she cursed Logan Sinclair. She shook her head, then grabbed at the nightstand for a handful of tissues, wiped away the tears, and blew her nose.

As it had with the previous dream, her heart felt as though it would burst from the sorrow of it all, and she let out a long sob. Such desperate loss, so profound . . . and so personal. Why would she feel the pain so acutely? This bordered on the insane.

Emma and Jacob Harte. Had they been real people, or had Logan planted those names in her subconscious by his so-called revelation? If they had existed, Logan's knowledge of them had certainly been gained by detailed research. If this Emma person had died a hundred years ago the night of the earthquake and fire, Andie could verify the fact just as easily as Sinclair.

But to do it thoroughly, she needed help.

The world as she knew it was teetering by a lunatic thread, and she wasn't sure who to trust anymore. Between Bostwick's blackmail and Logan Sinclair's lies—not to mention her own subconscious mind betraying her—this whole undercover operation had taken a bizarre twist, making her doubt her fellow officers, as well as her own sanity.

Though she'd rather take care of all this on her own, she considered herself wise and mature enough to reach out rather than stumble about blindly in the dark.

Scooping up her cell phone, she blew out a resigned sigh, pressed the autodial, and waited for the call to ring through.

Two hours later, across the table of the back booth at the Gold Nugget Cafe, green eyes that nearly matched her own narrowed in obvious skepticism.

"It's bullshit," Ethan snorted. "Whether Emma and Jacob Harte existed or not, this Sinclair guy is trying to con you, and you know it. Stick to the facts and do your job, Detective."

Always the hard-ass, Andie thought lovingly. Though she adored the eldest of her two brothers, Ethan could be a real snot sometimes.

Next to Ethan, Nate said dryly, "Stop the presses. I may actually agree with big brother here." He set his coffee mug on the table. After a moment's thought, his brown eyes went serious. "If it'll help, I'll ask Tabby to meet with you and try and interpret your dreams. Maybe she can find something significant—"

"Oh, right," Ethan scoffed. "Ever since you married a—you'll pardon the expression, *psychic dream interpreter*—you've really let those investigative skills slide, Inspector Darling."

Ever affable, Nate grinned. "And ever since you married a TV celebrity, your ego's more inflated than ever."

"Eat me."

"Prick."

"Dickhead."

"I can't take you boys anywhere!" Andie huffed. Flicking her gaze back and forth between them, she ordered, "Behave for once, will you?" She half expected them to elbow each other and end up in a tussle on the floor under the table.

The brothers glanced at each other. "She doesn't get it, does she, bro?" Ethan said with a smile.

"Nope." Nate chuckled.

Ethan faced Andie. "It's a guy thing."

Nate reached across the table and patted her hand. "Relax, baby sister. Keep your weapon holstered. We'll be good."

As her brothers returned their attention to their coffee, Andie quietly assessed them over the rim of her own coffee mug. Big, handsome, smart, and if the longing stares that followed them everywhere were any indication, hunky. Former SFPD detective Ethan and current SFPD detective Nate Darling had been at odds with each other for close to twenty years, ever since their parents had divorced and Nate moved away with their dad to Washington state, leaving teenaged Ethan alone to cater to a silly mother and help raise a very young sister.

But in the two years since Nate returned to the Bay area, something had changed between the brothers. From what was at first animosity born of misunderstanding, circumstances over the last several months had tempered their feelings, causing the bond they'd shared as boys to re-form and strengthen. Each happily married with babies on the way, they'd become men who now shared more similarities than differences. They'd each found their paths and were happy in their lives, devoted to the women they'd recently married.

If Andie didn't love them all so much, she'd probably be a little jealous. Still, they were going to make her an aunt twice over in July, so she really couldn't complain.

Okay, Ethan and Nate still chided and teased each other like the lamebrained juveniles they often were, but they seemed to have come to some kind of tacit understanding that when push came to shove, they'd watch each other's backs—or as it turned out a year ago, nearly die trying.

Because in the end, it was all about family.

"We don't have any ancestors named Harte, do we?"

The brothers glanced at each other, then at her, and shrugged.

"I mean, this Emma Harte," she went on. "She

couldn't be a great-grand-something to us, could she?"

Ethan's dark head tilted in thought. "Dad's sister, Aunt Shirley I think it was, did a family tree thing a few years back. No Hartes on it as I recall, and she went back all the way to when the Darlings emigrated from Ireland."

"Well, I think this Emma person is Irish, but Jacob Harte sounds American."

Ethan's gaze snapped to hers. "What do you mean *sounds*?"

Andie blinked. "I—In my dreams. She has an Irish accent, but he doesn't."

Nate straightened. "I still think you should have a session with Tabby—"

"I'll think about it," she lied. Nate might believe his wife was a psychic who could interpret people's dreams, but as much as Andie liked her new sister-in-law, psychic dream interpretation was total hogwash.

"Besides," Ethan said, his sharp green eyes boring into hers, "Sinclair thinks your name is Devon, so he's barking up the wrong family tree, so to speak."

Except for my dreams. I had the first dream before Logan identified the woman by name, so where does that leave me?

Andie wrapped her palms around her mug and peered into the flat surface of her black coffee. "Okay, that's Dad's family. What about Mom's?"

Nate's eyes narrowed as he ran his fingers through his short blond hair. "No Hartes there either. Mom's ancestors were mostly German who settled in Wisconsin and Michigan. Didn't move to California until after the First World War."

"I can run a background, see if there are any stragglers out there," offered Ethan. "I don't see what good it'll do, though."

"Yeah," Andie said, pursing her lips and nodding. "Yeah, why not? Put all that fancy-schmancy high-tech equipment you've got down at Paladin to work on it, would you? At the very least, finding no connection would close that avenue of investigation, and I can stop dwelling on it." Then she remembered . . .

"Oh, and uh, check on the name Emma Conner or Conner's Dry Goods on Van Ness, would you?"

"Why?" the brothers asked simultaneously.

She swallowed, licked her lips. "Uh, well, because, in that first dream, this Emma says something about her father's name being Timothy Conner, and he owns a dry goods store on Van Ness."

When they just stared at her, she charged, "Well, it's worth a shot, isn't it? Besides, with all your rummaging around, you might find something I can use to snare Sinclair."

A silence fell between them all as they sipped their coffees and contemplated their next moves. Finally, Andie finished and set her mug aside.

"There's one more thing I need to talk to you boys about."

Perhaps it was the tone of her voice that alerted them, but both Ethan and Nate raised their heads, waiting, looking at her as though she were about to announce the Second Coming.

"I'm in a bind," she began. "A very uncomfortable, unexpected bind, and the only way I'm going to get out of it is by asking blunt questions and getting straight answers. Okay?"

Solemnly, both Ethan and Nate nodded their consent.

"Okay," she breathed. Lifting her shoulders, she swallowed and straightened her spine.

"Ethan, I'm going to ask you something, and you have to tell me the truth."

"No problem," he said, his eyes burning with curiosity and a hint of trepidation.

"Okay, here goes. Rumor has it that the reason you retired from the SFPD was because you were forced to resign."

Nate's gaze flicked to his brother, then back to Andie. Ethan, however, remained silent, his eyes boring into hers like industrial lasers.

Andie licked her lips again. "Rumor also has it that the reason you resigned when you did was because . . . because . . . Shit, Ethan, did you murder a fellow police officer to cover up an illicit love affair?"

Chapter 10

Give us courage and gaiety and the quiet mind.

Robert Louis Stevenson

It was just past twilight when Logan pulled the Lexus to a stop in the curved drive outside Drew Mochrie's Sea Cliff estate and turned off the ignition. No van. Though he'd decided it might be a good idea to have Ollie present tonight, his partner seemed to be running a bit late.

That was fine. Gave Logan a few moments to collect his thoughts . . . thoughts that had been scattered like the winds to the far corners ever since he'd met Andie Devon.

Blast the woman with her cat's eyes and sassy mouth.

He swiped his freshly shaved jaw with his knuckles.

Andie Devon was beautiful and desirable, and he

wanted her. He'd wanted women before and had usually gotten them, but in Andie's case, he had to wonder—would having sex with her once or twice be enough to satisfy him?

He already knew the answer to that: It would not. This woman was different from all the rest, and the sense of connection he felt when he looked at her or thought of her was what had him staring at the ceiling each night as he tried to sleep. For most of his adult life, he'd not considered himself a one-woman man, but if he did, she could be that woman.

Andie Devon . . . Andie Devon . . . Andie . . . darling Andie . . . Andie, darling . . .

Who was she really? He knew what he saw when he looked at her, but it didn't match what his intuition sensed—*intuition* being his own personal euphemism for the "gift" of clairvoyance.

Gift. An obscenity was more the way of it.

For the first time in fifteen years, he considered lowering his defenses, allowing the voices to speak to him, but quickly rejected the idea. It would only serve to open a room he'd sealed off forever. Through that locked door lay not only madness, but the softer emotions he'd not let himself acknowledge, let alone enjoy.

As Ollie's van pulled up behind the Lexus, Logan flipped open his cell phone and punched in the secure number.

"Mr. Sinclair." The timbre of the woman's voice

was soft, her demeanor crisp and professional. "How may I assist you, sir?"

"How's the weather in London, Jilly girl?"

Her businesslike tone changed not at all. "Rather damp and a bit dodgy, sir. Aside from a weather report, is there anything else you wished?"

"Indeed, lass. I need a thorough background done, if you'd be so kind."

"I'll forward your request. I assume you want the information—"

"Yesterday. Aye."

"Your usual then."

"My usual." He allowed himself a quick smile before his stomach constricted into a hard ball. He should have done this before, as soon as he'd met Andie Devon, but something in him had wanted to trust her—though why he should be so foolish, he couldn't say. He knew she lied as easily as she breathed, and that suspicious part of him wanted to know what she was hiding.

"When you say thorough, sir—"

"I mean use every resource we've got. I want to know it all, from whether she was bottle-fed, to her favorite subject at school, to the name of the first boy she ever kissed. Everything, to right down to her DNA."

"Subject's name?"

"Andrea Devon." Inside his head, he saw her face, and that shocked and wary look in her eyes every time he called her—

"And Jilly my girl, in case you come up empty on Devon," he added slowly, "try this . . ."

He supplied a few more details, then finished the call. As he slipped the cell into his pocket, Ollie tapped on the window, then jerked his thumb toward the Mochrie house, where Drew stood in the threshold wearing a low-cut red dress and a sanguine expression.

Opening his door, he mumbled to Ollie, "Show-time, lad. Twenty quid says I get her to agree and have her baubles in my hands by noon tomorrow."

"Yer on," Ollie snorted. "Even you ain't that good—"

"Yoo-hoo!" Miss Mochrie sang from the porch, one hand fluttering in the air. "I'm ready for you, Logan!"

He flicked a quick glance at Ollie. "Ye hear that, lad?" he muttered. "She's ready for me."

Ollie scowled, as though he'd just seen his twenty quid sprout wings and fly off to the Highlands.

Logan stepped onto the porch. "You look lovely tonight," he said, taking the woman's outstretched hand. Bending his head, he placed a lingering kiss on her knuckles.

"Oh, Logan," she cooed. "I feel confident this evening will prove quite successful."

"I've no doubt of it, ma'am."

With Ollie in the lead, the trio made for the scullery and down to the wine cellar.

"May I take your arm, Mr. Sinclair?" Drew mewled. "I'm feeling a bit weak and need the support of your masculine strength."

"Anything to help ease you through this difficult time," Logan said, taking her hand in the crook of his arm.

Though he couldn't be sure, he thought Ollie snorted.

When they reached the spot where Tolley Mochrie had met his end, Logan took a deep breath, shook out his hands, rolled his shoulders, and tried to give the impression he was opening himself up to contact from beyond.

At his side, Drew Mochrie remained silent for a moment, then leaned toward his ear, and whispered, "When we're done here, Logan, perhaps you and I . . ." She cast a quick glance at Ollie unpacking his camera. "That is to say, just the two of us should go upstairs for a, ehm, nightcap?" She arched a brow and pursed her glossy lips.

"Indeed we can, lass. But first, let us attend to the business at hand." To Ollie, he said, "Ready, lad?"

His camera secured to the tripod, Ollie gave a quick nod. "Aye."

Closing his eyes, Logan let his head fall back. "Allister? Are you there? Can you hear me?" Inside his head, muffled voices tried to make themselves heard. He ignored them. "We call upon the spirit of Tolley Mochrie this night." His eyes still closed, he said, "Miss Mochrie, what is it you wish to say to your brother?"

"Oh, uh, yes." Her tone was impatient. "Well, tell him to move on then. That's all. Just, I don't know, go toward the light, or some such thing. I mean, no reason to linger, is there?"

"No, but—"

"Oh, blast!" she snapped. "Perhaps tonight isn't the best for contacting my late brother. Perhaps we could do this another time, and just go upstairs and have that drink now—"

"What's that, Allister?" Logan boomed over her invitation. "The Star of Avril?"

He opened his eyes, rubbed his temples as though plagued by a sudden headache. In a weary voice, he said, "Tolley is desperate to know whether that necklace is safe. He mentioned it last time, as I recall. He insists on knowing, and seems quite distressed about it."

Miss Mochrie blinked up at him, irritation plain to see in the depths of her calculating eyes. "As I said before, 'tis in a safe-deposit—"

"My dear, your brother insists on seeing it. That is to say, he wants me to see it and report to Allister that it is safe." He shook his head as though in a state of confusion. "Does this necklace have some significance for your brother, other than its pecuniary value?"

The woman came that close to stomping her foot. Crossing her arms under her breasts, her pouting lips turned down into a spoiled scowl. "Oh, but Tolley was always obsessed with the damn thing. Had it insured for a king's sum, he did. Never let me wear it for fear a thief would come along and snatch it. To him, possessing that necklace gave him some kind of credibility in the eyes of society. Or so *he* thought. Bah." Now she did stomp her foot. "Gems like that should be trotted out, displayed on one's décolletage for all to see, not locked away in some dusty bank vault."

"Ah, it makes more sense now," Logan said, nodding his head knowingly. "It seems that your brother will not rest in peace, however, until he's certain it's still in your possession."

Her scowl deepened, her mouth curving into a petulant bow. "And showing it to *you* will suffice, will it?"

Logan shrugged. "That is my understanding. 'Tis not my wish one way or t'other. However, if you agree to let me see it tomorrow, I can reassure your late brother all is well, and you and I can call it a night and go upstairs for that wee dram, if you so desire."

Emphasis on the word *desire*.

She angled her head just so and gazed out into space, apparently making an effort to look seductively indecisive. The effect was one of a woman who'd just fallen off a tilt-a-whirl and banged her head on a post.

"Aye, then," she cooed. Turning on her heel, she

headed for the stairs. "I wish no further communications with my dead brother tonight, but I am thirsty." One stiletto heel on the bottom step, she eased herself around to face Logan. "When you're packed up here, meet me in the drawing room, won't you?" To Ollie, she said dismissively, "'Twas nice seeing you again, lad. Good night."

Ollie shut off his camera and smiled cordially. When she had disappeared up the stairs, he said, "Ah, fock it. Twenty quid it is, then, but only *after* I see the goods."

Logan chuckled and shoved his hands in his pockets.

"Do you think she suspects anything?" Ollie asked, his gaze still on the shadows at the top of the stairs. "What if she gets the necklace from the bank and decides to skip with it?"

As Logan began climbing the stairs, he looked back at his partner and smiled. "She doesn't suspect, and she won't skip. You'll just have to trust me to deliver."

Ollie tilted his head and narrowed one eye. "Given what I know about you? Easier said than done, lad. Easier said than done."

Andie watched as Ethan's eyes narrowed on her. They glittered like shards of green glass, sharp enough to slice flesh clean to the bone.

"What did you say?" His voice was low, lethal,

and if she hadn't known him better, she'd have been afraid. "Where in the hell—"

"Relax, big brother," Andie said, then sat back against the padded seat. "Remember Brad Bostwick?"

Next to Ethan, Nate leaned forward and crossed his arms on the table. "*Commander* Bostwick?" He exchanged confused looks with Ethan. "What's Bostwick got to do with all this?"

Instead of launching into a full explanation, she said, "How much do either of you know about him?"

Ethan shook his head. "*Slick* Bostwick? I know enough to know I never liked the son of a bitch, sure as hell never trusted him. Married the commissioner's daughter and used it to climb the ladder."

Nate nodded. "I agree. He keeps a clean profile, no hint of scandal, nothing touches him. Rumors have persisted for years, but I've never known anybody—"

"Yeah, well, you do now," she said softly.

She raised her gaze to Ethan's. He hadn't answered her question, and in order to bring Bostwick down, she'd have to know the truth about everything. She couldn't risk any more surprises. She had to be prepared with answers for every accusation Bostwick might make. If he attacked, she had to parry, and had to make it stick. "Bostwick is blackmailing me."

Both Ethan and Nate were halfway out of their seats with their fists doubled when she said, "Easy boys. I'll explain in a minute. First . . ."

As Ethan eased himself back down and relaxed his shoulders, she pinned him with her gaze. His chin edged up, his eyes grew wary.

"Bostwick made the claim you murdered a fellow officer, and he has a coroner's report to back him up. I saw part of it. He's using it to coerce me into planting evidence in the Sinclair case. Said he'd go public with the report and ruin both you and me, and by association your famous wife—"

"Georgie knows what happened."

"It doesn't matter. The report appears damning, and he threatened to use it if I didn't help him." She stopped, sucked in a deep breath, squared her shoulders. "So I need to know. Did you do it, Ethan?"

He stared at her for so long, she thought he wasn't going to say anything. It was Nate who broke the silence.

"Hey, bro," he urged gently. "You trusted me. You can trust Andie, too. You know you can. Tell her the truth."

Ethan nodded slowly, looked briefly away, then met Andie's gaze. Suddenly, he looked older, tired, as though some invisible weight he'd been carrying a long time was crushing him.

"It happened over seven years ago." Lowering

his eyes, he continued, "Her name was Cathy Vandermere. She was an SFPD hostage negotiator, and my lover."

"And . . . and you . . . you . . ."

"Yes, Andie. I killed her."

Andie lay awake, her emotions in too much chaos to sleep.

What Ethan had told her . . . what he had *done*. Dear God, how could he live with himself? How could anyone put that kind of thing behind them?

Dammit, Ethan, why didn't you tell me about this Cathy? I would have understood . . . but typical male, he'd kept the torment to himself, the guilt. After everything her brother had done for her, all he had sacrificed to help raise her, and she had a chance to repay him with her love and compassion, but he'd denied her by not confiding in her.

She'd be furious at him if she didn't love and admire him so much.

Men! Men, men, men . . .

She closed her eyes for a moment. Logan Sinclair's handsome face immediately appeared, so she opened them again, doubled her fists, and slammed them into the mattress.

Damn the man. He was a crook, a charlatan, a liar, and a cheat, and maybe worse for all she knew. He deserved to be caught, but Bostwick's demand that she fabricate evidence against him had twisted itself into some bizarre kind of sympathy for Sinclair. Really, she *had* to keep her priorities straight, or this whole thing would blow up in her face.

Besides Ethan and Sinclair and Bostwick, not to mention Dylan Jericho, there was her mother. She hadn't called Mom in days, and with her mother's emotions as frail and flighty as they always were, Andie suddenly felt guilty for just being alive.

Then there were the babies. Nate and his wife Tabitha were expecting a baby in July; Ethan and his wife Georgie were also expecting a baby, also in July, as luck would have it. Her two seemingly forever-bachelor brothers had married within months of each other, and were now about to become daddies, while Andie . . .

She scrunched her eyes closed and pressed her lips together in an effort to keep her emotions under control. She wanted a career, not marriage and not motherhood, and even if she did want those things, not now! She had a professional reputation to build, things to prove, strides to make for herself and all of womankind.

True, the feminist movement was long over, and women had rights and opportunities they'd never had before, but even so, the fire was in her to prove herself capable as a person—neither male nor female, nor married or single or whatever. Just a damn fine police officer above and beyond, and not in spite of being female.

She tugged the covers up under her chin. Sure, husbands and babies were wonderful things, and she wanted those things, too, the same as any woman. But they could wait . . . there was time . . . there was always . . . time . . .

Drifting down, she saw the little house come into view, and she relaxed . . .

Home . . . family . . . love . . . yes . . . oh, yes . . .

The house on Vallejo Street is smallish, but it suits the two of us just fine. It's in need of a slap of paint, but me fine young husband assures me the work'll be done well before the chill of winter settles on the city, well before the most blessed of events.

Of course, the house ain't what I'm used to, as me father has been sure to point out on the rare occasions he comes by to see how his newly married daughter fares.

"Well now," he blusters, taking in the cramped kitchen with a view of nothing more than the lines of fluttering bed linens hanging from the wash line in the yard next door. "You've made yer nest, haven't you, Daughter! And now you'll be lying in it a good long while." His face, which has always reminded me of an eagle's, all sharp-eyed and hook-nosed, contorts into a sneer. "You'll see, when the going gets rough, me girl, where marrying for love will get you, and I'm sayin' you'll be

sorry. When you come crawlin' back, I might, I say might, take you in."

"I won't come crawlin' back, Da," says I. "I love Jacob, and he loves me. We'll be happy. He's what I've always wanted—"

"Stupid girl!" Da shouts, slamming his bowler hat against his trousers. "What are you now, twenty? What in the hell does a girl your age know about anything? I didn't pawn everythin' I owned to come to America to make me fortune, to have me daughter throw that fortune in me face, now did I? Time and again, I arranged for you to mingle with some of the most eligible young bucks in San Francisco, and what did you do but ignore them. An insult to their families, and to me!"

"Stop shouting, Da." Me corset pinches and I put me hand to me stomach to try and ease it a bit. "I appreciate your efforts, but marrying the stuffy son of some stuffy banker . . . this is America, Da, not Ireland, and women here choose fer themselves, if they've a mind. I'm pleased you've become a rich man, I am. You've given me a good life, and I'm sorry if I'm a disappointment, but I fell in love with Jacob—"

"He's a policeman, for the sake of Christ!" Da shouts not two inches from me face. "And a beat cop for all that! He'll never be able to provide you with the kind of life I have. And when the babies come, what then, eh?"

An odd look crosses his face, putting a glint in his eye what bothers me.

"Why," he says slowly, "I wouldn't be surprised if your Jacob doesn't just up and die in the line of duty one day—"

Chapter 11

Absences are a good influence in love and keep it bright and delicate.

Robert Louis Stevenson

"The body's this way, Inspector Darling."

Nate followed Officer Rusty George up the drive, maneuvering past an aid car, the ME's sedan, two unmarked vehicles, two SFPD patrol units, a crime-scene van, and four TV station trucks complete with slicked-up reporters, greed in their eyes, microphones in their hands.

Yeah, this one would make the nightly news, all right.

"Were you the one who called it in?" Nate said to the uniform's back.

"Yes, sir," George answered over his shoulder. "Secured the area, tried to minimize contamination, followed procedure to the letter, Inspector."

Nate smiled. "Thanks, Officer. Good job."

George turned his head in Nate's direction. The officer's cheeks were slightly flushed as he gave a curt nod. "Thank you, sir." When he turned away again, Nate caught the hint of a grin on the man's face.

As were most crime scenes, the ambiance was one of quiet chaos—flashing red and blue lights, men and women in blue uniforms or gray suits milling around, their heads bent as they took copious notes. They asked questions, told jokes, renewed acquaintances. *How's the wife and kids? When'd you transfer out of Central? Don't this weather suck?* Cars on the street cruised slowly by, their curious drivers hoping to get a glimpse of the action.

Nate took the wide porch steps two at a time. Passing through the open double doors, he noted the handcrafted stained-glass window arching above the entrance, the black Italian marble floor in the foyer, and three CSIers already at work processing the scene.

He held up his badge. "Any sign of forced entry?" he said to the uniform standing just inside the threshold.

"Not that I've heard, sir." The officer shrugged. "Pretty big house, though. Guess we'll see."

As Officer George continued on through the foyer, Nate followed, noticing a large bouquet sitting on a table in front of an enormous gilt-framed oval mirror on the far wall. To no one in particular, he mumbled, "What are those, roses?"

Behind him, the sound of a woman's heels rapidly tap-tap-tapping across the polished floor grew louder, then came up beside him, matching his stride.

"I see we didn't get our flower arranging merit badge in Boy Scouts," said the familiar voice. "Actually, the big poofy magenta ones are peonies. And just in case you're totally clueless, the white ones are daisies, and the green ones are ferns."

He turned his head toward his new partner. "Thank you, Betty Botanist," he drawled. "I *know* what daisies and ferns are." Pushing his glasses up on his nose, he returned his gaze to the flowers. "Pretty. Maybe Tabby would like some. I bring roses home to her all the time. You think she'd like, what'd you call them, *p-e-e-e-yonies*?"

Inspector Glenna Matthews, stunning redhead and single mother of four boys, appeared to be in her mid-to-late forties, though Nate knew she was older. With her hair and her sassy, take-no-prisoners attitude, every guy in the department—older or younger—had his eye on her. For her part, however, she seemed oblivious to their overtures, and in the three months she and Nate had worked together, if she'd given any of them a tumble, he was unaware of it.

"They're not pronounced that way," Glenna scolded, "but close enough I guess. Listen, whether you take your pregnant wife peonies, roses, or crabgrass tied together with dental floss, it makes no difference."

As they passed a long row of original oil paintings probably worth more than Nate's yearly income, he said, "Why not?"

She looked at him like he'd just asked why the sky was blue. "Because bringing your wife flowers of any kind is physical evidence that, at some time during the day, you thought of her." Her eyes sparkled as she brushed back a stray lock of hair. "That's all a woman really wants, to know the man she loves, loves her, too, and that he thinks of her even when they're not together."

He straightened his spine, lengthening his stride as if to catch up with Officer George. "I knew that," Nate mumbled. He took flowers to Tabby because he loved the hell out of her. Wasn't it a given that he thought of her throughout the day? Did he need to provide proof? Is *that* how she interpreted the bouquets? God, women were so complicated.

Entering the kitchen, Nate said to George's back, "Who discovered the body?"

The officer halted and turned to face Nate and Glenna. "One of the maids came back from the grocery store just after lunch. Her head's twisted funny."

"The maid's?"

George chuckled. "Nah, the vic. ME says it could be a broken neck."

"Did you touch the body?" Glenna had taken a small notebook from her pocket and begun writing.

"Just to check for a pulse.'"

Nate's gaze wandered around the kitchen. "Anybody move her?"

"No, sir. Maid comes into the kitchen, load of groceries in her arms. She sees the cellar door's open and takes a gander down the stairs. Sees the body lying at the bottom, screams bloody murder, and dials 911."

"She didn't check to see if the woman was alive or not?"

George stuck out his lower lip and shrugged. "Says she thought the woman looked pretty damn dead and didn't want to touch her. Knows the drill, she says. Big *Law & Order* fan, she says."

Nate stepped aside as Glenna brushed past the two men and began descending the stairs into what appeared to be a basement pantry. "Where's the maid now?"

"She was all hysterical-like. My partner, Officer Dawson, is with her in the study."

As Nate followed Glenna down the stairs, he took care to move with caution around the dead woman's legs resting lifelessly on the bottom step. She'd landed on her back, her spine contorted awkwardly, her arms flung out to her sides as though she were waving down a passing motorist. One foot was bare, while the other bore a red stiletto heel.

Her clothing was expensive-looking—gray-wool slacks and a white silky blouse. A string of pearls encircled her slim throat. Her blond head arced at an unnatural angle, her blue eyes were wide open, frozen forever in shock as though someone had just leaped in front of her and shouted *surprise*!

He began scribbling in his notepad. "Vic's name?"

Officer George referred to his own notes. "Drew Muriel Mochrie. Age thirty-one. Moved here a couple of years ago from Scotland. Single. No known relatives. Lives alone."

"What about staff?"

"Two maids, a cook, and a gardener. But they don't live in."

"Mochrie?" Glenna repeated. "That name's familiar."

"Yes, ma'am," George said. "Sister of the late Bartholomew Mochrie who died a year ago in exactly the same way."

Nate's head came up. "No shit?"

"None, sir."

"Her brother fell down the wine-cellar stairs and broke his neck?"

Officer George tilted his head and gave Nate a sly look. "Like they say in the movies, 'fell . . . or was pushed.'"

Glenna crouched over the body. "I remember that case. Mochrie's death was ruled accidental, but there was suspicion the sister had given him a hefty nudge down the stairs so she could get her hands on all the goodies. DA's office didn't have enough evidence to indict, so no charges were ever brought."

Giving the cellar one more glance, Nate said, "I'm going to talk to the maid. You want to handle this, Matthews, while I go upstairs?"

"Knock yourself out," she said absently, as she pulled an evidence bag from her pocket.

A few minutes later, Nate found himself upstairs, sitting on a plush velvet sofa in the spacious study, while a distressed Estelle Langley blew her nose and wiped her puffy brown eyes. Officer Dawson, the policewoman who'd been keeping an eye on the maid, sat beside her, holding a large box of pink pop-up tissues.

"I'm sorry for your loss, Mrs. Langley," he began.

Dressed in a conservative white-cotton shirt and black pants, Estelle Langley was an attractive woman of medium height and build who appeared to be about fifty. Her graying hair had been pulled into a tight bun at the back of her neck, and she wore no jewelry save for a narrow gold wedding band. At Nate's remark, she raised her head, a bewildered expression on her face. "What loss?"

"Well," he said softly. "The death of your employer, of course. Your grief is understandable—"

"Grief!" she snapped. "'Bout the only thing I'm mourning right now is the loss of my paycheck! That bitch owed me five weeks' salary, and I doubt I'll ever see it now! I got bills to pay, and a sick husband to boot who's been out of work these last six months. What in the hell am I s'pposed to do now?"

Her face crumpled, and her bottom lip quivered. Covering her eyes with soggy tissues, she burst into another round of gut-wrenching sobs.

Nate exchanged helpless glances with Officer Dawson, who pulled a handful of fresh tissues from the box and shoved them into one of Mrs. Langley's fists.

"If Ms. Mochrie was so rich," Nate said, "how is it she owed back pay?"

Estelle scoffed into her growing clump of tissues, then raised her head. "Rich. Right. She went through her brother's money like an elephant on ice skates careens across Lake Michigan."

Officer Dawson's brow furrowed, and she looked off into the distance, as if trying to imagine such a scene.

"Hmm," Nate offered. "Interesting metaphor. You from the Midwest?"

"Detroit. Go Lions."

"Okay then. So you're saying Ms. Mochrie was broke?"

This time, Estelle snorted. "Well she couldn't pay

me, is all I know. When I complained, said she was down on her uppers, said she was going to collect on some insurance thing real soon. I don't know for sure what she meant, but I do know that one day, when I was cleaning around her desk, I come across a copy of a claim form to some insurance company overseas."

"She was attempting to collect on a loss?"

Estelle eased back on the sofa and let her head rest on the cushions. Rubbing the bridge of her nose, she closed her eyes. "Yeah, far as I could tell. Some expensive necklace she says was stolen when her brother died a year ago. My eyes 'bout bugged out of my head when I saw the numbers."

"You mean the value of the claim?"

She blinked. "Five million pounds she was asking. I looked it up. That's close to ten million bucks!"

Nate scowled and reviewed his notes. "My understanding was that her brother died from a fall down the wine-cellar steps. I hadn't heard there was a robbery involved."

Estelle's brown eyes glittered, and her mouth quirked up on one end. "Uh-huh. Acc'dent. Like the *Titanic* sinking was a acc'dent."

It was Nate's turn to blink. "The sinking of the *Titanic was* an accident. It hit an iceberg—"

"Sure." A knowing glint shone in her eyes. Nodding slowly, she said, "That's just what they *want* you to think."

"Ms. Langley," he said, trying to get this interview back on realistic ground. "Do you remember what the date was on that insurance claim? Maybe the name of the company?"

She shook her head. "Dated back a few months ago, I guess. Don't remember the name of the company, but their logo, I think it's called, was printed at the top of the page. It was a red lion with big claws, standing on its hind legs, and pawing at the air. Anyway, Ms. Mochrie came in the room just then and seen me looking at it. Got real pissed. Grabbed it from me and stomped out of the room. Never saw it again."

Nate made a few more notes, then said, "Did Ms. Mochrie have any visitors last night or this morning?"

Mrs. Langley sat straight up, clasped her hands in her lap, and got a dreamy look in her eyes. "Oh, aye," she said. "Aye, Mr. Logan Sinclair it was. A handsome devil."

Nate's brow lifted at the maid's impromptu attempt at a Scottish brogue. "Logan Sinclair? The clairvoyant?"

The same Logan Sinclair Andie is cozying up to?

What were the odds this was the same Scottish Logan Sinclair who was currently the subject of an undercover investigation for robbery and fraud, and who Brad Bostwick was resorting to blackmail to snare? Jesus, it had to be the same guy, and didn't that just throw a monkey wrench into the tapioca pudding.

The maid's lashes actually fluttered. "Aye," she sighed. "A charming man. He arrived about seven, and they was all still here when I went home at half past."

"*All?*"

"Mr. Sinclair, Ms. Mochrie, and Sinclair's assistant; younger guy, didn't catch his name. They all went traipsing down to the wine cellar."

"It took three of them to pick out a bottle of wine?"

"No. Mr. Sinclair was here to help Ms. Mochrie try and contact the spirit of Mr. Mochrie." She rolled her eyes and scoffed. "She was real big on that sort of thing."

With a straight face, he said, "Do you know why she wanted to contact her dead brother?"

She lifted a shoulder in a casual shrug. "Couldn't say."

"What time did you arrive for work this morning, Mrs. Langley?"

"About eight."

"Was Sinclair still here?"

"No." She blew her nose again and wiped it so aggressively, Nate thought she was trying to remove her upper lip from her face. "Ms. Mochrie went out early, about ten or so. Didn't say where she was going, but when she got back, she was carrying a black-velvet box, you know, the kind they put expensive jewelry in."

Nate exchanged glances with Officer Dawson. "How big was the box?"

Estelle's lower lip protruded as she considered the question. "'Bout the size of a three-ring binder, you know, like the kids use in school."

"Do you know what she did with it?"

"Last I saw, it was on her dresser in the bedroom."

"Is there a safe anywhere in the house?"

"If there is, I don't know where it would be. Never seen one, not in the wall neither, because I dust all the paintings and such. Ms. Mochrie always was the careless one though. Left things layin' around all the time."

At the maid's words, Officer Dawson nodded to Nate, stood, and set the tissue box on the sofa before hurrying out the study door.

Returning his attention to Estelle, he said, "What time did you go to the grocery store?"

"Um, just after twelve. Was gone about two hours. Would've been back sooner, but I ran into Marge Drexler who's a domestic over to the Spauldings' estate a few blocks down? We been friends since forever, and I was asking her if they had any openings over to her place, Ms. Mochrie being such a cheap bitch and all, and me having my husband laid up and not getting paid—"

"What happened when you returned?" Nate interrupted.

"Oh. Well." She sighed. "I let myself in through the kitchen—"

"Was the door locked?"

She shook her head. "Minute I come in, I see the cellar door's wide open. I go to close it, and well, I guess you know the rest."

As he finished jotting the information down in his notepad, Dawson returned from upstairs. He already knew what she was going to say.

"Gone," he stated, as the officer took her seat next to Estelle.

"With the wind. Sir."

Absently tapping his pen on the spiral wire of the notebook, he muttered, "Only if that wind's name is Logan Sinclair."

Andrea Rose Darling
Thirty-one
Single
Father: former police officer, now deceased
Mother: age 62, resident of San Francisco
Brother: Ethan Darling, age 38, former SFPD
     detective, currently owner/operator Paladin
     Private Investigations; spouse Georgiana née
     Mundy
Brother: Nathan Darling, age 35, SFPD homicide
     detective; spouse Tabitha née March.
Education: Criminal Justice, BS

Logan's eyes scanned the data, the words on the screen in front of him practically burning his eyeballs. He took a sip of brandy, set the glass down, wiped the dampness from his lips.

. . . joined SFPD out of college . . . distinguished service . . . recently made detective . . . Investigative Bureau . . . currently undercover ops . . . fraud . . . Logan Sinclair . . .

Christ Almighty, she was a *cop*, and she was investigating *him*. Well, if that just didn't damn well put a *fankle* on it.

He leaned back in the desk chair, tenting his fingers under his chin as he let his gaze wander across her image on the computer screen . . .

While the photo was of a stern young woman almost glaring in defiance at the camera, there was no mistaking it was Andrea "Devon"—beautiful, intelligent, determined.

He read the file again and snorted in spite of himself, letting amusement warm his blood.

So she thought to snare him, did she? No wonder she was so keen on getting him to play along with her séance, insisting on a dinner engagement, continuing to see him even after the Haggis Incident, as he'd come to think of it. And finally, demanding to know how he faked his clairvoyance.

Had she worn a wire? Probably.

He took another sip of brandy and considered the big picture. Why had she been sent undercover? What did the SFPD suspect him of, hope to learn about him—that he was a rogue and a charlatan? A thief? A murderer?

Sure, he was all those things, and damned if he wasn't.

His chair squeaked as he leaned back, clasping his hands behind his head. He could confront her, come clean, put all his cards on the table, or whatever term the Yanks used.

Or . . .

A slow grin curved his mouth as a much more appealing thought began to take form inside his head. He could play her game, see how far she'd take it, how far she'd go—in the line of duty—to get her man. According to the file, her brothers held distinguished service records. He'd be willing to bet she was out to best them; it would be just like her, or what he knew of her—and he fancied he knew a lot at this point.

He pursed his lips. Giving the adorable Andie Darling the runaround might prove interesting. After all, he now knew who she was and what she was up to, but she knew nothing of him, save for his reputation and whatever information the SFPD thought they had.

He powered down the laptop. By rights, he should be angry as hell at being played like this, but the allure of getting his hands on a woman who was pledged to find whatever means she could to get close to him was simply too fascinating to resist.

This was going to be fun, damned if it wasn't. If he kissed her again, would she let him? If he ran his hands under her clothes, would she protest? How far was she willing to go to get him to spill his secrets?

Sliding his cell phone out of his pocket, he flipped it open to dial her number, when a knock on his hotel room door stopped him. He made sure the computer was completely shut down, then went to the door.

A man and a woman stood there. The man was good-looking, blond, midthirties, wore rimless glasses and a nicely tailored blue suit. Though he looked vaguely familiar, Logan was certain they'd never met before.

The woman waited a step or two behind him. Forty-something, maybe older, but she was eye-catching, and no mistake. Red hair, beauty-queen bone structure. Full lips that did not curve into a smile.

The man raised his hand. A brass shield flashed in the light of the hallway.

As if these two didn't have *cop* written all over them.

"Logan Sinclair," the man said.

"Aye."

The man grinned, and Logan could have sworn he'd seen that smile somewhere before.

"I'm Inspector Darling, and this is my partner, Inspector Matthews. We'd like a word with you."

Logan stared at the badge, then at the man. Same color hair, same cheekbones, same smile. The color of their eyes was different, but there was no mistaking this was one of Andie's brothers.

The voices inside his head began to chatter, competing with each other to be heard. Jesus, had something happened to her?

Panic quickened his heartbeat as he stepped back, opening the door wider to allow the two entry.

"Always happy to cooperate with the police, Inspector . . . *Darling* did you say?"

Behind the lenses of his glasses, the detective's brown eyes narrowed. "Best not to go down that road, Mr. Sinclair."

Logan nodded. "Understood."

In a solemn tone, Andie's brother said, "You're acquainted with a woman named Drew Mochrie, correct?"

Och. So this was about Drew. Well, best to play along, not stray too far from the truth, and say no more than required.

"Miss Mochrie is a client of mine."

"Client?"

"Aye. I'm a clairvoyant. I'm helping her to encourage the spirit of her brother to leave this world behind and move on to the next."

"That so? When did you see her last?" Inspector Matthews eased forward and all but glared into his eyes.

He lifted a shoulder in a casual shrug. "Last night. And again this morning, as a matter of fact."

"Where?" Darling said.

"At her home last evening. This morning, we met for tea in a café in Union Square. Why? What's all this about?"

The detectives exchanged quick glances.

"What time this morning?" Darling said.

"Close to eleven thirty, I should think," he said, not bothering to hide his impatience. "Are you going to tell me what this is about, or do I have to resort to mental telepathy?"

When Darling's mouth flattened, Logan said slowly, "Just what division of the police department are you with, Inspector?"

"Homicide." Darling's gaze intensified.

"Hom—What in the hell? Has something happened, then?"

Inspector Matthews raised her chin, locking her gaze with his. It was obvious she didn't want to miss his reaction, whatever it might be.

"Ms. Mochrie was found dead earlier this afternoon at her home," she said.

"*What?*" Drew was *dead*? What in the hell had happened? "How did—"

"Early reports," she interrupted, "indicate a broken neck suffered in a fall down the cellar stairs. We won't know for sure until the ME's had a chance to perform an autopsy."

Drew broke her neck in a fall down the same cellar steps as Tolley? Logan swiped his hand over his jaw and mumbled, "Jesus Christ."

Inspector Darling cleared his throat. "Also, a valuable necklace is missing. You wouldn't happen to know anything about any of this, would you, Mr. Sinclair?"

Chapter 12

I've a grand memory for forgetting.

Robert Louis Stevenson

Andie watched Nate pace the floor of her living room. Her house on Russian Hill was small, but even so, on a cop's salary, if Ethan hadn't helped her out with the down payment, she never would have been able to afford the charming, single-story tongue-and-groove.

Nate was a big guy and covered the carpeted area in five long strides before turning on his heel and pacing back again. Shoving his glasses up on his nose, he said, "Without probable cause, we couldn't do a search of Sinclair's room, and the necklace sure as hell wasn't sitting out in plain view." He scrubbed his jaw with his knuckles.

Andie eased herself into the floral wing chair by the bay window that overlooked her tiny and very precious rose garden. "What about prints?"

Her brother's brow furrowed. "Even if we lifted some latents, he admits to having been at her house. Doesn't prove anything."

"You said the maid talked about a second man."

"According to Sinclair, the guy's name is Oliver Kerr. He films the sessions."

"Well, is he a witness, an alibi, or an accomplice?"

"Sinclair could have named him as a witness to his innocence, or his alibi, but didn't, so I'm looking at accomplice. Or I will, when we find him. Apparently, he hooked up with a girl, and Sinclair doesn't know where he is."

"You try his cell phone?"

He gave a quick nod. "Voice mail."

Andie closed her eyes for a moment. This new information on Logan—that he was implicated in robbery and murder—began to overlay, color, even distort what she knew about him. And what she didn't know.

Was this why Bostwick was so eager to collar him? Did the commander have information on past crimes, maybe including a homicide . . .

Damn. Something nagged at the back of her brain—something insistent yet indistinct, like the buzz of a mosquito under a blanket. Then she realized what it was. The idea of Logan's killing a woman to rob her didn't jibe with her perception of him. Sure, he was charming, he was smooth, he was a con man head to toe—but a stone-cold killer?

"I don't know, Nate," she said thoughtfully, tenting her fingers under her chin. "I figured him for a lot of things, but this. My gut tells me no."

Nate put his hands on his hips. "It's obvious you're letting your personal feelings sway your judgment."

She raised her head and scowled. "I don't have any personal feelings one way or the other about Logan Sinclair!"

Her brother's lips curved downward as though he'd just been asked to believe in the Easter Bunny.

"I see the look in your eyes when you talk about him, Andie. Maybe you don't realize it, but he's not just a suspect to you, and this isn't just a case. Something inside you has gotten too close, made it personal."

When she began to protest again, he raised one hand. "Hold on," he growled. "I know what I'm talking about because the same thing happened to me. I recognize the signs. But if you think you need a second opinion, ask Ethan, because the same damn thing happened to him!"

"You're wrong. You're dead *wrong*, Nate."

Now he lifted both hands in the air, palms up, as though he were pushing an invisible box across the room. "You can deny it all you want, but I think it's time you took a good hard look at what's going

on inside your head. Hell, maybe even your heart
for all I know. Either you stay detached, aloof, im-
personal, or you admit you have inappropriate feelings for this Sinclair and ask to be removed from
the case. Do you really think you can be effective if
you have a crush on him?"

She thrust herself to her feet, her arms rigid by
her sides. "What am I, fourteen? I do not have a
crush on Logan Sinclair!"

"Don't you?" he shot back. "I've talked to him.
He's good-looking and charming, smart, smooth
. . . hell, if I wasn't straight, even *I'd* fall for the
guy!"

Crossing her arms over her stomach, she turned
away from her brother. Fury and confusion
formed a battleground inside her head. Nate
was wrong. Wrong, wrong, *wrong*. She was as
professional and detached as any cop she knew.
More. Nate didn't know what in the hell he was
talking about.

She dropped her gaze and examined the detailed
pattern of the Oriental rug beneath her feet. "Does
Sinclair have an alibi for the murder?"

A moment passed while Nate apparently decided
whether to continue with his line of attack or ad-
dress the question at hand. Finally, he said, "It's
not a homicide . . . yet. We won't know until we get
results of the autopsy whether she was murdered—
and maybe not even then. Sinclair says after he had
tea with her, he went for a drive—alone. He says

he doesn't remember where he went or how long he was gone."

Andie licked her lips, turned the information over in her head. "When will the results of the autopsy be available?"

"Few days."

"Really? That fast?"

"Yeah. Apparently, Commander Bostwick called in a few favors to get it bumped to the head of the line."

She rubbed the back of her neck, then brushed a piece of lint off her jeans. It was Saturday, her day off, and she'd planned on spending it at the library doing research on Jacob Harte and Emma Conner. But now, with Logan implicated in a homicide, finding out about the players in her ghostly dreams would have to wait a little longer.

Turning to face Nate, she said, "Look. I'm sorry I yelled. You're right. I need to examine my priorities. I . . . I don't have a crush on Sinclair, at least, I don't think I do, but he's . . . well, it's hard to keep a safe distance from him emotionally. He's very . . . attractive, likable. It's difficult to imagine him as a cold-blooded killer."

Nate paused a moment, then walked toward her and grasped her shoulders. She raised her head and looked into his kind brown eyes.

"Look, you were just seven when Mom and Dad split up," he said softly. "Hell, I was only fourteen, and if I hadn't moved to Olympia with Dad, I'd've been around to see you grow up. Maybe you and I would have the same kind of relationship you have with Ethan." The dull gleam of regret shone in his eyes. "But that's twenty years' water over the dam, baby sister. Since I came home, I've tried real hard to reconnect with you, Andie. You and Ethan."

She gave him an understanding smile, then arched a brow. "How's that working out for you?"

He looked a little sheepish. "Peaks and valleys, kid. Peaks and valleys. Anyway, I'm sorry if I come across to you as harsh or judgmental. I don't mean to be. Honest. I love you. Always have, even when you were an irritating little brat who kept trying to butt in to whatever Ethan and I were doing." He smiled. "I hope that the next twenty years brings us back to where we should be, know what I mean?"

Wrapping her arms around his waist, she gave him a tight hug. "I know *exactly* what you mean."

She released him and stepped back, clasping her hands in front of her.

"When I was little, I . . . I worshipped Ethan. And you, too, what I remembered of you. And Daddy. But you and he were so far away. Cards, letters, phone calls, they were enough to stay in touch, but not enough to really know your father and your brother."

"Yeah."

With a hard swallow, she said, "Did, uh, did Daddy talk about me much?"

"All the time," Nate whispered, chucking her under the chin with his knuckle. "All the time."

She felt hot tears well up in her eyes and fought to dispel them, but they came anyway, stinging her lids, rendering her vision to a watery blur. "Wish I'd seen more of him."

"I know he wanted that, too, but he wasn't much for showing his emotions or asking for what he needed. Besides, he hardly ever took vacations. And what with putting in extra hours to have enough money to send to Mom for you and Ethan, keeping an eye on me during my wild years, and then the cancer came . . ."

She sniffed and swiped the tears from her cheeks. "Yeah. The cancer."

"Sorry. I didn't mean to stir up bad memories."

Shaking her head, she said, "You didn't. When I was younger, time had no meaning. There was always today, and after today, there would be tomorrow, and after that, another tomorrow, and on and on. When you're a kid, you don't realize that eventually, some people run out of tomorrows, and you can't get them back, and you can't do anything about it. I just wish I'd known him better, that's all."

Nate nodded, swallowed, shoved his hands into his pockets.

They stood in silence for a moment, and she knew they were each lost in their separate pasts. She really had no idea what his childhood had been like, and he had no idea of hers, and there was no way to go back and make things right.

Her thoughts drifted to memories of days spent, time wasted, opportunities missed.

"I—I want to know you better, Nate," she stumbled, raising her head, catching her brother's gaze and holding it. "I want to know you much better, and your wife, Tabby, and the baby, too, when it comes. I don't want anything to come between any of us, ever again."

He grinned down at her and angled his head. "Even if we disagree on how you feel about Logan Sinclair?"

She palmed away the rest of her tears, then sniffed. "Well now, it's not really a problem, since you're so obviously *wrong*." In the kitchen, her cell phone chimed to life. "Excuse me for a sec," she said as she hurried from the living room.

Her phone rested on the kitchen table; the readout displayed Logan's number. "It's him!" she shouted.

In a moment, her brother was by her side as she picked up the phone and put it to her ear. Nate leaned in, cocking his head, trying to listen.

She cleared her throat. "Hello?"

"What are you wearing?" Logan murmured.

Nate slid her a wry look.

"What's it to you, pal?" she quipped.

"I've a mind to indulge m'self in a bit o'haggis

and whisky for supper, and wanted to know if you're dressed for the occasion."

Her nose wrinkled. "There isn't enough whisky in the wide wide world to induce me to eat haggis again."

He chuckled, and she steeled herself against an involuntary melting of her resolve. "*Och*," he said. "Where's yer sense of adventure?"

"Not in my stomach, laddie." She exchanged glances with Nate. "But that doesn't mean I wouldn't be interested in . . . getting together."

Nate nodded his approval, but Sinclair seemed to hesitate.

"Hmm," Logan said. "No haggis and whisky, eh? Well, I don't know. Maybe I'll just spend the day curled up with a good book."

He wasn't *interested*? She locked eyes with Nate, who looked confused.

"Okay," she said casually. "Since you're the only expert on the spirit world I know, I was hoping to talk to you about those dreams I've been having, but I guess it can wait. Enjoy your book. Buh-bye."

She held her breath. She was that close to pressing the END button, when he spoke.

"Well, lass," he said slowly, as though it were an effort to form the words. "I *might* be able to spare some time today." His tone was one of an arrogant potentate granting the wish of a desperate serf. "When can I pick you up?"

"I'll meet you."

Nate nodded his approval.

"Suit yourself," Sinclair said. "I'm at the St. Francis. Room 422. Three o'clock."

Silence.

Andie flipped the phone closed. "He hung up on me!" she huffed. "The conceited bastard, instructed me on when and where to meet him, then he hung up!"

Nate's mouth quirked. "Seems pretty sure of you."

"Sure of him*self,* you mean!" Glancing at her watch, she said, "All right, fine. Go away now. I only have an hour."

His brown eyes grew serious. "This guy is under investigation for fraud, and maybe homicide. Wear a wire, and I'll—"

"And you'll nothing. You have no evidence he killed that woman, and I'm working undercover on a separate case. Let me do my job my way. If he's involved in the Mochrie murder, I'll know it soon enough."

"I don't think it's a good idea for you to—"

"Stop making noises like an overprotective brother!" she huffed. "I know how to take care of myself. I know how to do my job. Now go away and let me do it."

When he started to protest again, she said, "I understand your concern, Nate, but I'm going to try a different tack today, and I'd be worried about him becoming suspicious as to why I'm so ardent in my questions. If he discovers the wire, he'd make me as a cop, and that would be that."

"And just how would he discover a wire hidden on your body, Andie?" He actually glared at her.

"I'm a big girl now, so don't go there, okay? Listen, I'm trying to get him to trust me, confide in me, let me in a little. To do that, the woman in me has to appeal to the man in him."

"Andie, I—"

"Let me grow up, will you? I'm not that seven-year-old girl anymore tagging after you and Ethan. I'm a woman with a job to do, so let me do it the best way I know how."

He shoved his hands into his pockets, closed his mouth, nodded.

"Besides," she continued more softly. "I've got my cell phone, and my knee, and I know how to use both. He doesn't suspect anything, and I'm going to keep the conversation on those stupid dreams I've been having. It's going to be casual, all the way. There won't be any trouble. None at all, Nate. I promise."

Though the downtown parking garage was nearly full, Andie finally found a spot on the fourth tier. Locking her car, she checked her watch, hurried to the elevator, and pressed the button. She heard the gears engage, and a minute later, the door slowly slid open. Entering the small compartment, she went to press the button to take her down, when a man's form appeared in the doorway. Quickly, he stepped inside and faced her, blocking her exit. The door rattled closed.

He widened his stance, clasping his hands in front of him. The navy blue suit he wore was exquisitely tailored. He looked polished and professional. With a slight grin, he said, "Made any progress yet, Inspector?"

Commander Bostwick. The elevator began its noisy descent. She was alone in a small compartment with a man she had once admired and now loathed, even feared. A man she thoroughly distrusted.

Suddenly she wished with all her heart and soul that she'd worn that damn wire.

"Sir," she said, meeting his gaze head-on. "What in the hell are you doing here?"

His grin widened, but in no way could be construed as friendly. "Right to the point, eh, Inspector? Well, I was just checking up on my favorite lady cop." His smile vanished; his eyes gleamed with malice. "I asked you if you'd made any progress."

"Some. Nothing much to report yet, though. I'm meeting Sinclair in a few minutes."

The elevator settled to the street level, and the door ambled open. Without taking his eyes from her, he reached behind him and pressed a button.

The door closed again, and the elevator began to rise. So they weren't done yet.

"What floor did I press?" he said, clasping his hands in front of him once more.

"Six."

He nodded as though satisfied. "Good. That's probably all the time we need. I understand there's been an unexpected . . . complication."

Behind her, the wood paneling felt too hard, too cold, like the inside of a cheap coffin. The fluorescent light overhead was harsh, distorting Bostwick's features. For the first time in her life, she felt claustrophobic.

"A woman's been murdered," she said. "And you consider that a little complication?"

"I do. Sinclair's responsible, of course."

She swallowed. "I doubt that."

He looked surprised. "Defending him, Inspector? Has he charmed the pants off you, too?"

Ignoring his innuendo, she said, "There's no evidence to indicate he had anything to do with the Mochrie woman's death. My understanding is, the coroner hasn't even—"

"Evidence can be misleading," he interrupted. "It can be conclusive or it can be vague. You already know how I feel about evidence, don't you, Inspector?"

"You want it whether it exists or not."

His mouth descended into a bitter-looking

scowl. "No time to get flip, Andie. I have to say, I'm displeased with your progress. I expected more expeditiousness from someone with your . . . ambitions."

The elevator stopped, and the door opened. Behind Bostwick, three people stood, but when they attempted to enter the elevator, the commander waved them off and pressed the button for the ground floor. As the door closed, Andie heard angry yelps of protest, but Bostwick seemed oblivious.

When he returned his attention to her, she said, "Sinclair's a hard nut to crack. He doesn't give much away. He's just starting to trust me, and I'm getting close—"

"Get closer, and soon," he snapped. "Or a nasty rumor will begin to circulate about your partner, and you know how rumors are. They tend to grow and take on a life of their own. You don't want that, do you, Inspector?"

"Dylan and I were never involved, and you know it. Neither he nor I have done anything wrong—"

"I. Don't. *Care*," he snarled, leaning toward her so his face was only inches from her own. "Think about it. Who has more credibility, my dear, a sexy blond bombshell and her famously womanizing partner, or a commander with a spotless reputation?"

Andie remained silent, unsure what to do, what to say next. The air inside the elevator compartment was stale, thick with poisonous tension. She had to get out of there, get away from Bostwick's viperous presence.

"To make sure I get what I want," he said softly, "I'm upping the stakes."

"What are you talking about?" Her words rode on an exhaled breath, soft, almost not there at all.

"Not only do I want evidence of Sinclair's fraud," Bostwick said, "I want it on the homicide. Sinclair killed the Mochrie woman to get his hands on a very valuable necklace. Finding it in Sinclair's possession would just about seal the case. Retrieve it for me, and all the unpleasantness goes away."

"But the homicide is being worked by—"

"Your brother. Yes I know. Very convenient, don't you think?"

"You . . . did you have something to do with Nate's being assigned to the Mochrie case?"

He shrugged. The elevator settled on the ground floor once again, and the door opened. This time, he stepped out.

"That's neither here nor there," he said softly as he backed away from her. "Find that necklace. I don't care who you have to betray to get it, but find it and give it to me. I want Sinclair's ass in a sling and you're going to help me put it there. Find the necklace, Inspector, or life for you and for all those around you is going to get very, very unhappy very, very fast. You have forty-eight hours."

"*Forty-eight hours!* That's ridiculous—"

"Let me repeat. I. Don't. Care. I need this taken care of now. You're lucky I don't make it twenty-four hours."

Anger and astonishment edged her words. "What if Sinclair didn't kill the woman? What if he didn't steal the necklace? What if—"

"He did, and we both know it! I don't want to hear any more excuses. Do this job right, or suffer the consequences!"

A car door slammed, people jabbered about something, footsteps echoed through the parking garage as a man and a woman began strolling toward the sidewalk.

Straightening his tie, Bostwick sent Andie a generous smile. She would have thought it sincere, except for the lethal gleam in his eyes.

As he turned and walked away, over his shoulder, he said congenially, "Forty-eight hours, Andie. Understand?" then pushed through the double glass doors to disappear into the bright San Francisco sunlight.

"Yes, sir," she mumbled. Her eyes never left those doors as she felt her blood turn to ice. "I understand completely."

Chapter 13

It is the mark of a good action that it appears inevitable in retrospect.

Robert Louis Stevenson

Logan went to the door expecting to be dazzled by Andrea Darling. He'd tug her into his room, kiss her, test her resolve, her resistance—and her repertoire of creative avoidance techniques. The fact was, he'd lined up a number of expectations for their encounter today, and he intended to either fulfill each one, or amuse himself at how she'd squirm out of them.

He assumed she'd dress alluringly. After all, it was her job to snare him, get him to let down his defenses, tell her all his secrets. Since meeting her, he'd learned to anticipate the cool look in her eyes, the squared shoulders, the determination.

But when he opened the door, what he saw nearly knocked the breath from his lungs. Instead of the

sassy, confident, give-as-good-as-she-got undercover detective, he felt sucker-punched at the unexpected look of vulnerability in her eyes.

Aye, she covered it quick enough, but it was there
all the same, and it affected him faster and more
effectively than a poison arrow straight through
the heart.

When she said nothing, just stood there like a
fragile doll, he reached for her, gently curling his
fingers around her shoulders. With the slightest
motion, he pulled her into his arms, lowered his
head, and kissed her.

At first, she did nothing, neither resisted nor
yielded. But when he tugged her closer into his
body, she seemed to relax, let go. She made a soft
whimper at the back of her throat, then flung her
arms around his neck and opened her mouth for
him.

Kissing him back, she gave as good as she got.
Her mouth was soft, but her kisses teasing, coaxing, sexy as hell. She slid her tongue against his,
and he grunted in satisfaction, tightening his embrace. He could feel the length of her body touch-
ing his in all the best places. Her nipples were hard
against his chest, her hips firm to his own, and he
had to resist the primitive urge to back her against
the wall and thrust into her, make her gasp his
name, moan her release, pant for more.

It wasn't the sex he wanted so much; it was *her.*
Her and her and her and all of her, and more. *Her*

until he couldn't think, couldn't speak, couldn't walk. *Her* until the world no longer existed, and it was just the two of them alone with no distractions—no wretched memories, no stained past or complicated present, no uncertain future. Only *now,* this very moment. Give and take and man and woman and primal and hot and passionate. Her, only *her* in his heart and in his soul.

She had the power to heal him, to make it all right again, allow him to forgive himself, make him whole. Maybe it was just some cruel cosmic joke, an illusion his weary and desperate mind had created to try and find absolution where there was none.

Something about her made him believe he'd paid long enough. But did he well and truly *deserve* this second chance she was unwittingly offering? Could he risk it? *Should* he? If he did, and she walked away, would the pain of it be too great to bear?

His brain twisted and spun until only one thought, one word remained. *Andie, Andie, Andie . . . what you do to me, lass. Christ, what you do to me . . .*

He kicked at the door until it closed, then went for the buttons on her blouse. The fabric parted. Instantly, his mouth was on her breast. He yanked down the lace of her bra until one dark nipple popped free, and he covered it with his mouth, suckling, teasing with his tongue until the nub was hard and he heard her fighting for breath. She choked his name, then pushed her palms against him, trying to shove him away.

He stopped. Lowering his head, he fought to recover his own breath. The room was silent, except for the sounds of their breathing. After a moment or two, his brain cleared a little, and common sense returned.

Slowly tugging her bra back in place, he made a feeble attempt to close the front of her blouse, but she brushed his hand away.

She didn't speak, didn't move past him, just stood with her head against his shoulder, her eyes closed. He could feel her body trembling, and he wasn't so full of himself that he didn't realize it wasn't his mere kisses that had set her nerves on edge.

Stroking her silky hair, he whispered, "What's wrong, darlin' Andie?"

A moment passed. And in that moment, he withdrew his defenses and let the essence of her seep deeply into his core. He did not resist, but welcomed the union. Relaxing further, he let the sorrow and confusion she sought to hide from him, mingle with his own energy. He inhaled, breathing in her scent as though it was life-sustaining, and for this very moment, maybe it was. Closing his eyes, he absorbed all she was into all he was, making her a part of his own flesh and bone and soul.

Against his chest, her heart beat slow and heavy, and he held her closer. "Please," he murmured. "Tell me what's wrong."

She took in a breath and he felt her rib cage expand, her breasts move against him, her spine straighten.

"If you really were clairvoyant," she muttered, "you'd know."

Raising her head, she captured his gaze with her own.

So we're back to the game, are we, lass? Good for you . . .

Logan wanted to laugh out loud in sheer joy, but instead, used his free hand to cup the nape of her neck. He brought his mouth down hard on hers, and she opened for him without hesitation this time.

Letting his tongue seduce her mouth, he ran his hands down her sides, over her hips, down her rump where he splayed his fingers and pulled her tight into him. When she moaned into his mouth, he slowly let his hands glide around to her belly.

Aye, she was clean; no wire. He'd thought not. So she was playing it fast and loose, eh? He stifled a smile as he kissed her harder, letting his hands roam over her body.

She pulled back a wee bit, panting. Her green eyes were misty with unmistakable desire. "I'm not . . . going to sleep with you."

Lowering his head, he bit the side of her neck, licked her there, then nuzzled her ear. "But you want to."

"I also want world peace, but it's not going to happen."

"You never can tell, lass. What with the proper negotiations and incentives . . ."

She stepped back from him and crossed her arms. And wasn't that body language at its most expressive.

Looking down for a moment, then meeting his gaze, she stated, "I came to see you because I'd like your help."

"Done," he said without hesitation. "What do you—"

"I want you to help me," she began, then paused. Biting her lower lip, she inhaled deeply then laughed sharply. "I can't believe I'm going to say this, but I want you to help me contact that woman in my dream. Can you?"

He stared at her, swallowed.

I can do it, lass, but I don't want to. Dear God, don't ask it of me. I've already sacrificed enough to get close to you. After all these years, my feelings for you have me lowering my defenses. You have no idea what you're asking . . . no idea at all.

"I'll think about it."

Anger flashed in her eyes. "You'll *think* about it? Hey, it's what you *do*, isn't it? The truth is, you really are a fake, aren't you? What, haven't you had time to research Emma, so you can use whatever facts you uncover to trick me into believing in your powers? What happens after you tell me some cock-and-bull story that ensures my trust and blind devotion? Are you going to ask for money? Sex? *Both?*"

He looked into her upturned face and felt his emotions begin to fray around the edges. When— exactly—had she become so important to him? What moment was it when she ceased to simply be an attractive woman and become his obsession?

"Sex and money," he said lightly. "Neither to be underestimated, darlin' Andie."

Doubling her fists, she lurched toward him, slamming her hands into his chest.

"Tell me!" she bit out through clenched teeth. "I need to *know*, goddammit! I need to understand if you're on the level or not! You don't . . . you have no idea . . . I . . . damn, just *tell* me!"

The lass was either a very good actress, or her distress was real. She was nearly hysterical, and he wondered, did she want to know for herself, or to ensure an indictment?

Placing his hands over her balled fists, he said, "You have it nailed, lass. I'm a fraud, through and through."

Her delicate brows furrowed and she looked like somebody had just tossed her bannocks into the Findhorn.

"You *are* a fake?" she whispered. Slowly, she shook her head as though in disappointed disbelief. "You really *are?*"

With a shrug, he dropped his hands, freeing her fists. She kept them in place against his chest.

"I am," he admitted. Without warning, he felt the old bitterness rise in his throat, and the truth came out before he could stop it.

"A man's got to make a living, lass. When I was a wee lad, I discovered I had the Powers and used them willy-nilly. Pretty full of myself, I was, and in the end . . . it cost me more than I ever wanted to pay."

The images played through his head, the memories, the loss. With a quick shrug, he said, "When I discovered it was not so much a gift as it was a cruel joke, I decided to use the Powers, instead of them using me." Self-loathing soured his mouth. "I did readings, got a name for myself, wrote a couple of books. The rich and famous clamored after my services. The tabloids loved me. I became the Paris Hilton of the psychic world. All very grand."

Shoving Andie's balled fists off his chest, he stepped back, away from her warmth, her furrowed brow, the disillusionment in her eyes.

Her chin lifted as she seemed to assess him, but was it the seductive Andrea Devon who watched him so closely or the secretive Andie Darling?

She reached for him, placing her open palm over his heart. "I'm sorry."

He scoffed. "Don't feel sorry for me, Andie. I'm sleepin' in a bed of my own making."

"Tell me about it."

He nearly did, nearly confessed everything. Instead, he let his head fall back, and he laughed. Even to his own ears, it was a harsh sound, edged with self-recrimination. He took her hand between his and she made no effort to escape. But of course, she wouldn't. This was a game to her, one she obviously intended to win. How could she know he'd changed the rules?

"I'll make a deal with you, lass."

A glint of caution flared in her eyes. "Go on." She swallowed, and he was certain she feared the kind of deal he'd propose.

"I share with you my deepest, darkest secrets . . ."

She licked her lips. "And the price for that information is?"

He reached for her hand, bringing her slowly to him. She raised her face, and he lowered his mouth to hers. He kept the kiss gentle, letting her know without words how he felt, rather, how he wanted to feel if he let himself.

She responded, kissing him back as though she felt it, too, felt their connection, their undeniable oneness.

If it was an act, he didn't want to know, so he closed his eyes, and let himself believe . . .

A moment later, against her open mouth, he whispered, "The price is simply that you tell me about your dreams."

She pulled back, blinked hard, then blinked again. "You want to know about the *dreams*? That's why I came to see you. I already told you that."

"Then the price will be an easy one to pay, will it *nae*?" He smiled and slid his arm around her waist. "Tell me, and leave nothing out."

Her head tilted a bit to one side as she gazed up at him. "All right."

"You look decidedly disappointed, lass. Were you expecting some . . . other price for my secrets?"

"No. Um, no, I wasn't."

"Fine then."

"Yeah. Fine."

Still holding her hand, he moved toward the bar, and she had no choice but to follow. "I'd wager a wee dram will help us both relax a bit, don't you think?"

"Sure," she said. "A wee dram. As long as it's not a dram of haggis."

He snorted a laugh. "No, lass. You've done yer duty, so far as the haggis goes. Perhaps a glass of wine would suit ye better."

She nodded, and he let go of her hand to fill their goblets with rich burgundy. Handing her a glass, he picked up his own and walked to the window.

The view from his hotel room faced west, and this time of day, the distant Golden Gate Bridge shone brilliant red as the sun dissolved into the sea on the other side of the world. Gigantic container vessels reduced to the size of toys skimmed across the bay, its puckered surface turned deep green with the coming of the evening.

Without turning to her, he said, "How many dreams have there been?"

For a moment, she said nothing, then, "Three."

"Tell me about them."

He heard her move toward the small table next to the bar, pull out a chair, and sit. As he poured the wine, she said, "Well, at first, they seemed almost like scenes from a movie that I was watching."

Her tone was quiet, uncertain.

"But then I began to feel as though they were much more personal, and I was actually participating in them. They weren't dreams anymore, more like . . . memories. I hear this Emma talking like she's not only telling me what's happening, but is living the events for the first time. Sometimes, I feel like I'm her, living her life, loving the people she loves."

She shook her head in a gesture of helplessness.

"There's nothing of the abstract, like in regular dreams. They're too organized, too linear. And so . . . well, real."

"Linear?" He placed her wineglass on the table in front of her, then took the other chair at the small table.

She nodded. "The first one showed me how Emma met Jacob. The next, their wedding night. The last one was a visit from Emma's father. He didn't like Jacob and was furious she married him. And . . . and each time I dream of Emma, I . . . I wake up crying."

"Why?"

She licked her lips, ran a finger up the stem of her glass. "Because . . . well, there's just something so sad about her. I feel it . . . here." She placed her open palm over her heart. "I actually *feel* it, as though whatever's happening to her is happening to me."

Her words reverberated inside his body. Letting his breath out, he relaxed into his thoughts, let them come, let them work—and then, he knew. Without question, he *knew*. He was also sure Andie wouldn't like it; she would resist. Carefully, he said, "I believe you and Emma are related in some way."

"But I'm *not*," she said quickly. "I asked my . . . I mean, I did some research. There are no Conners or Hartes in my family history."

Logan shook his head. "Doesn't matter. Yer a blood relative, lass. Somehow."

Her mouth turned down. "You're way off, swami. It's just not possible."

Okay, if she was convinced she and the ghostly Emma Harte weren't connected, he'd let it go . . . for now.

Outside the window, the San Francisco skyline had faded, kept alive only by the pinpricks of a million office lights. Behind the darkening silhouette of the buildings, the sky succumbed to the indigo night.

Logan took a sip of wine and watched Andie watching him. "You ready to tell me what's got you so upset, lass?"

"I'm not upset."

He challenged the lie with a steady on gaze. She didn't so much as bat an eye.

"Liar. I saw it in yer eyes when first you arrived. Besides, your aura's not its usual color."

"And just what color is my aura, usually?"

"Oh, it's run the gamut since the day we met, darlin' Andie. But up until today, it's been predominantly a deep red."

"Which means . . ."

"Which means you are grounded, realistic, active, strong of will. A survivor."

"Damn. I hate it when my aura gives away all my secrets. Guess I'm going to have to wear a coat all the time."

He smiled across the table at her. "It wouldna matter if you did."

She diverted her gaze past his shoulder to the window. "You said up until today. What changed?"

"When you first arrived," he said, when he was sure he had her undivided attention, "it was a very clear red indicating power, energy, competitiveness, sexuality, and passion. Then it changed to yellow, almost the color of a lemon."

"That can't be right."

"And why not?"

"Because I look like hell in yellow. Turns my complexion sallow."

He took a lock of her hair between his fingers. It was silky. He slipped it over her ear. "Nothing could make your complexion look sallow, lass. A yellow aura often manifests when someone is struggling to maintain power and control over some situation. They fear losing that control, the prestige, respect . . . and power that goes with it."

Before he could move his hand, she reached up and curled her fingers around his. When she spoke, her voice was pitched low, husky, sexy.

"I don't believe a *word* of it," she murmured. "You make this stuff up, and gullible women buy it. Well I'm not gullible, and I think you're despicable for cheating people, defrauding them, lying, taking advantage." The words sounded sultry, more like an invitation than a condemnation.

He leaned across the table and kissed her lightly. Then, looking deeply into her eyes, he said solemnly, "I've been as honest with you today as I've ever been with anyone, lass. Every word of it true."

"But there's more, isn't there."

"Aye, but that's a tale for another day. You still have *nae* told me what's bothering you."

Pulling away from him, she said, "You're right. Something happened. I was . . . I *am*, very upset.

When I was getting coffee at Starbucks this morning, I bumped into the maid of an acquaintance of mine. Apparently, my friend died recently, unexpectedly." She lifted her lashes to stare into his eyes.

Inside his chest, his heart tightened and missed a beat. Suspicion crawled up his spine. "You have my condolences. You and this friend were close?"

"I suppose. In the way that wealthy women often are. She and I played tennis together, did lunch, that kind of thing. And now she's gone. Poof. Just like that. Life takes such odd turns, don't you think?"

"I'm sorry you're suffering so. Perhaps I can help."

"Perhaps you can. The maid told me the most shocking thing."

"It's my belief that maids know all the best gossip."

"Oh, this isn't gossip," she said, her eyes wide in astonished innocence. "The maid said the police think she was murdered for her necklace. Isn't that *awful*?"

Logan sat very still, his gaze locked on Andie's. "What else did this loquacious maid have to say?"

"Actually, she mentioned you. Said you'd been to see Drew a couple of times."

"You knew Drew Mochrie?"

"Small world, huh."

"And getting smaller."

She tossed her head. "Well, when I told the maid I knew you, she warned me to be careful. That *you* could have killed Drew and stolen the necklace."

"Anything's possible now, isn't it?"

Sitting back in her chair, she clasped her fingers on the table in front of her. With a small shrug, she said, "I told her it was ridiculous. I mean, you're charming, and you certainly con women out of their money and possibly their virtue, but really, you're not a jewel thief and a murderer . . . are you, Logan?"

Chapter 14

The devil . . . can sometimes do a very gentle-
manly thing.

Robert Louis Stevenson

Andie all but held her breath. She knew she was
riding a fine line with Sinclair, giving him partial
truths, not pulling any punches she didn't have to
pull. The mantra of undercover ops was *Stay close
to the truth, vary only when you can't avoid it.
Keep it as real as you can for as long as you can,
and when that doesn't work, lie like hell and pray
the bad guys buy it.*

She'd sensed early on that if she tried to cozy up
to Logan, ply him with flattery, try to seduce her
way into his confidence, he'd close ranks, keep his
secrets under tighter wraps, and she'd end up getting nothing at all from him, let alone an arrest
and conviction. Even though deceit might be his

stock-in-trade, he valued honesty when it came to his private life.

Sure, he might never come to trust her enough to give her the whole story, so she had to take whatever she could get—a candid comment, a slip of the tongue—something, anything that would give her an inkling where to dig deeper, maybe even deep enough to build a case.

Not for her—for *Bostwick*. She was fast coming to the conclusion that the commander was out to get Logan for reasons having nothing at all to do with the obvious, but something more subtle. With Bostwick, it was personal, and it ate at her that he was using her to do his dirty work.

Especially if Logan was guiltless of any wrongdoing. Hell, for all she knew, maybe he *was* everything Bostwick claimed him to be, and maybe he *was* the world's best con man, but damn, she didn't see it. The way Logan spoke to her, the look in his eyes, the tone of his voice, he'd been telling her the truth.

Sure, there was more, something under the surface that might prove damning, and she wished to hell she knew what it was, but Logan Sinclair had an honor about him, a code, for want of a better word. He wasn't slimy, and he wasn't a jerk, and— God help her in case she was wrong—he was *not* a killer.

But for the moment, at least, she was stuck going about business as usual. Until she came up with a way out of this mess, she was going to have to play along with the commander and just keep her fingers crossed and her wits about her. If she were smart, she'd find a way to roll over on the bastard, and the sooner the better.

The clock was ticking and she had yet to figure a solution to outing Bostwick. There was no way she was going to let the little shit manipulate her, or hurt anybody she cared about—including Logan.

But first she had to get the *real* goods on Logan, if there were any to get. She had to know what she was dealing with. Once she proved him innocent, she'd have some ammunition, some leverage. She could go to Internal Affairs and lay it all on the table, bring charges against the commander.

But if Logan had a skeleton in his closet, she needed to know about it in advance, or risk having everything blow up in her face.

It was the only thing keeping her from asking him outright and from telling him the truth. On the outside chance he really was guilty of something, she had to be cautious and keep her mouth shut, for the time being. If the moment ever arrived for her to lay it all out for him, she'd know it. Until then, she had to suck it up and do her job.

The dilemma was like a snakebite—painful, frightening, and maybe even fatal.

She and Logan sat across from each other as the tense silence started to feel like a physical object between them, a weight one or the other of them would have to move.

Finally, he eased away from the table and stood. Looking down at her, he said, "If you think me a thief and a murderer and have the bollocks to ask me about it to my face, you're either a very brave woman or a very foolish one."

She stood and faced him squarely. "Just tell me you didn't do it. That's all I need to hear."

He assessed her for a moment. "I did not do it. I first heard of it when the police questioned me. A detective by the ridiculous name of Darling." He laughed. "I'll just bet the bad guys go knocking in their knickers when Detective *Darlin'* comes callin'."

A glint of . . . something . . . lit his eyes, bringing to mind a calculating cat just before it pounced on some hapless rodent.

A good guy would declare his innocence and level with her; a bad guy would keep the game going.

Her stomach went queasy, and she suddenly felt more miserable than she ever had in her entire life.

She watched in silence as Logan moved across the room to stand at the window, his back to her. Over his shoulder, the city on the other side of the glass was nothing more than shadows and pinpricks of light. In the distance, sirens blared and blended into a weird kind of harmony.

"The necklace that was stolen," she ventured. "I heard it was fabulous. Worth millions. Did she ever show it to you?"

He turned, crossing his arms over his chest. And for one brief, insane moment, she saw him as a Scottish warrior, big, brawny, bold. She felt drawn to his warrior's heart, seduced by his warrior's courage, and she figured that in a past life—if there really was such a thing—he had to have been the leader. The image suited him perfectly.

With an unsettling gleam in his eyes, he raised his chin. "Aye."

"She did?" Her surprise wasn't feigned. "You saw the Star of Avril? When?"

He was watching her, watching for her reaction. Why should he examine her so closely? she wondered. What *was* he up to?

"As a matter of fact," he drawled, those eyes of his locked on her face. "I saw it the morning of the day she died. Why, I was probably the last person on earth to see that necklace before it . . . disappeared."

Logan watched as the interest in Andie's eyes flared.

He waited for her to say something, but for the longest time, she didn't. When it finally looked as though she were about to speak, he said, "Ah, but we've run off the track a bit, now haven't we? You wanted my help with yer *ghaists*."

She looked like she wanted to grab him by the throat and shake him, but all she said was, "Since you didn't take the necklace, I'm curious to know what happened to it. Can your spirit guide find it, or would it be better just to resort to MapQuest?"

"Allister and I can give it a try."

"Then let's get to it, shall we?"

Lowering his head, Logan closed his eyes and placed his knuckles on his temples.

"Are you all right?" she asked in a dry, sarcastic tone. "Are you going to faint . . . I mean, *black out* again?"

"Allister?" he said, as though he hadn't heard her. "Are you there? Aye, I can hear you now."

Even with his eyes closed, he knew Andie was glaring at him. He could feel the waves of heat coming off her body, sense the tension thrumming along her nerves.

In a flat tone, Andie drawled, "Tell us, oh swami of the magic lamp, where is the necklace? Hold on now, let me guess. It's in a dark place, safe, secret. It waits to be discovered by the true king—"

"Ah, lass," Logan interrupted, opening his eyes. "You wound me deeply, making light of my gifts—"

"Cut the crap, Logan. I've had enough. There is no Allister," she accused. "It's you, so give my intelligence a break here and bypass the double talk, okay?"

He lowered his hands, let the smile fade from his lips. In a dead serious voice, he said softly, "All right."

"Can you help me locate the necklace?"

"It's a police matter, I should think. Why would you look for it?"

She shrugged. "Just doing my civic duty. Besides, maybe there's a reward."

For the second time that day, Logan came that close to telling her the truth, but if he confided in her now—and she went straight to his enemy with the information—all would be lost. No, for the sake of the friend he'd once loved like a brother, he fought past his need to confess. The game would have to go on a little longer, but the time might come, and soon . . .

"I cannot help you with the necklace, lass," he said. "But I believe I can make some headway with your dreams."

Irritation flashed across her face, and she scowled up at him, then smiled. "Well, okay, sure. Why not."

She sat once more at the table and clasped her hands in front of her. "I've told you about the dreams, so if you have comments, let's hear 'em."

He dropped into the seat across from her and let his tense body relax. As he did, the humming inside his head began, the voices urging him to let them out, let them speak. Blinking, he clenched his jaw and fought them off, but the effort cost him. The dizziness began again, and he had to close his eyes.

"Logan?" Andie said. "You've gone a little pale. Are you okay?"

He nodded, unable to speak.

Tell her for me . . .

How could he let in only a little and keep the rest out? Reaching for the table, he grabbed the edge and held on.

Yer the only one can do it. Tell her, tell her, speak fer me, would you now . . .

"J-Jacob Harte," he muttered. "Lived. He was a real man. He . . . He, um, died in the line of duty. Shot straight through the heart at the age of thirty . . ."

The images and words began to bombard him now. Damn, he'd been strong for so long, what had changed? Had he simply grown tired of fighting it, or was it more than that? Was it that something about this woman made him want to lower his defenses, maybe even need to? Or maybe the story Emma Harte had to tell was so powerful, it had crept into his brain like a mind-altering drug, setting everything in motion, forcing him to deal with what he'd fought long and hard to keep his heart and mind closed to.

Andie's voice penetrated his brain. "Logan? Are you okay? Is there more? Logan?"

More?

He clenched his teeth as he felt the sweat trickle down his back . . .

A pretty blond woman, crying, desperate, torn between two men . . .

The baby, where's my baby? I can't go without knowing . . .

A staccato blast fills the air, the scent of gunpowder . . .

A young man in a blue uniform falls into the woman's arms . . .

No! she screams. Jacob, no! I did this! I killed him! How can it be, how can it?

But I cannot go without him . . . without Jacob . . . without Sean . . .

I cannot go . . . will not go!

What have I done? Dear God, what have I done . . .

Logan opened his eyes to see Andie crouched at his feet, her eyes genuinely worried. His clothing was saturated with cold sweat, but his mouth was dead dry.

"Thirsty," he whispered.

She leaped up, and in a moment, was back with a glass of water. He drained it, then wiped his mouth on his sleeve.

"You are connected to her, Andie," he panted. "To Emma Harte."

"But how?"

He licked his lips. "Don't know . . . only know, she did it. It's why she's still here."

"Did it? Did what?"

"Killed her husband. Killed the man she loved. Shot him. His spirit went on without her, so she lingers . . . looking for him . . . waiting for him to come find her, take her with him. There's more."

"Tell me."

"They had a wee babe. A son. Sean. She's desperate to find him. Looking, looking, for a hundred years. Lost and looking . . . never finding. It's why her spirit remains. She's looking for her dead husband and her baby son."

"But she loved Jacob. I mean, in my dreams, she . . . she adored him. Why would she *kill* him?"

"I don't know," he muttered, letting his weary head fall back. Closing his eyes once more, he whispered, "I don't know."

Chapter 15

We are all travelers in the wilderness of this world...

Robert Louis Stevenson

Ethan gestured to the file in his hand. "Officer Jacob Harte died the night of the earthquake. Firemen found him inside a shop they were about to dynamite."

Andie glanced down at the folder. "But his death wasn't a result of the quake."

"He'd been shot through the heart." A sheepish grin tilted his mouth. "I guess there's a joke in there somewhere."

When Andie didn't return her brother's smile, he handed her the folder. "Sorry. A little gallows humor there. Nobody was ever charged with the murder. It was assumed he was shot by a looter."

"Assumed?" In her fingers, the file felt smooth, the

paper cool. She wanted to hug it to her body, warm it, somehow give it life. "What about Emma?"

Ethan shoved his hands in his jeans pockets and lifted a shoulder in a small shrug. "*Nada*. She seems to have fallen off the face of the earth that night. Things were frantic after the quake and fire, and documentation is sketchy at best. She was probably killed in the quake and her body never identified. Or maybe she just left town."

"She didn't," Andie whispered absently while her mind tried to reconcile the dreams with the reality she now held in her hands. "She never went anywhere."

"How do you figure?"

The waterfront where they stood was windy and cool. Andie watched as a breeze off the bay ruffled Ethan's hair. He turned his head toward her, and she saw her own reflection in his dark glasses.

She took in a breath, blew it out. "I just *know*."

Maybe Emma's body had died that night, but her spirit remained; without doubt, Andie knew it was true. Her dreams of the woman, the events of her life a hundred years ago, were too vivid, the story they told, too real.

A cold chill slid to the base of her spine as though somebody had run an ice cube down her bare back.

Though she had never before given the paranormal a second thought, the events of the last few weeks had changed all that. Emma's ghost—or spirit or soul, whatever in the hell people called the remains of a person's energy—lingered. Apparently, the woman had a message for Andie—though the nature of that message, and why Emma had chosen Andie to receive it, was confusing and thoroughly unclear.

Logan seemed convinced Emma and Andie were connected, related in some way. But how could he make such a claim when he didn't even know her real name.

Or did he?

. . . darlin' Andie . . . Andie darling . . .

Damn, had he made her as a cop? He was a smart man; he must have either figured it out or had access to high-level resources.

Wait, wait, wait, she admonished herself. She was getting off track. For the moment, she would set those thoughts aside and examine them later. Right now, she had another mystery to solve.

"Andie?" Ethan said, rousing her from her thoughts. "What do you mean you just *know . . .*"

"I don't know *how* I know, Ethan, I only know she died that night, too. She just . . . *did*."

Andie had rendezvoused with Ethan in front of The Cannery on Fisherman's Wharf, grabbed some to-go coffee, then crossed Jefferson to walk out on the Hyde Street Pier. Touristy as hell, but she didn't care. She adored San Francisco, especially the waterfront.

Approaching a weatherworn bench, still a little damp from the morning fog, she sat with the file resting on her lap. She took in a deep breath of brisk salty air while she let her fingers slide over the file. Ethan remained standing, his stance wide, his attention focused on the bay behind her, where Alcatraz sat like a crazy kind of battleship anchored on a choppy sea.

The file on her lap seemed to grow heavy. She knew it contained photographs. Would the faces she was about to see match those of the people in her dreams?

What if they didn't? Would she feel relief . . . or disappointment? And if they did match, would it mean her subconscious had been invaded by the spirit of a woman who had died a hundred years ago?

Her fingers trembled only a little as she eased opened the file; her breath snagged in her throat, and she nearly gasped out loud. Blinking back tears, she let the shock run its course as she tried to focus on the photograph of Emma Harte.

On barely a breath, she whispered, "Oh my God, it's her."

Though the tintype's ecru-and-khaki hues had faded, the young woman who stared serenely up at Andie from a world that existed a century ago was the very woman of her dreams.

Andie let her gaze run over the picture. Emma Harte was lovely. Her hair had been brushed back and up, pinned into the Gibson Girl style of the day. Her light eyes gleamed with intelligence and undisguised mirth. She had a full mouth that curved into a smile, as though she knew some secret she was bursting to tell. Inside Andie's head, she heard Emma's voice, her Irish accent sweet and rich and honest.

Though she'd only seen Emma in dreams, looking down at her photograph now, she felt the woman was familiar in a way she hadn't realized before. Something about her forehead perhaps, or the set of her jaw. And maybe a little something around the eyes. Though it was an elusive familiarity, it couldn't be denied.

Had what Logan said been true? Were she and Emma Harte related? If so, it must be a distant connection, since neither Ethan nor Nate had been able to find a direct link.

"It *is* her," she said flatly. "I can't explain it, Ethan, but this is the woman I've been dreaming about."

"Okay." Ethan stared down at her for a few moments, then said, "What about the man?"

Taking a deep breath, Andie slid Emma's photograph off the top, revealing a second picture.

Jacob Harte wore a policeman's uniform and bowler hat. His handlebar moustache all but obscured his mouth, but the line of his strong jaw was clear. He had a fine nose, high cheekbones, dark hair. And he was handsome.

Andie glanced up at Ethan, then down again at the photograph of Jacob, then back up at Ethan. "Did you, uh, notice anything odd about this picture?"

"Maybe," came the curt reply.

"*Maybe?*" she drawled. "Ethan, he looks just like *you*."

Removing his dark glasses, he rubbed the bridge of his nose. With a slow nod, he said, "I thought it was just my imagination."

"No. He looks exactly like you."

"And the woman," he said. "You look like her."

Andie shook her head. "I-It must be our imagination. We're trying to find a resemblance, trying to make it fit, that's all. We're not related to these people."

Ethan shoved his dark glasses back on, put his hands on his hips, set his jaw. "I don't know. I guess we could be. Maybe Grandpa Jack's father had a brother—"

"That would explain why you look like Jacob, but not why I look like Emma."

Ethan rubbed his jaw. "Why does it matter? If the family tree gets a little confusing way back when, what does that have to do with now?"

Andie studied the two photographs. "Well, it doesn't, except for my dreams and the possibility that this Emma Harte is trying to . . . uh . . . send me some kind of message." She closed the file and shook her head. "There's no way I can say that without sounding totally loony."

For a moment, Ethan gazed out across the bay, then rolled his lips together and shrugged. "A couple of years ago, I would have agreed with you. But my wife . . . I mean, you know, Georgie . . . well, like, okay, here's the deal. For Christ's sake, I'm married to a woman who makes me carry a green-silk hankie in my pocket so I'll stay healthy. And, what's even weirder, I actually *do* it."

Andie smiled up at her brother. "It's only because you love her so much."

He shrugged, then a faraway smile turned his mouth into a that-close-to-being-silly grin. "Yeah," he said quietly. "But that's beside the point. I mean, while I still don't buy her whole feng shui thing, I have come to accept certain, um, elements of it, I guess you'd say, and if my wife thinks my carrying a green-silk hankie will keep me safe, I don't have a problem with that. So if you tell me you have dreams of a woman who looks like you, who lived a hundred years ago, who's trying to send you some kind of message, well hell, who am I to throw stones?" He shrugged again. "I mean, maybe Nate's right. Maybe you should go see Tabitha and have her help interpret your dreams. It can't hurt, can it?"

A blessed event, they call it! Blessed when it's over, and that's a fact!

With my belly swollen twice the size of California, my knees up and spread wide, all dignity has vanished, and I feel vulnerable and even shamed. I've never seen a babe born, so this is new to me, and perplexing. I'm used to knowing what I'm about, but this has stolen my self-assurance from me and replaced it with bewildering doubt.

Sure, and I'm giving a heave and a push, but I may as well be trying to roll a barrel of nails up Telegraph Hill with me little finger, as shove Jacob's son into this world.

"Emma," Mary darlin' says to me . . . like I could hear a word she says above my own yellin'. "I can see the baby's head now." Her eyes are wide, her pretty mouth curved into a bow. "Soon, now, Emma. Very soon. Do you have anither push in you, gal?"

"Anither push?" I'm yelling. Though I love her dearly, 'tis a truly stupid question she's askin' me, and don't I know it! "I'll give you anither push . . . me doubled fist in me husband's handsome snout, the rascal! If he ever comes near me again with his bulgin' pole, I'll be slammin' it flat with me cast-iron pan, and that'll teach him to be sweet-talkin' me come a foggy Sunday mornin'!"

But Mary, she smiles. "Ah, yer sayin' that now, gal, but it'll be different come by and by. And when yer holdin' yer own sweet babe in yer arms, you'll be glad of that Sunday mornin', and wishin' fer anither."

A pain the likes of which I've never felt seizes my spine, and my belly tightens. Placing my sweating hands atop the mound, I heave to, letting loose with a yelp that sets my own ears a-ringing. I collapse onto the bed, the linens near soaked as they are with sweat from my own poor body.

"That's fine," Mary whispers. "Here he comes, and fine he is, gal. Ooh, there you are my sweet lad. And a slippery little angel, to be sure . . ."

I barely hear what it is she's going on about, so glad I am for the pain to have eased.

The pain . . .

"Is he out, then?" I ask, my voice no more than a squeak. "Is he here? Why can't I see him? Why can't I hear him?"

My son is dead! My own wee babe dead! Why is he not wailing like a banshee? My heart ceases to beat as terror grips at me like the very fist of Death. My fingers claw at the damp bed linens, and I try to rise. "Mary . . . tell me!"

"Lay yerself down, gal," says Mary, calm as you please. "'Tis a strapping lad, Emma, but yer not done as of yet. Give us anither quick push."

I muster a bit of energy and do as she bids. In a distant sort of way, I feel something slide out of my body. The bloody bits that come after the baby, must be.

Over my still-swollen belly, I see Mary pick up my sewing scissors. A bit of a snip, and my wee

*babe and I are parted, one from the other, for now,
and for always.*

*That's when it happens . . . that's when the tears
come. Tears mix with sweat on my cheeks until I
can no longer tell which from which. I try to catch
a glimpse of my newborn son, but my sobs jerk
my body so, and my eyes are too blurred to get a
lasting look.*

*For these long nine months, I've carried his tiny
life inside my body. He and I were close as two
people can be, and now he's out into the world,
and we're separate. How can I protect him?
Already, he's an arm's length away, just born
though he is. We'll never be so close again, and
I feel that. Feel the ache of it in my heart, and I
wonder, how can such a joyful day be so sad at
the same time?*

*And now I hear them, my son's cries. The first
one comes soft, like he were chokin' on a fish bone.
Then* anither *wee squeak. Ah, but that was just
the warm-up. Now comes a lusty bawl that nearly
shakes the windows.*

*"And there he is then," I choke through my tears.
"Jacob's son, and my own."*

*I raise my head just as Mary wraps a thin blan-
ket around the lad and lifts him up for me to see.
And I grin, wide and laughing through my tears.
He's beautiful, with his red face and dark, damp
hair. Gently then, Mary sets the noisy bundle into
the crook of my arm, and I hug him close.*

"*And welcome to the world, Sean Jacob Harte,*" *whispers I to my babe.* "*You sure took yer time gettin' here.*"

His face scrunches up, and he yowls his agreement.

"*Put him to yer diddie, gal,*" *says Mary,* "*while I get all this cleaned up. Go ahead. He'll know what to do.*"

For the first time, I look hard at Mary, her own eyes red with tears.

"*I'm sorry,*" *says I.* "*I'm thankful of yer help, and glad for yer abiding friendship, but . . . I'm also sorry. I hadn't thought how hard on you this would be . . .*"

With a clean rag, Mary wipes the tears from her pale cheeks. "*'Tis no matter,*" *she says lightly, and I know she's lyin'. Now that I have a wee babe of my own, I understand her loss so much better.* "*'Twas a long time ago,*" *she says, stronger now.* "*And God's will for all that. Besides, I can pour all my lost love onto this wee one of yours. That'll be joy enough.*"

I smile into Mary's kind eyes, and she smiles back at me. Then I cup my hand around Sean's head, his hair so fine and soft, and the same dark shade as his da's. Easing up, I move him to me, and slide my soaked nightgown off my shoulder. Mary helps me put him to my breast. He nuzzles me there, opens his wee mouth, and latches on right away. The strength of his sucking takes me by surprise, as does the pain that follows as my milk lets down for the first time.

As my wee babe suckles his first meal, I gaze down at him in wonder. My son, mine and Jacob's. Does every new mither feel her heart double in size, the first time she lays eyes on her newly born child?

The birth of my son has made of us a family, me and Jacob and Sean. My life is complete now, and I can't imagine how much happier I could ever be. I only wish Jacob could've been here to witness his son's first moments, but he'll be home from work soon enough, and then the two men in my life and I will be together.

Joy, unlike anything I've known, fills my heart to near bursting, and I feel hot tears slide down my cheeks and into my mouth, and I don't care. Let them come. I'm a wife and I'm a mother, and it's nothing I'd dreamed of wanting so much, but realize now, I could never have lived without.

I feel a strange fierceness well up in me then, an anger, a fury of sorts, and I know that, without a doubt, I'd fight to the death to protect my wee babe from harm, and my husband, too . . .

Aye, to the death . . . and more.

Andie opened her eyes to meet her sister-in-law's gaze. "So, Tabby," she said flatly. "You're the psychic dream interpreter. What did that dream mean?"

Tabitha March Darling, Nate's wife of nearly two years, gently placed her hands on her swollen belly and closed her eyes. The maternity top she wore was thankfully devoid of pink bunnies and arcing rainbows, but was somewhat elegant, and the same vivid blue as her eyes. Until she'd actually met Tabby, Andie had wondered why sensible Nate had fallen for a New Age type, but in the ensuing months, discovered her sister-in-law was smart and sweet and fun, and obviously head over heels in love with Nate. They made a cute couple, and in July, they'd be a family.

The memory of Emma Harte's words played through Andie's head like the strains of a lost melody.

Tabby's lashes fluttered, and she opened her eyes again, a look of confusion furrowing her brow. Absently, she curled a lock of strawberry blond hair over her ear.

"It . . . I mean, the dream you related to me," Tabby began, her words halting, her tone uncertain, "didn't mean anything."

Andie felt her mouth turn down. "So this was a waste of time." She'd known it would be, but both of her brothers had urged her to give it a try, so she'd only done it just to assuage them.

"That's not what I mean," Tabby said, gently rubbing her tummy with her open palms. "What I should have said was, what you related to me wasn't a dream."

"Sure it was. Last night—"

"Andie," Tabitha interrupted. "As I explained,

the way this works is, I hold your hand, you tell me your dream, and I can see it as you relate it. Then I can interpret it. At least, that's how it usually goes." She shook her head. "But I didn't see any dream. Instead, I received information psychically, more like a radio transmission than HDTV."

"I don't—"

"Bottom line, what you related was not a dream. It was more like somebody telling a story around a midnight campfire. Dreams are representational, this was a page from a psychic diary. It was linear, rational, and it was, well, it was *real*."

Andie shot out of her chair, her hands curled into fists at her side. "No! I can't buy that. *Don't* buy it. No. A ghost has *not* invaded my head."

Holding her belly, Tabitha rose to her feet like she was trying to balance a melon on her lap without dropping it.

"It's okay, Andie," she panted softly. "You are free to believe what you want. I'm just telling you what I got from it, and what I got was that this Emma Harte has chosen to tell you her story. The problem for you is, she's revealing it to you scene by scene. You can't ask her questions or fine-tune the transmission . . ."

Her brows lowered, and she looked thoughtful for a moment. "Or can you?" she said. "There's a man in your life, right? Um, a tall man with black hair. He speaks with a brogue. He can help you."

"Logan Sinclair?"

Tabitha's lips formed a happy smile. "Yes! Is that his name? Yes, Logan can help you. He can talk to Emma, ask questions. He can—"

"How do you know about Logan? Did Nate put you up to this?"

Tabby looked a little bewildered. "Nate? No. I got Logan from you. He's in your head, and in your . . ."

Lowering her lashes for a moment, a small smile crept over her lips.

"Um, you're connected to him, and he to you. You've known each other through many lifetimes. You must feel it, Andie. Feel that connection. You and Logan are, well, you're true soul mates—"

"We are not!"

God, she was shouting. *Soul mates.* What a ridiculous idea. Here she'd come to see her sister-in-law for some advice—advice she was admittedly prepared to ignore—and her silly crush on Logan was being thrown in her face. When she got her hands on her brothers, she'd ring their necks for suggesting she talk to Tabitha!

In a more measured tone, she said, "We can't be soul mates. Logan is under investigation for . . . things. He's a suspect in . . . things. He is *not* my soul mate."

Tabby slowly eased herself back into the chair. Clasping her hands on top of her stomach, she said, "My job was to interpret your dream. Whether you believe me or not is totally up to you. As for Emma, she's revealing her story to you, but my feeling is, when she's done, it won't be resolved. For that, you're going to need Logan's help."

Andie grabbed her purse from the coffee table and headed for the door. "I doubt it. Logan is a fraud, and maybe worse. I've tried to accept him as a good guy, but he has too many secrets. I seriously doubt we're soul mates, and I'm positive I'll never ask for his help."

Tabby smiled but said nothing.

As Andie wrapped her fingers around the doorknob, she stopped. "Look, I appreciate your taking time to help me. I know you believe what you told me, but I don't."

"That's your right. It's not my place to judge you, Andie. Only you know what's best for you. Your instincts will guide you, as they always have."

Andie nibbled on her lower lip for a moment. Then, gesturing to Tabby's swollen tummy, she said, "You doing okay? My niece or nephew comfy in there?"

"Very comfy, but I'll be glad when he or she decides to make his or her appearance. My bladder will be grateful, and my ankles will rejoice."

"So, um, what's it like to be pregnant? Aren't you afraid, you know, of childbirth?"

Tabby rubbed her tummy again while a thoughtful smile played over her lips. "Being pregnant is complicated, emotional, scary, and fabulous. Sometimes my body feels like the enemy, and I can't get comfortable, but just as often, I feel great, like all is right with the world."

She raised her brows. "Yeah, I have to admit I'm a little afraid of childbirth, worried from the horror stories I've heard about the pain and all." Her lashes lowered. "I guess my biggest concern is that I'll disappoint Nate somehow. I love him so much. I want this baby for *me,* but I also want to give him this gift, for want of a better word. It's, um, it's sort of hard to explain."

Turning the knob, Andie opened the door and stepped into the threshold. She hesitated, then met Tabitha's calm gaze. "I think I understand. I don't believe in your psychic dream-interpretation thing, but you're a very cool sister-in-law. Nate's a lucky man."

"Thank you," Tabby said with a laugh as she pushed herself to her feet. "Look, I have to get out of these damn shoes, find some chocolate somewhere, and go to the bathroom, and not necessarily in that order." Her expression turned serious. "Andie, it doesn't matter to me whether you're a believer. It's not my call, it's yours. But I would request one thing of you."

"Name it."

"The next time you see Logan, ask him who he *really* is. Why he *really* came to San Francisco."

Andie blinked hard. "Who he . . . why he *what*? What are you talking about?"

"Just ask him. Hell, he might even be ready to tell you."

Chapter 16

The saints are the sinners who keep on trying.

Robert Louis Stevenson

"In other words . . ." Andie shifted the cell phone from one ear to the other and turned into the parking garage near Logan's hotel. "Drew Mochrie died of a broken neck."

"That's what I said." Dylan's deep voice sounded indignant. "Spinal fracture and cervical-cord transaction at C1, yada, yada, and just for good measure, yada."

"I want to see a copy of the coroner's report myself."

"Granted. But it's gonna say the same thing when you read it, except for the yada stuff."

Andie's tires squeaked, the sound echoing through the cement cavern as she rounded the first turn and began the approach to the next parking level. Even through her closed windows, the scent of spent exhaust with nowhere to go irritated her nose.

"Anything else?" she asked as she began looking in earnest for a parking spot.

"There's a very nice paragraph here devoted to external signs of trauma, which basically translates to the fact that somebody put his hands around her throat, snapped her neck like a dry twig after a long hot summer, then tossed her down the cellar stairs."

"A dry twig, Dylan?" she drawled.

"Yeah, well, I'm taking this creative-writing class at night. So many similes, so little time."

"Don't I know it."

Andie shifted the cell phone again, then spotted a vacant space and slowed. "So Drew Mochrie was murdered." She slid neatly into the parking space between a red PT Cruiser and a silver SUV. "Coroner's report say anything else we can use?"

"Nah, that's pretty much it, but I think it's obvious that whoever has the necklace is our perp. So, as the French say, *Cherchez les* rocks."

"Are you taking a French class at night, too?"

"Hey, you got it, didn't you, so stop criticizing."

Andie turned off the ignition, then checked her reflection in the rearview mirror. Absently finger-combing her hair, she said, "Okay, Dylan. Let's put aside for a moment the fact that your French totally stinks, I disagree that whoever has the necklace is the killer. Even if it's recovered, I don't think the DA's office will accept possession as evidence enough to prosecute a homicide, do you? I mean, whoever has it could say they found it in an alley or bought it on eBay or something, not realizing it was stolen. We need to deliver motive, opportunity, and means."

"Seems to me your Mr. Sinclair had all three."

"Sure, but maybe he wasn't the only one. It wouldn't be good detective work to focus in on one suspect who may be innocent, while the trail to the real perp grows cold."

Why was she defending Logan? And why did she have to explain "good detective work" to her partner?

Bostwick's instructions oozed into her brain. *No evidence? No problem. Create evidence. I want Sinclair's ass . . .*

"Um, Dylan?"

"Yeah?"

She sat back in her seat and lowered her head, the phone to her ear as she tried to decide how to broach the subject. "Is there, I mean, has anyone . . . uh, has somebody like, say, Commander Bostwick, tried to influence this investigation? Maybe put some pressure on you to hurry things up or maybe misinterpret evidence . . ."

The connection was silent for a moment, then Dylan gave a sharp laugh. "Nope. I just figure that the woman was murdered for the necklace, so whoever has it probably killed her. Sinclair was known to have associated with the vic about the time of the homicide and robbery, so I'm just saying we should focus our attention there first. That's all I'm saying. I'm not saying anything else." He cleared his throat. "Are we okay on that, Inspector?"

She nodded. "Okay, yeah, sure." Raising her head, she said, "But you know, if you *should* encounter any kind of, uh, situation, I hope you'll talk to me about it, because I—"

"If I do," he growled, cutting her off, "I will. Until then, we have nothing to discuss. Copy that?"

Did she ever. "Dylan, are you *sure*, because there's something—"

"Positive." Andie heard him take in a deep breath and blow it out. "Okay, so where are you now, and what are you up to?"

She let a moment of silence pass between them. Something was most definitely up, and he most definitely didn't want to talk about it. She figured she pretty much knew what it was, and she also knew her partner well enough that if he wasn't ready to talk about it, pressuring him would do no good.

"Let me just say one thing, Dylan."

"Shoot."

"If the same thing that's happening to me is happening to you, we need to do something about it. Bring this to an end. Do you copy that?"

"Copy. Let's move on now, all right?"

"Uh, yeah, okay. Well," she stumbled as she

closed and locked her car. "At the moment, I'm at Sinclair's hotel. I've never had a chance to do a search of his room, so maybe a look-see will turn something up."

"Where is he? Is he there?"

"I don't know. Doesn't matter. I can get the maid to let me in. If the necklace is there, I mean, if there's any evidence at all linking him to the homicide or how he bilks his clients, I'll find it."

There was a momentary pause, then Dylan said, "So . . . what if there's nothing to find?"

"Then I won't find anything."

More silence.

"Dylan? What are you implying?"

Another pause. Then, "I, uh, nothing. Forget it. Listen, I've got to interview a mess of witnesses on the Staunton case. It's really heating up, and it's going to need my undivided attention for a while. Can you handle the Sinclair case solo for a few days?"

"Knock yourself out."

There was silence for a moment, then he said slowly, "Hey, uh, listen. Don't do anything stupid, like . . . uh, never mind. Just don't do anything stupid."

Andie felt her brows snap together. "What in the hell does that mean—Dylan? Don't hang up on me, Jericho. Hey! Hello?"

In frustration, she slapped the cell phone closed and dropped it into her purse. Where did Dylan get off admonishing her against doing anything stupid? Stupid how? What on earth was he talking about?

She pressed the redial and instead of Dylan, got his voice mail. Damn the man. He didn't want to talk to her, so he wouldn't answer until he was good and ready.

Bostwick's used-car-salesman grin popped into her brain. Had Dylan been warning her against the commander? Or was it Logan he was talking about?

Just how and when had this all gotten so complicated? She'd been sent undercover to gather evidence in a fraud case. Difficult, but fairly routine.

Yet overnight, the whole thing had blown up in her face and now included homicide, robbery, possible conspiracy, bribery, and harassment. Throw in the fact she was maybe being haunted by the spirit of a woman who'd died a hundred years ago, and that pretty much put the icing on the Weird Cake!

A few minutes later, she exited the elevator on the fourth floor of the St. Francis Hotel and began walking down the thickly carpeted hallway. She'd planned her visit to coincide with the maid service, and was relieved when she spotted a service cart just outside Logan's open door.

Finally, a lucky break. She'd been prepared to show her badge to gain entry, but this was better.

Peeking inside, she saw the maid just finishing up

with the bed. Andie planted a concerned look on her face and entered the suspect's room. "Excuse me."

The maid stopped what she was doing and turned in Andie's direction.

Smiling, Andie said, "Has my husband been here? I did a little window-shopping this morning, and we were supposed to meet in the lobby downstairs, but I must have missed him."

"No, ma'am. Haven't seen anyone."

"Hmm, well. I wonder where he could be then." She shook her head as though she felt helpless. "*Men*, you know?"

The maid rolled her brown eyes and laughed. "Do I ever. After two husbands and four sons, I could write a book."

Andie set her purse on the bar next to Logan's laptop and wondered for a second if she had time to access it. "I promise not to get in your way. Hopefully, he'll come looking for me. We're going to go to the Wax Museum on Fisherman's Wharf. Have you been?"

The maid's face lit up. "Oh, yes, ma'am. My boys just love it. The Chamber of Horrors is the best part. Make sure you and your husband don't miss it."

"Thanks," Andie said. "We won't."

After giving the bed pillows an extra plumping, the maid nodded a good-bye and scurried out of the room, closing the door behind her.

Okay, first question: Where was Logan and when would he be back? Technically, that was two questions, but they were equal in importance so she figured the Question Police weren't going to show up and cite her.

Moving quickly to the nightstand beside the bed, she opened the only drawer. A Bible, a notepad, a phone book. She hurried to the desk and turned on the lamp. Another drawer, another notepad, a room-service menu, and a handful of literature on goods and services the hotel provided.

The TV set stood on a small chest of drawers. In the top drawer she was greeted by the usual men's things, neatly folded. She felt around, but nothing untoward presented itself. The other two drawers were empty.

The closet. Sliding the mirrored door open, she quickly checked the pockets of the three suits hanging there. Nothing. She inhaled and caught his scent, then decided to ignore her response to it.

His suitcase sat on the floor of the closet. How many minutes had passed? Would she have time to unzip it and put it back in order before he returned?

Two minutes later, she had checked it out and found nothing.

Pressing her luck, she hurried to the bathroom. Men's toiletries sat on the marble counter, a white bathrobe hung from a peg on the back of the door.

The bathroom was small, no place to really hide anything.

Then she thought of the toilet tank. The idea was absurd. He'd be a fool to keep anything of value there. Everybody knew that's where crooks hid things in hotel rooms, didn't they?

Even so . . .

She approached the toilet and stared at it. To check inside the water tank would be a silly and amateurish thing to do—yet now that she'd thought of it, she knew she had to look.

The white porcelain was cool to her touch. Lifting the lid a couple of inches, she peered inside the tank. Nothing but the black ball float met her gaze. As she was about to let the lid settle back into place, something in the bottom corner of the tank caught her attention.

Reaching into the cold water, she slid her hand past the float to grasp the plastic bag. Curling her fingers around it, she pulled it out and simply stared.

No. Her stomach felt queasy, her head light. *No. It can't be. He isn't a killer, he isn't.* What she knew about him, what she knew about herself, wouldn't allow it. Logan Sinclair's being a cold-blooded killer went against every instinct she'd ever had. There was no way she'd ever fall for a murderer the way she had for . . .

But the truth, she reminded herself, the reality of what she held in her hands could not be denied.

She had to get out of there before he returned. Without probable cause to search his room, the evidence she'd found would not be admissible. It hadn't been in plain sight, so she couldn't claim she'd stumbled on it. From this moment on, she had to be very careful . . .

Bostwick. He'd told her he wanted the necklace, that when she found it, she was to bring it to him, but if it was proof Sinclair has been involved in the Mochrie homicide, she had to leave it in place until she could obtain it legally.

Damn. She didn't want to give the necklace to Bostwick. Nor did she want to think about the ramifications of defying the commander and not turning it over. She stared down at the wet baggie in her hand.

She didn't want to find evidence Logan was a killer. She didn't want to question her feelings or her instincts or her carefully ordered world.

What she wanted was for Logan to be a good guy, for there to be some rational explanation for his having possession of the necklace, for his fake clairvoyance, for his reputation as a con man, for . . . *everything*.

And she sure as hell didn't want to be caught in the middle of this mess, but dammit, she was.

A slight shuffling noise behind her made her freeze in place. A moment ticked by, then another. The bag containing the stolen necklace weighed heavily in her hand as she turned to face the bathroom doorway . . . and the man who stood there.

"I see you found that clever hidin' place," he whispered. In his fist, the .38 he held pointed straight at her heart. Extending his free hand, palm up, he ordered, "Give it over, lass."

"Not so clever," she drawled. "I found it, and I'm not that bright."

He smiled, revealing a chipped front tooth. Greed and malice shone in his black eyes as he wiggled his fingers to silently reiterate his request.

"I'm curious," she said. "Who exactly are you?"

"Give me the fockin' necklace. Who I am is no concern of—"

"His name is Ollie."

Both Andie and the man named Ollie jumped in surprise at the softly spoken words. He whirled around, pressing his back against the open door. With both hands, he raised and aimed the gun at Logan, but before he could squeeze off a round, Logan's doubled fist shot out, slamming into Ollie's wrist, nearly knocking the gun from his hand.

"Ollie," Logan growled. "Give me the gun . . ."

"The bloody necklace is my share!" he yelped. "I've earned it, ye damn bastard!"

Grabbing a struggling Ollie by the collar, Logan dragged him away from the bathroom and tried to strong-arm him to the floor. But Ollie was skinny and tough, and though Logan was bigger and fast, the younger man squirmed out of his grip.

Logan lunged, wrapping his arms around Ollie's knees, taking him to the floor where they thrashed around. A table lamp teetered and fell. One of the chairs at the table toppled over backwards. A fist came up, followed by the sound of knuckles meeting flesh. A moan, a groan, gnashing teeth . . . the fight went on with no man the clear winner.

Andie hurried past them to her purse sitting on the bar. She popped it open, reaching for her weapon, but before she could grasp it, a muffled shot split the air, and the acrid bite of cordite flared in her nose.

Except for Logan's panting, silence filled the room.

On the floor, Ollie and Logan stared into each other's eyes. Then Ollie groaned and slumped into Logan's arms.

"Stupid son of a bitch," Logan gasped, his voice low and raspy. "Had to go and get greedy. Greed'll kill a man, Ollie. *Damn* you, I *liked* you, lad, I liked you! Why'd you have to go and pull a stunt like this?" His voice ended on a whisper, and it was so filled with regret, Andie felt a sense of pity wash over her.

Kneeling beside the wounded man, she went to put her fingers on the side of his neck, but Logan brushed them away, replacing them with his own. He was silent for a moment, then muttered flatly, "He's gone."

Over his heart, Ollie's white shirt bloomed dark with blood. His young face held a look of surprise, his eyes wide and unblinking, staring up at the ceiling as though something fascinating held his attention. His thin mouth formed a frozen O. His dead hand still clutched the .38.

"Um, we have to call the police," she mumbled.

"No police," Logan growled, still crouched over the body. "Even if somebody heard the shot, they'll not come running. One shot only, they'll think 'twas their imagination or a loud TV show."

"A man is dead," Andie snapped. "We *have* to call the police—"

"No!" His blue eyes flared with fury. "Let me handle it. I just need to think about this for a bit."

Across the barrier of Ollie's body, she glared at Logan in shocked wonder. Her first instinct was to pull out her badge—and her weapon.

Logan's dark hair was mussed, his forehead beaded with perspiration from the struggle. With the back of his hand, he wiped it away, then reached for her. Wrapping his fingers around her wrist, he rose to his feet, bringing her with him. "Get yer things. We have to leave."

She shook him off. "I'm not going any—"

"Ye'll do as I say. Now get yer things."

"No!"

"Andie—"

She stalked toward the bar, opened her purse, and reached for her weapon. Turning, she flashed her badge. "Inspector Andrea Darling, SFPD. Now sit down and shut up while I make a phone call."

His lids lowered a bit, and he shoved his hands into his pockets. "So, you're a cop."

"Aye," she snapped. "But you already knew that, didn't you."

He shrugged. "Remember, I am a clairvoyant."

"Bullshit."

A smile slowly spread across his face. "All right. I'll come along quietly. Make your phone call and haul me in, then." He raised his arms and pressed his wrists together as though waiting to be cuffed.

Flicking a glance between Logan and the dead Ollie on the floor, Andie narrowed her gaze and let the wheels roll around inside her head.

She motioned to the bed behind Logan. "Sit."

Logan lowered himself to the edge of the bed, his face unreadable. As she held her weapon on him, she sidled closer to Ollie's body. Watching carefully, she waited.

Finally, her patience paid off, and she pressed her lips together in a satisfied smile. Cocking a brow, she looked meaningfully over at Logan . . . who was scowling.

"All right, Ollie," she said. "You can get up now."

Logan crossed his arms over his chest. "Andie—"

"*Ollie*," she interrupted. "This game is over."

The "dead man's" eyes slowly shifted, and when they met hers, he grinned.

"An Oscar-winning performance," she said dryly. "Funny thing, though, about fake dead people. They have to breathe eventually." She wiggled her weapon in the direction of the bed. "Go sit next to your partner."

Ollie pursed his lips, then rose and did as instructed.

Andie eyed the two of them. "Logan Sinclair and Ollie . . . what's your whole name?"

"Oliver Kerr, ma'am."

She cleared her throat. "Logan Sinclair and Oliver Kerr, you're under arrest for maybe murder, definitely being in possession of stolen property, unlawfully discharging a weapon, and pretending to be dead—"

"Since when is that against the law?" Ollie said, his tone one of outrage.

"Since right now," she snapped. "You have the right to remain silent—"

"Before you get all wrapped around the axle with your arrest, Inspector," Logan interrupted. "I have something to show you."

She arched a brow. "I'll just bet."

"I'm going to stand up, and I want you to reach into my back pocket."

"Bribery won't work," she growled. "I don't know what the two of you were doing with your little murder scene here, but . . . hey!" As Logan defied her order, she yelped, "Sit! Stay!"

He raised his arms above his head. "Back pocket, left side." He turned to give her access.

She eased forward and dipped her hand into his pocket, then immediately stepped back out of range. Without her telling him to, he sat back down.

She flipped open the leather folder and stared down at the crown-and-crest badge. Around the perimeter, it read—

"*Scotland Yard!*" Her eyes wide, she choked, "Scotland Frickin' Yard?"

He smiled shyly. "Aye. Seems we have something in common, Inspector. Now if you wouldn't mind holstering yer weapon, I believe the question-and-answer portion of our program is about to begin."

Chapter 17

The cruelest lies are often told in silence.

Robert Louis Stevenson

Forty-eight hours were up; time for him to put his money where his mouth was. Failure to follow through created doubt, and he couldn't have that. He'd promised dire consequences for not complying with his wishes, and now it was time to deliver. Empty threats would gain him no rewards, but fortunately, he had never had a problem with talking the talk, then walking the walk.

Brad Bostwick pulled his car to a stop, flipped down the driver's side visor, and checked himself in the mirror. Straightening his tie, he spotted a bit of lint on the lapel of his navy wool suit. Irritated, he plucked it off with forefinger and thumb, then flicked the offending particle away like a dead bug. He lifted his clean-shaven chin and admired how professional he looked. Excellent. Ten minutes ago, he'd been at one of his wife's notoriously boring charity fund-raisers. He'd excused himself to make an important phone call—*de rigueur* for such an important man. But instead, he left the restaurant and drove to the park. If things went as planned— and they always did—he'd be back before anyone was the wiser.

This late on a weeknight, Golden Gate Park was nearly empty and generally quiet. He'd hoped a cold fog would roll in, hampering visibility, aiding him in his desire to keep this meeting on the QT. But the evening was shaping up to be clear, with a full moon and even a few stars winking overhead. No problem since he'd been careful to choose an isolated spot near a thick stand of trees, where two men having a rendezvous would not be observed or disturbed.

Exiting his car, he meandered down the narrow path that led through the trees to Stow Lake and the squat, green tile-roofed Chinese red pagoda. He'd left his car east of the lake and instructed his visitor to park on the west side. In the off chance somebody who recognized both men's cars should happen by, awkward questions might be raised that Bostwick most definitely wanted to avoid.

He had no doubt his orders would be followed to the letter. After all, his visitor's career was at stake, and both men knew it. True, he didn't really *want* to ruin the other man—he'd rather have results, but since those hadn't been forthcoming . . .

Conveniently, every man had something in his past that made persuasion so much easier. Years ago, Bostwick had discovered that holding a man's little peccadilloes over his head guaranteed a positive outcome, and this situation was no different.

He wanted Drew Mochrie's necklace; he would get it.

As the commander walked along the path, he thought about what he would do when he obtained the gems . . . more to the point, when he had the money selling them would get him.

Freedom. Ah, sweet freedom.

He would leave it all behind, all of it.

No more son-in-law to the former police commissioner.

No more husband to the socially prominent Gloria Bostwick.

No more father of two overindulged—by their mother, of course—ungrateful daughters.

And the pressures his career had placed on his shoulders over the years would be lifted. He'd fly away to Mexico, or maybe the Caribbean. With the millions the sale of that necklace would bring, he could buy a new identity and never look back. Perhaps Italy was a better choice. A villa on the Italian Riviera with hot and cold running maids—wouldn't that be nice? Warm, sunny Italy . . . and peace and quiet for the rest of his days.

From the moment he'd first seen that necklace, he'd known it was his ticket to a new life. Still, it had taken nearly two years and a very circuitous route to obtain it. He was closer now than ever, and nothing . . . *no* one . . . was going to screw this up for him.

He stopped, smiled to himself, and closed his eyes for a moment.

Sure, some would say he was a monster, but he wasn't. He was just a simple man who'd done a good job for a lot of years and deserved to reap the rewards and settle into a comfortable retirement.

Ten million dollars would certainly do that.

The sound of footsteps reached him, bringing him out of his woolgathering, and he opened his eyes. Moving quickly off the path, he eased out of sight around the trunk of a large willow tree. From the shadows of the lush, overhanging limbs, he watched as the form of a man emerged from the darkness at the top of the hill and began down the path to the lake.

Just as the man reached the willow, Bostwick stepped out, startling his visitor.

"Relax," Bostwick said with a chuckle. "Did you come alone?"

"Of course I did," the man snarled. "You think I want anybody to know about this?"

Bostwick smiled. "You wearing a wire?"

Holding open his Western-style denim jacket, the man said, "Hell no. You can check if you want."

"Hey, if you can't trust a cop, who can you trust, right?"

"Eat me."

Bostwick clicked his tongue a couple of times. "Temper, temper."

In the deepening shadows, he could see the gleam of fury in his visitor's eyes. "Let's get on with this, shall we? You have status for me?"

The man shoved his hands into his jeans pockets and growled, "Nothing to tell. The necklace hasn't surfaced yet."

"That is *ridiculous*," he hissed. "It can't have disappeared into thin air. I'll bet *she* knows where it is. I'll bet she's in cahoots with *him*. That's the only explanation, unless you're lying to protect her!"

The man shrugged. "I'm not lying. I don't know where in the hell the damn thing is. Can I go now?"

"Not until I'm satisfied with your answers."

"Look, Bostwick. If she has it, she sure hasn't said anything to me."

The commander slowly nodded, then blew out a long sigh. "Well, no matter. What I have planned will encourage her to come forward." He paused. "But in order to make it work, I need your help."

"I've already helped you all I'm gonna."

"It occurred to me you might say that." Another meaningful pause. "Let me preface this by saying I informed the lady that if she didn't find—and hand over—the necklace within forty-eight hours, something horrible would happen."

He raised his brows and looked into the other man's eyes. When his visitor began backing away, he knew his meaning was beginning to dawn. Reaching inside his jacket, Bostwick withdrew his weapon.

The other man froze, his gaze locked on the barrel of the gun in the commander's hand. "I told you, she doesn't have it!" he shouted. Taking two steps back, he raised his palms as though begging a favor. "Don't do this, Bostwick. You don't have to do this. Give me a little more time to talk to her. Look, I've done everything you've asked. Sold myself down the river, my career, my fucking *honor*. I'll be damned if I let you—"

The Glock made a pop-popping sound as it discharged three times into his visitor's chest. Without emotion, he watched as the man fell to his knees, then slowly slumped to the ground.

Lifting his head, the commander stood still and listened. All around him, there was silence. No shouts, no screams, no whistles or sirens or alarms. Good.

Taking a clean handkerchief from his pants pocket, he wiped the unregistered gun, then walked to the edge of the path and threw it into the lake. When he heard the deep-sounding plunk a few seconds later, he returned to the body.

"Sorry to blindside you like that, but if taking you out will buy me a new life . . ." He paused, grinning to himself. ". . . I'm willing to make the trade, Jericho."

By the time he reached his car, he was feeling damn good. Sliding behind the wheel, he thought, yeah, life was pretty nice, and about to get a whole lot nicer.

She checked his badge, read his credentials, made him empty his pockets. Even though it was the wee hours of the morning in the UK, she called the London office, then the office in Edinburgh, then Ethan, who knew somebody who knew somebody who knew somebody at the Yard, and had them check. She did everything she could think of to prove Logan was a phony, but she couldn't because he wasn't.

Logan Sinclair really was a police officer— Detective Chief Inspector Logan S. *Macmillan* of the New Scotland Yard CID.

"And the clairvoyant thing?" Andie said, tossing his passport and badge onto the bed.

Picking up the items and returning them to his pocket, Logan smiled. "I told you the truth about that, lass. As much as I could at the time, at any rate. Just after university, for a while, I plied my trade and made a name for myself as clairvoyant to the stars. But I didn't want to sully the family name, so I forwent Macmillan and used my middle name, Sinclair."

"What about when you became a police officer?"

"Well, rather than tossing all that work down the proverbial loo, it was decided that my former glory, such as it was, might work to advantage in certain circumstances."

While the decidedly not-dead Oliver Kerr excused himself to go wash the fake blood off his hands and change his shirt, Andie fought to understand and control her emotional mix of outrage, relief, and delight. She paced the hotel room several times, finally stopping in front of Logan.

Part of her wanted to scream at him for his duplicity.

Part of her wanted to sink to the floor in thanks.

Part of her wanted to fling her arms around his neck and kiss him.

In the end, she went with Option Four—doubling her fists and slamming them into his chest. "Goddammit," she huffed. "Why didn't you tell me you're a *good* guy?"

He covered her hands with his own, and bent his head to gaze deeply into her eyes. "Sorry, lass," he said softly. "There's nothin' good about me, and that's a fact. What I am is on the right side of the law is all."

"But you haven't always been."

"True enough." He kissed the tip of her nose. "I used to be a lawless cad."

"What turned you around?"

A sad look came into his eyes. A look of loss and grief and melancholy. "A friend," he murmured. "A good friend. Saved my life. Kept me going during my darkest days, he did. He was steadfast and true. Rare and elusive qualities in this world. I do what I do now because of him, and in honor of his memory."

"His memory? He's . . ."

"That's all the explaining I mean to do, Andie. The rest is best left for another time." He kissed the tip of her nose again.

"All right." She eased her body up against his, craving the closeness she'd denied herself since she'd met him. "But I'm still furious with you for lying to me."

His voice held a note of fake outrage as he said, "And you were on the up-and-up the whole time with me, were you, Inspector Andrea Darling of the San Francisco Police Department?"

"I was just doing my job."

"And I was just doing mine."

"I . . . I have a lot of questions," she stumbled. "About why you're here, what you're after."

"Ask away. I'll tell you what I can."

She licked her lips. "The most immediate question is . . . are you going to kiss me now—"

The "or not" part got lost when Logan's lips met hers

She went up on her toes as his arms slid around her waist. He pulled her tight, tighter, until their bodies were aligned, and she could feel the steady beat of his heart against her breast.

His mouth was soft, his kiss tender, as though he'd been waiting to kiss her like this from the beginning. No secrets now, no obstacles. Just two people in each other's arms, the long waiting and wondering over, the time for honesty at hand.

He tugged on her lips, then pulled back a fraction to smile down at her. "So you were sent undercover to get the goods on a con man, eh?"

"Aye," she murmured against his mouth. "A fake clairvoyant who cheats wealthy women out of their money or their virtue." She smiled up at him. "They figured you targeted Drew Mochrie as your next victim. I was supposed to find out how you got your inside information. Guess I know that answer to that, Mr. Secret Agent man."

She lowered her lashes and remembered her immediate—and unprofessional—attraction to him. Her brother's warning, the commander's blackmail, the murder, the necklace, even her bizarre dreams.

"It seemed a simple enough assignment at the beginning," she said. "But things have gotten more complicated than anyone would have imagined."

His aquamarine eyes turned stormy, all mischief gone. "Aye. And likewise."

"So," she said. "Tell me why you're here. What did you come to the U.S. for? Who are you after, Chief Inspector Logan S. Macmillan?"

A look of raw emotion passed over his face. "I'm after the man responsible for the murder of a countryman of mine."

"A countryman?"

"Aye. And a friend. Tolley Mochrie."

"Mochrie?" Andie's brow furrowed in confusion. "I thought Drew killed her brother."

Logan shook his head, then eased Andie out of his embrace. Stepping away, he went to the window and crossed his arms over his chest. With his back to her he said, "Drew may have been a willing accomplice, maybe not, but it was another who did the deed. He's the one I'm after. *He's* the one I'll have."

"Who, Logan?"

He turned then, his stance solid and fierce. Once more, she was reminded of an ancient warrior, armed and ready for battle. And very, very dangerous.

He searched her eyes and she got the impression he was debating whether he could trust her. The air between them grew thick, time slowed, stopped. The rage in his eyes made her want to look away, but she didn't.

"Who, Logan?" she whispered. "Who killed Tolley Mochrie? Who is it you're after?"

Through tightly clenched teeth, he bit out, "Your boss, it is, lass. Bradley Bostwick."

Chapter 18

Give us grace and strength to forbear, to persevere.

Robert Louis Stevenson

Ollie stepped out of the bathroom, took one look at the expression on the lass's face, and said brightly, "Right then. I'm off to grab a bite. Can I bring you two anything?"

Logan shook his head, then said to Andie, "You?"

But she was simply staring at him, jaw slack, eyes wide, like a kitten surprised by a Doberman.

"Well then," Ollie said. "I'm off."

As the door closed behind the departing Ollie Kerr, Logan said, "I've broken several regulations by telling you what I'm about, especially since you could turn right around and alert your Commander Bostwick."

"I won't," she whispered, then lowered her head.

"Trust me. I won't." She ran her fingers through her hair, then went to the bed and sat on the edge. "You . . . you have hard evidence that Bostwick killed Mochrie?"

Logan eased himself down next to Andie. He placed his elbows on his knees and tented his fingers. Without looking over at her, he said, "If we had hard evidence, the bastard would be behind bars."

She blinked a few times, then turned her face to him. "Well then, how do you know he did it? I mean, the guy's a genuine, diamond-plated son of a bitch, but homicide . . ."

"I can only reveal so much, lass—"

"So let me get this straight." She looked a bit dazed. "My going undercover was all for *nothing*. This whole case is for . . . *nothing* . . ."

Her voice trailed off, but he hadn't missed the anger entangled with dejection in her words.

Sliding his arm around her shoulders, he said, "I'm sorry that I'm not a crook, Andie. Would it make you feel better if I stole something?"

When she just stared blankly at him, he smiled sheepishly. "I have something in mind right enough. Something I've wanted from the first. Very valuable it is, and locked tight away, I'd say. It'll be a challenge to steal, but it's a prize beyond measure and definitely worth the effort."

Ignoring his innuendo, she studied him for a moment, then shrugged out of his embrace. Standing, she began to pace the room again. Her frown told him all he needed to know about what was going on inside her head.

When finally she halted, she said, "How long have you known who I am, Logan? Was it from that first time we met?"

"*Nae.* I didn't know you were a detective until I had the home office run a background a few days ago."

Her mouth flattened, her eyes narrowed. "But how could you when you didn't even know my real name?"

He pursed his lips. "In a way, lass, you told me by your reaction every time I called you darlin'. So I did a check on Devon, which turned up nothing, of course. But I also had them check Andrea Darling, which was quite informative."

Her pretty mouth went flat. "That was quite a leap. Not many people would have made it."

"Call it instinct, if you will."

"Or clairvoyance?" Her sarcastic words were punctuated when she angrily crossed her arms under her breasts.

"*Nae.* Never that, lass. I don't go there anymore, remember?"

She started pacing again, rubbing the bridge of her nose as she moved slowly back and forth through the room. Halting in front of the TV, she said, "I'm assuming you did not kill Drew Mochrie."

"You assume rightly."

"Then how did you get the necklace?"

"The fact is, she gave it up willingly. When I met her at the bank, I told her who I was, and that we knew what she was up to. I explained that if she turned over the necklace, the Crown Court might go easier on her. The insurance company might even drop the charges. I didn't make any promises, but she became so agitated, she took the necklace out of the box, burst into tears, and shoved it at me, then ran out of the bank. That was the last time I saw her."

"And she was killed later that day."

"It appears so, yes."

"Why," she said, drawing out the word into five syllables, "didn't you explain who you were to the detectives who interviewed you?"

"You mean yer brother?" He stood and walked to the bar, where he poured himself a club soda. When he gestured to her with the bottle, she nodded, so he filled another tumbler. Adding ice from the minifridge, he handed one to her, then took a drink of his own. "I had to maintain my cover and didn't know who I could trust. Didn't know who would go running to Bostwick. The time was not right for full disclosure."

She seemed to think about it for a second, then blew out a tight breath. "Okay, I can buy that. But what was this elaborate hoax all about? Why pretend to shoot Ollie?"

He took another gulp of his drink. "I wanted to get Bostwick's attention. He killed Tolley Mochrie to get the necklace, but failed. Then he killed Drew—"

"*What!* Bostwick killed . . . are you *sure?*"

He swallowed more sparkling water to try and get the sour taste out of his mouth, but it didn't work. His hatred of Bradley Bostwick polluted every atom in his body. "He killed her, yet still failed to get the necklace. I wanted him to know I had it."

She whispered, "Oh, my God. You want him to come after you."

"I couldn't just go walkin' into his office and introduce myself, now could I, lass? That's about all I can tell you for now." He wondered what she'd say if he told her the truth . . . the entire truth. "There are things . . . complications to this case I can't discuss, for the time being."

They stood only a few feet apart, but he could feel the heat from her body as her anger began to rise. "You *used* me. You staged killing Ollie so I'd haul your ass in, and there are 'things' you can't tell me?"

He looked steadily into her eyes. "Aye, lass. Had to. I'm sorry—"

"Well there are 'things' going on that I can't tell you about either, and between your things and my things, my career just may well end up in a rathole!"

"Truly, I'm sorry, but you have to realize, I didn't know where you stood—"

"There's the necklace," she accused. "Finding it in your possession would have been enough. You didn't have to frame a fake murder to get my attention, or Bostwick's."

Her eyes flashed with fury. With her fists doubled at her side and her mouth a tight line, she looked like a woman a lesser man would think twice about crossing.

"I didn't count on your being such a damn fine detective," he cajoled. "You weren't supposed to find it, only witness a killing, then haul my ass in, as you say."

She lowered her head for a moment, and when she raised it, she said, "But Ollie isn't really dead. I don't understand how—"

"I'd planned on getting you to leave the room, then Ollie was going to walk out. When the cops arrived, there'd be no body. I mean, I couldn't really kill the lad, now, could I? Not that he hasn't deserved a good kick in the nuts on the odd occasion—"

"What a stupid plan!"

He shrugged, then chuckled to himself. "True, it's not without its flaws. But when I discovered you were one of Bostwick's direct reports, we decided to use that knowledge. A bit on the fly, I'll admit . . ."

Slamming her tumbler on the bar, she huffed,

"We're done here, pal. I have to go to my superiors and tell them what I know. This has all gotten too weird, and since you're a cop and not a crook, then I have no purpose staying undercover."

"You're going to tell Bostwick about me."

"Don't you see, I *have* to! If I don't, I mean, there's nothing I can do. I mean, like, everything has changed and I . . . oh, damn! I don't know what to think anymore!"

She ran her fingers through her hair, fiddled with an earring, returned to the bar, and took another sip of her drink. "Look, Logan," she groused. "I hate Bostwick. But I can't help you. I need to go to Internal Affairs and you need to come with me. If I keep quiet about what I know, I could lose my job. Whatever's left of my career after this would be shot to hell. Now that I know what's going on, I *have* to tell them."

Rolling his glass between his fingers, he studied the small bricks of ice floating among the tiny, effervescent bubbles, then raised his eyes to pin Andie where she stood.

"I don't *want* your blasted Internal Affairs involved," he growled. "I don't *want* to relinquish this case to you Yanks. I don't *want* to sit by and watch the slimy son of a bitch slip the knot. I didn't travel over five thousand miles for naught."

In three large gulps, he drained the tumbler, then set it carefully down on the bar.

"Bradley Bostwick murdered two citizens of the

United Kingdom, and I intend to see him pay. I came here to get the bastard, and I mean to do just that. And nothing is going to keep me from it, lass," he rasped. "Not even you."

Not even me? Andie thought. *Yeah, well, we'll just see about that, pal.*

She stepped away from him, not out of fear, but frustration.

"I think we may have a jurisdictional problem here, laddie," she accused. "I haven't seen anything yet that says you're authorized to conduct a criminal investigation in the U.S. Or arrest and extradite, should you uncover evidence that Bostwick is guilty of the murder of Bartholomew Mochrie. As for Drew, that homicide is currently under investigation and has nothing to do with you." She raised a brow and waited for his response.

"You know who I am," he snapped. "You've seen and verified my credentials."

"Yeah, you're a detective, all right, but if you're here to investigate Mochrie's death for Scotland Yard, I'd like to see some documentation to that effect, please."

Again, she waited.

Narrowing his blue eyes on her, he said, "I don't have to show anything to you. It's for your superiors to see, but since I don't know who Bostwick has in his pocket yet, I'll only say I havena made an official approach."

She watched him, his eyes, his mouth, the tension in his body. He was lying.

"Who is Ollie, exactly?" she said. "Is he Scotland Yard, too?"

Logan averted his gaze, then shrugged. "If you must know, he's . . . Ollie's here . . . in an unofficial capacity, you might say."

"*How* unofficial?"

"If I tell you, will you help me get Bostwick?"

"No. But tell me anyway."

If looks could kill, she'd be on death's door, but instead of grabbing for her throat, he said, "If ye must know, he's my cousin. My father's sister's son, and a good lad for all that."

His *cousin*? Andie shook her head in wonder. As she watched him, things began to make sense. A picture began to form in her brain, and when it was complete, she said, "You have no authority, no jurisdiction to do what you're doing, am I right? You've gone rogue or something, haven't you?" When he said nothing, she raised her voice. "What in the hell are you up to, Logan? And before you open your mouth, no more lies and half-truths, okay?"

As they stood facing each other, across the room, Andie's cell phone chirped to life. She raised her hand to Logan. "I have to get that. When I'm done, I want some answers, Chief Inspector Macmillan."

She walked to the bar, opened her purse, and

checked the cell's readout. Her heart rate picked up and her throat tightened. Lowering her head, she flipped the phone open and put it to her ear. "Yes, sir?"

"Inspector Darling."

"Commander Bostwick . . ."

In two steps, Logan was beside her. Edging slightly away from him, she said, "What can I do for you, Commander?"

"I hate to be the bearer of bad news, Inspector . . ."

As his voice trailed off, Andie felt her stomach turn sour. Something like panic thickened her brain. Her palms dampened. She would have swallowed, but there was no moisture in her mouth.

"Bad news?" she said. "What kind of bad news?"

On the other end of the line, Bostwick let out a heavy sigh. "When was the last time you saw or were in contact with your partner?"

"Jericho?" she said as evenly as she could manage. "Has something happened to Dylan?"

"I really couldn't say. I mean, when I spoke with you forty-eight hours ago, he was fine. Now he seems to have . . . disappeared. Hasn't reported in, and can't be reached by phone. I truly hope he hasn't fallen victim to foul play. I know how close the two of you are."

"Bostwick," she whispered. "I swear to God, if you had anything to do with—"

"Now, now, Inspector," he said heartily. "I'm

sure he's fine. Just on a bender or holed up in some motel with his latest conquest. He'll turn up sooner or later."

"Bostwick . . ." Her voice was a mere breath, barely audible. "Bostwick, I—"

"In the meantime, I hope you're on task, Inspector Darling. I look forward to hearing from you very soon and that you've closed that case you're working on so diligently. The timetable has been accelerated, and I now expect results within the next twenty-four hours. I hope we're clear on that."

The line went dead. She lowered her hand, closed her eyes. *Dylan*. What had the son of a bitch done to Dylan?

"Andie?" Logan growled, his voice filled with concern. She felt his hands cup her shoulders as he turned her to face him. "Andie? That was Bostwick? You look pale as a *ghaist,* lass. Tell me what's wrong, darlin'."

The tears that filled her eyes were not tears of sorrow or regret, but fury and helplessness.

Dylan. Dear God, what had Bostwick done?

Raising her face, she locked gazes with Logan. He looked worried, anxious. He ran his thumb gently across her flushed cheek, wiping away a tear that had managed to escape. "Jaysus, lass. What's wrong? You look like you've just lost yer best friend."

Slowly, she nodded. "I think maybe I have."

She took in a deep breath, blinked away the tears, then straightened her spine. Inside her chest, her heart hardened with resolve.

"All right, Logan," she said softly. "I'll help you get Bostwick, but it's not going to be easy. The situation is very complicated, he's covered his tracks well."

"But we can get him anyway, aye, lass?"

She gave him a curt nod. "Aye."

Chapter 19

You cannot run away from weakness; you
must sometime fight it out or perish.

Robert Louis Stevenson

When the police arrived, Logan put a sardonic
look on his face while Andie answered the door.

"Inspector Darling," she said to Nate, then
nodded to the two uniforms who had accompanied
him. "Sinclair's over there."

Over there was the little table by the window,
where he sat finishing a mug of coffee. As Nate approached, Logan flicked his gaze to meet the detective's eyes for a split second. Understanding passed
between them.

The game had begun.

"Inspector Darling has explained to you why I'm
here," Nate said. "Come along quietly, and there
won't be any trouble."

Logan pursed his lips, crossed his arms over his

chest. Cocking a brow, he said, "Am I under arrest, then?"

"No, but it's early yet." Nate motioned for the uniforms to approach. "We just want to have a word with you at the station, Mr. Sinclair. These officers are simply here to make sure it all stays official."

As in witnesses. Aye.

An hour later, Logan sprawled uncomfortably in an aluminum chair, watching while Andie's brother went through the motions. The wall to the left was a two-way mirror, and he knew on the other side of the dark glass, Andie stood observing the proceedings, her fingers crossed, her career on the line.

And Bostwick. Aye, Bostwick would be there as well, his greedy eyes taking it all in.

This had to work. If it didn't, all would be lost, and Andie would suffer for it more than anyone. He couldn't, *nae,* wouldn't, let that happen.

After what she'd told him about Bostwick, what the man had demanded of her and how he was blackmailing her to get it, it was all Logan could do to restrain himself. Given the chance, he'd crash through that mirror and grab the bastard by the throat as payback for what the commander was doing to her.

And her partner. Where in the hell was Dylan Jericho; more to the point, what had Bostwick done to him?

"Listen up, Sinclair," Nate growled, interrupting Logan's thoughts. "We know you killed Miss Mochrie. We know you stole her necklace. It'll go a lot easier on you if you confess and tell us where you hid it."

"You can accuse all you like, Detective." Logan sighed. "But the truth of it is, you have no evidence linking me to the crime at all. No prints, no witnesses, and no Star of Avril."

And thank God for that. If Andie had indeed done as Bostwick ordered and manufactured evidence against him, he'd be behind bars right now, and even the truth of who he was wouldn't have made a difference.

It would have been easy enough for her to do; cops planted evidence all the time. Bad cops, they were, or maybe just overeager or maybe lazy.

But she hadn't done as her commander ordered. Of course she had not. She'd defied the man because she was brave and honorable, and he realized he loved her for all that, and more.

"Even if I did it," he said, easing back in the horrible little chair, "while I'm not entirely clear on the methods you Yanks use to obtain convictions, I'm pretty certain you need a little thing called evidence. How many times do I have to tell ye? I've kilt no one, Detective, and stolen nothing."

Before Nate could respond, the cell phone in his pocket played a tune Logan didn't recognize. He watched as Darling retrieved the phone, flipped it open, and put it to his ear.

"Yes, sir. Yes." His brown eyes met Logan's, then quickly looked away. "Yes, sir. I'll inform him."

Slapping the phone closed, he let it drop back inside his pocket.

"Well Sinclair, it looks like you've attracted some powerful attention. Commander Bostwick will be joining us in a moment. Wants to have a word with you, personally."

And the hook is set . . .

Logan nodded as though he could not have cared less. Inside his chest, his heart rate bumped up a couple of notches.

"Bostwick, you say? A commander? I'm hardly worth the effort, for all that."

For a flash, Logan locked eyes with Nate, then each man blinked and looked away. Logan slumped in his chair, pretending nothing unusual was about to happen while every nerve ending under his skin felt raw.

A moment later, the door to the interrogation room squeaked open. Logan worked to maintain his casual air as Bradley Bostwick sauntered in. After he passed through the threshold, someone reached in and closed the door behind him.

Too important to close yer own fockin' door, eh, bastard?

Bradley Bostwick looked exactly like his file photo, only more obsequious in the flesh. A self-important, preening peacock who undoubtedly felt that puffing out his chest would compensate for the fact he probably had a dick the size of a stubbed toe.

Slowly, Logan rose from his chair. Before him stood the culmination of months of planning and convoluted maneuvering. But his patience and hard work had all paid off; now the circle was complete.

So here he was, Bradley Bostwick, the man Logan had crossed twelve months' time and thousands of miles to face down . . . and kill.

Though she knew Logan couldn't see her, Andie stood motionless, focusing on him through the glass, hoping he would feel her encouragement, hear what was in her heart and mind—and fearing Bostwick somehow could.

At the moment, Logan and the commander were engaged in a staring contest, neither man speaking, each one just taking the other's measure. And in that second, that fraction of a heartbeat, she feared for him, for what Bostwick might do to him if he suspected what Logan and she were up to.

With a slight shake of the head, she dismissed her fears but found herself unable to detach herself from her newly acknowledged feelings for Logan.

She wasn't in love with him; there had been no time for her to fall . . . had there? Nate had accused her of a crush, and she couldn't deny she found Logan charming, but love? Desire maybe, coupled with intriguing possibilities.

No, probably not love, but something most definitely circling the neighborhood, and closing fast.

She recalled the candid conversations they'd shared when he'd been honest about his background. He'd kissed her so tenderly. Had it only been physical need she'd been responding to? Or was there more to it? Had he felt something for her in return?

Her gaze drifted to Bostwick, and her eyes narrowed. She felt her nerves tighten and that sick feeling return to her stomach.

The whole time Nate had been talking to Logan, the commander stood behind the glass next to her, watching mutely, his eyes dark and cold, his fists clenched. As the interrogation proceeded, he became more and more agitated until, finally, he seemed to snap.

Without looking at her, he snarled, "You have fucked this up beyond belief, Inspector. You have failed to get any hard evidence against Sinclair, *and* you've somehow managed to let the necklace slip through your fingers."

He turned to her then, his eyes glazed with fury. "Screwing with me is a big mistake, Andrea. A very big mistake."

On barely a breath, she choked, "Where's Jericho?"

He grinned at her but said nothing. With one last threatening look, he took out his cell phone and told Nate he wanted to talk to Logan, then left her to enter the interrogation room.

Now, on the other side of the glass, the two men stood facing each other, while Nate continued asking questions that Logan continued to evade.

She watched him watch Bostwick and tried to get inside Logan's mind. Something had changed, and it puzzled her.

Something about his stance . . .

A new look, a feral one, had come into his eyes.

His demeanor had altered, and he suddenly looked like a wolf gauging its prey . . .

Or maybe like a man who had come face-to-face with a hated enemy . . .

Sure, they'd agreed on a plan to get Bostwick, but something more was going on here. It was almost as if . . .

Suspicion hit her then like a kick to the head. She thought back over all the things Logan had said, his refusal to be up-front with her about why he hadn't gone through official channels, how he had no investigation or extradition papers, how he'd circumvented authority . . .

She blinked, mentally scrambling and unscrambling the pieces until they began to fit. Yes, yes, that was it.

Holy shit.

She opened her cell phone and pressed the speed

dial. When Ethan answered, she said quickly, "I need a favor."

"Done."

"Run a check for me and run it now. Logan Sinclair Macmillan. He's the detective with Scotland Yard."

"The clairvoyant guy? I already checked out Logan Sinclair and gave you the data . . ."

As she watched Logan's face, it became clearer by the minute what was going on, and what had begun as a nagging suspicion grew into a full-blown epiphany.

"No time for questions, Ethan. Just get me as much as you can on Macmillan and call me back. This is bad. This is very bad."

Patience, lad, Logan said to himself. *Not here and not now. Patience . . .*

"Take a seat, Sinclair," Bostwick ordered, gesturing to the chair Logan had recently vacated. "We may be here a while, and I wouldn't want you to collapse from exhaustion."

"No worry there," Logan said evenly, then smiled. "I am at your disposal, Commander."

Thanks to an e-mail only hours before Tolley had been murdered, Logan knew some of what had happened and guessed the rest. Tolley's note had spoken of his discomfort with his flighty sister's "relationship" with a married man named Bostwick, a Yank policeman who showed an inordinate amount of interest in the family's most precious possession, the Star of Avril. Tolley distrusted Bostwick and his intentions toward Drew and the necklace.

I'm going to confront the ballsy bastard tonight, Tolley wrote. *A married man, and a high-ranking police official, for all that. He's not a fellow to be underestimated, Logan, so if I come out of this one the worse for it, look to Bostwick to have done the deed. I trust you'll find a way to set it right.*

Nate hovered in the background while Bostwick seemed to assess the situation. Finally, he said, "So you're Scotch."

"*Nae,*" Logan replied dryly. "*Scotch* is a whisky. What I am is a *Scot*. Period."

Bostwick shrugged casually as though he didn't care a whit for the distinction.

"Drew Mochrie was a Scot," he said, his tone haughty. "Did you know her back in Scotland?

So sure of himself, he is, thought Logan. *And so high, and about to topple on his shiny ass.*

"Aye. We were acquainted."

Bostwick's head came up, and his eyes snapped. "You . . . what did you say? You knew her *before*?"

"Aye. And her brother, too, the unfortunate Tolley," Logan said slowly, holding Bostwick's gaze captive.

From behind the commander, Nate's surprised eyes drilled into Logan's, but he said nothing.

Bostwick's brow began turning damp with beads of sweat. Crossing his arms over his chest, he said, "So you must have known about the necklace, and come all the way to the U.S. to steal it. When Drew got in the way, you killed her. That about it, Scotchman?"

Logan ignored the slur, and instead said, "Maybe I didn't have to kill her. Maybe I didn't have to steal it. Maybe she gave it over to me of her own free will."

The blood drained from the commander's face. His eyes darted around the room, then came back to Logan. "Are you saying you have the necklace in your possession?"

Logan smiled. "I'm only saying maybe, that it *could* have happened that way. In which case, I wouldn't have had to kill to get it, like some might, eh, Commander?"

Bostwick glared at him as Logan prepared his final blow.

"Funny thing, about that necklace," he said lightly. "Just before Tolley died, he wrote to me. Told me his sister was seeing some slimy guy, a married man it seems. Tolley was worried the cad would do his sister wrong and get his hands on the necklace. And maybe that's exactly what happened, in which case, as you Yanks are so fond of saying, yer barkin' up the wrong tree."

Both Nate and Bostwick stood as though frozen

in place, but the commander's face had gone from white to red as fast as that.

"You're lying," Bostwick snarled. "You're lying, and I'm going to—"

"Say what you will," Logan interrupted. "I'm just saying, there's more than one man who might could've done the deed. Oh, and one more thing, Commander."

When Bostwick remained silent, Logan said, "Tolley asked me, should anything happen to him, to make it right. As a point of honor and revenge. I'm sure as an officer of the law, you understand my meaning, don't you, Commander?"

Logan waited while Bostwick rolled this information around in his head. Abruptly, he turned and walked swiftly toward the door. Over his shoulder, he said to Nate, "He's free to go. Get him the fuck out of here."

"Yes, Commander."

Bostwick flung the door open, but before he stepped out of the interrogation room, he turned back and glared into Logan's eyes.

"If you know what's good for you," he bit out, "you'll be on the next plane back to Scotland."

"I'll keep that in mind," Logan said. "Before I go, let me say, it's been a distinct pleasure, Commander. But I have a feeling our paths will cross again someday soon." He smiled. "*Very* soon."

Chapter 20

You can give without loving, but you can never love without giving.

Robert Louis Stevenson

By the time Logan exited the station, night had fallen, and a foggy one it was. The parking-lot lights looked like fuzzy yellow balls floating overhead as he walked out the gate onto the busy street. He went a couple of blocks, then turned a corner, listening for her car to pull up behind him. When it did, he glanced up and down the quiet, empty street, then quickly opened the passenger door and got in.

Andie said nothing to him but drove in silence for a few blocks. Just when he was beginning to think she'd planned on staying mute, she said, "You weren't completely honest with me, were you, laddie."

"I was as honest with you as I felt I could be at the time. I'm sorry if—"

"You came to the U.S. with the express purpose of killing Bostwick, didn't you? For what, for revenge?" She flicked on her turn signal and took a left.

"There was no way I could explain beforehand. It's too complicated—"

"And you didn't feel you could trust me with the truth, is that it?" She sent him a meaningful look, then turned another corner and started up a hill.

"It's like I said, complicated. Not a matter of trust."

"The hell it's not!" she snapped. "I told you everything. What Bostwick threatened, how my career was on the line, and I thought you'd leveled with me."

"I did."

"But you left a few details out. Details such as how Tolley Mochrie was your best friend. How you're in the US on your own time, not Scotland Yard's. And how you'd vowed to make Bostwick pay for killing your friend."

He looked over at Andie, trying to keep his temper under control. He had every right to do what he was doing. He owed Tolley.

"And what about *your* friend, Andie?" he said. "This Dylan Jericho fellow who's disappeared. Do you think the commander is responsible?"

Her tongue darted out to moisten her lips. "I know he is."

"And what do you plan on doing about it?"

Slamming her fist into the steering wheel, she bit out, "I don't know! I don't know where to begin looking! They've checked his apartment, his usual haunts. He's gone. I'd like to tear this town apart, but I don't know where to start! I'd like to shove Bostwick up against a wall and knee him in the groin, but that wouldn't do any good! I have no proof he did anything to Dylan."

She took in a deep breath and made a sound at the back of her throat. Anger, frustration, helplessness were all taking their toll on her, and he wished he knew how to comfort her . . . if she'd even let him.

Finally, she rasped, "I have no proof of anything . . ."

He watched her profile as she returned to silence. The interior of the car was dark, but light from passing cars and streetlamps illuminated her golden hair, high cheekbones, straight and honest brows. She swallowed, then said, "What do you think Bostwick's going to do now?"

Settling back in his seat, Logan considered the question. "He knows I have the necklace, but he also knows I'm a threat on more than one level. That'll make him more desperate, and dangerous. He'll have my room searched, if he hasn't already, of course. And he'll undoubtedly put a tail on me."

"Nobody's been following us," she said, glancing in the rearview mirror. "We can't go back to your hotel room, and he'll probably have somebody watching my house as well, not to mention my brothers' places."

"Well," he drawled. "There must be somewhere we can go that nobody will think of . . ."

She nodded, then took the next corner. "You're right. There is."

The night was moonless and dreary, the fog heavy and oppressive, and as they turned into the long driveway, Andie imagined the mansion had been waiting for her to return. She tried to put her sense of foreboding aside to focus on the fact she and Logan needed a refuge, and this was about the only place in town nobody would think to look. She still had a key; the place was still at her disposal until the case culminated, so why the hell not make use of it?

She parked behind the house so anyone driving by from the street wouldn't notice her car. Unlocking the back door, she went inside, Logan silently following. Without a word, she walked down the hallway, turning on lights only as necessary, ones that had little chance of being seen from the outside.

When she reached the library doors, she paused. Turning to Logan, she said, "We're going in here. Are you going to faint again?"

His gaze met hers. "*Nae,* lass."

She nodded, swallowed, then opened the doors and switched on the light. Instantly, the room was flooded with an amber glow. Nothing had changed, the books still marched along the walls, the table still held the Ouija board, but the air was different, not as musty as before, and much colder. Rubbing her arms, she said, "We might as well make ourselves comfortable. Are you hungry? There's food in the fridge, and we can . . ."

That was when she noticed it—the whirring inside her head. An insistent, low humming through the walls, as though the neighbors were playing their TV too loud.

But there were no neighbors, no TV, only the buzzing in her brain.

She rolled her shoulders, trying to relax, but the drone increased. How could she think through all the damn noise? She wanted to talk to Logan about the case, about Dylan, about everything, but her mind seemed to have been taken captive and wasn't responding to her own desires.

Facing Logan, she began to say something, then stopped and only stared at him. His eyes were locked on her, a look of concern on his face.

"What's the matter, lass?" he said. "What's happening?"

Slowly, she shook her head. "I . . . I don't . . . I feel . . . sleepy or . . . or . . ."

Instantly, his arm came around her waist. He helped her to a chair, where she sank down and let her head fall back.

"Don't resist it," he urged softly. "Let it happen, let the images come. Trust them. I'll be here. You'll be safe, lass. I promise. You'll be safe . . ."

His palm cupped her cheek, and she looked sleepily into his eyes. She watched his mouth move as though he were speaking, but whatever he was saying was lost under the voices inside her head.

Relinquishing control, she let her lids drift down and down . . . allowing Emma Harte to invade her senses once more . . .

And what's all the ruckus, I'm wondering? Sounds like the world is coming apart! 'Tis not Jacob, home so early of a morning, just after five as it is. He's on the night shift, and not due back 'til six.

I hear my Sean cryin', so I fling off the bedcovers and try to make my way to his crib side, but the floor shifts beneath my bare feet, and I stumble and fall against the doorjamb, wrenching me shoulder. Taking hold of my senses, I realize now it's more than just the bed shaking, it's the floor and the walls and maybe even the very air set to trembling, such as like an angry giant is come trudging up the street.

Pushing forward, I try to get to Sean in his little room just off the kitchen, but the shelf in the hallway tumbles over, and books fly about. I reach for the lamp pull, but when I tug at the swinging chain, nothin' happens. Underlying it all is a terrible sound, like the earth has a belly set to groanin' for a meal. Other noises reach me ears . . . glass windows bursting to bits, bricks crumpling away from their foundations, and from the sound of it, the very streets twisting and cracking.

San Francisco is a bucking wild horse, trying to toss its rider into the bay.

I reach my Sean, and whether he's squallin' out of hunger or fear, I can't tell. I bundle him up quick and hold him tight to my body while I lurch back down the hall, me bare feet pressing into a bed of broken glass. Pain, hot as fire, spreads across the flesh. Then I remember the pair of slippers I left next to the commode, so I scuffle into the water closet, and even though I know my soles are bleeding, I shove them onto my feet, ignoring the sharp jabs of glass embedded in me skin.

Though I can barely make it out in the darkness, the far wall makes a wrenching sound as it tumbles forward, and the roof above me head showers chunks of plaster on my face and into my hair.

The house is disintegrating, and I must get me babe outside to safety.

I'm pantin' now, tryin' to catch a breath, but 'tis hard, so fearful as I am. I manage to stagger to the front door, throw the lock, and pull it open. Outside, people in their nightclothes are running from their houses, same as me, some with babes in arms, others carrying jewelry boxes or books or photographs. Children scream and cry and cling to their mothers' flannel gowns.

As I turn, my small house—mine and Jacob's and Sean's—crumbles before me very eyes into a jagged heap of rubble and dust. I realize I'm cryin', but I can't stop the tears. I hug Sean tighter as the rumbling stops, and I look about, gasping from the shock of it all. This is just a dream, is it not? This is not truly happening? My home is not gone, my world destroyed, is it? Let me wake up, dear Lord. Let me wake up now!

Next door, Mrs. O'Darrell is in her nightgown, on her knees, clutching her favorite porcelain vase to her breasts, while her husband stares blankly at what remains of his house. Across the street, Mr. Bernstein is pullin' at a pile of boards, yelling Mrs. Bernstein's name and beggin' for her to call out to him . . . but she does not.

As for m'self, I'm numb. Sean is quiet now against me own racing heart.

I think of me dear Jacob. Now that the earth has ceased its terrible quakin', I'm desperate to find my husband. I look up and down the street, and all I can see is people and rubble and smoke and smoke and more smoke. A yellow glow lights the debris . . . the city is on fire.

Down my street, a main has burst, sending a towering spray of water high into the air, drenching everyone near it, turnin' parts of the street to mud. I hear shouts, cries, pleas, but I think only of Sean, and Jacob.

Will he come home now, I wonder, or is he trapped under bricks and boards, like poor Mrs. Bernstein?

I want to stay and help, but I can't. I have to find Jacob.

And me da, what of him in that big house made of stone and plaster and brick? There'll be no one but me to come lookin' for him all alone in that crumblin' mansion.

My feet begin to move. I trip on broken cobbles, but keep going. My eyes are blind with tears and smoke and grit, but I can't stop, I won't.

Up the street and down, I stumble, me babe in me arms.

I don't know how long it takes, but by the time we arrive at me da's house, the sun is up and I can see the mansion has stood against the quake in fine form, and thank God for it.

The front is open, so I take the steps, me poor cut feet ablaze with pain. Inside, I hear voices . . . two men . . . I recognize 'em . . . me da, and Jacob.

"You're under arrest, Mr. Conner," says Jacob. "I saw what you did—"

"Blast you to hell!" shouts Da as I tiptoe down the hall toward the library. "I've an investment to protect, ye dumb bastard. Now get yerself out of here and leave me be!"

Peekin' 'round the corner into the library, I see

Da and Jacob standin' and glurin' at each other. I want to rush in, throw my arms around my husband, hug me da, but I dare not. They both have weapons drawn on each other, and it's a blood-thirsty look I see in me da's eyes.

"I've no earthquake insurance!" Da yells. "Hell, man, there's a fire big enough out there. Nobody'd be the wiser. If I don't torch me own place and collect the insurance, I'll be ruined! I can't be ruined, Jacob. I've worked too hard all me life, built somethin' from nothin', to have it all come crashin' down around me like this."

Jacob holds his ground. "But I've orders, Mr. Conner. Looters and fire starters are to be shot on sight. You're lucky I'm only going to arrest you. I'll speak up for you in court, if that'll help, but I have to do my duty."

I slip into the room and set my darlin' sleeping Sean on the floor in the corner where he'll be safe, and walk toward me husband.

"Jacob," says I, and he whirls 'round.

"Emma!" he shouts, relief and joy plain to see on his face. His hair's mussed, his uniform scorched and torn, his face near us grimy as mine, but he's handsome, all the same. He moves toward me and hugs me tight, and me life begins again.

"I went to the house," he murmurs into me bedraggled hair, "but you and Sean were gone. I thought . . . dear God, I thought. But they said you'd taken the baby and left, so I went looking *for you at your father's store. Where's Seanie?"*

I send a look to our own wee babe sleepin' like an angel wrapped in his soot-stained blanket. "He's fine. Not to worry—"

"Are you all right, Emma?" Da interrupts, though he makes no move to embrace me.

"Yes, Da." I kiss Jacob's cheek, then step away. "Is what he says true? Did you fire yer own place for the insurance money?"

"I did," says he, waving his pistol around. "But I won't be arrested and taken in fer it—"

"I'm sorry, Mr. Conner," Jacob says, then starts to move past me. "I have my orders."

I don't know why I do it, but the next second, I reach out and put me hand on Jacob's wrist, shifting his arm so his pistol is trapped between us. "Jacob," I say. "Can ye not make an exception, given the circumstances?"

He looks away from Da, and into my eyes, and I see compassion there, and love, and how his sense of duty is battlin' it out inside his own tormented heart. For a moment, he glances up, then grabs me, the pistol in his hand still between us. He starts to turn, starts to shove me behind him. I hear a blast, and pain rips through me own chest as though me heart has just burst.

For an infinite second, Jacob stares into me eyes, then slides to the floor, and I go with him, bearing him up in me arms as best I can. I rock him like a babe, his head cradled against me chest. I don't know what to do, what to say as the red of his blood spreads across his proud blue uniform.

Me heart feels like it's going to break, the pain nearly beyond bearing.

He smiles up at me as I gaze down into his eyes.

"Jacob," I whisper, for there's barely a breath left in me body. "Don't go . . ."

His lips move then. I love you . . . and then he's . . . gone. I haven't enough breath to scream . . . there's no air left in the room, no time, no time, no time . . .

The pistol in his hand . . . my hand on his wrist. Dear God, I must have done something to make it discharge! And now I've killed him . . . I've killed me own sweet Jacob!

"No!" I cry, but me throat is empty and no sound comes out, and all I can do is mouth a silent, "No . . . no . . . no . . . no . . ."

Chapter 21

A busy person never has time to be unhappy.

Robert Louis Stevenson

"Andie, darlin'?"

His voice drifted into her subconscious from far away, a murmur carried through an open window by a summer breeze. As the sound of it seduced her to wake, inside her chest, her heart felt like it was in splinters. With every breath, the razor-sharp shards lanced her soul.

She opened her eyes to stare into his face, a face she only vaguely recognized. Blinking several times, she finally lowered her lids, then slowly raised them again, allowing him to come fully into focus.

Logan . . .

A sob escaped her throat as tears rolled down her heated cheeks. He reached up and wiped them away. Gently, he said, "What was it you saw, lass?"

"She k-killed him. She didn't mean to, but—" Looking into Logan's sympathetic eyes, she whispered, "I think I understand it now. This was her father's house, Timothy Conner's, and had been her home growing up. She came looking for him after . . . after . . ."

Realization slammed into her like a fist to the ribs.

"God, Logan," she choked. "Emma Harte really was *real*. I . . . I never wanted to believe it before, despite the file Ethan gave me, but . . . oh, how she must have suffered! She died that night, filled with guilt over killing the man she loved. I . . . I can't imagine the grief, the regret . . ."

His lids lowered and he seemed to go inside himself for a moment, and when he sought her gaze again, he whispered, "I can." Squeezing her hand, he said, "But how did *she* die, then?"

Andie licked her dry lips, dabbed at the tears that continued to track from her eyes down her cheeks. "I don't know. I came out of it just after she realized Jacob was dead. He . . . he died in this room." She felt her throat close up, her eyes burn. "And so did she. I'm certain of it."

"Maybe, in her grief, she took her own—"

"*No*," Andie protested, shaking her head. "No. She wouldn't have. She was a young mother; she had a child. And she was Catholic. No matter her guilt or grief, she wouldn't have done that, wouldn't have left her baby son behind. I *know* it. Maybe it's

why she haunts the place. Maybe she's looking for
. . . oh, God, what am I saying! That I believe in
ghosts? I'm a police officer. I only believe in facts
and evidence. There's no way I can accept—"

"Trust yer heart, Andie," Logan coaxed. His
voice was low, tender, infinitely compassionate.
"It'll guide you through your confusion. The facts
are there, the evidence plain to see. Don't shove
away what you know in your heart to be true. The
real world, the one you live in, can and does coex-
ist with the other, the spirit world. Sometimes the
two worlds cross. Emma has sought you out for a
reason. She believes in you, lass; you need to believe in her."

As Andie considered Logan's words, the dream
began to fade into memory. The hard edges softened, the pain subdued, the guilt diminished until
she felt her body go limp. The adrenaline rush she'd
experienced retreated like an ebb tide, leaving her
feeling raw, stripped bare of defenses, exhausted.

"But you told me you don't believe in the spirit
world—"

"I never said I didn't believe in it, lass," he cor-
rected. "It's because I *do* that I shut it out."

Too exhausted to think about that, she closed her
eyes, willing herself to recover, not wanting Logan
to see her so . . . vulnerable . . .

When she heard him stand, she thought he was
going to leave, but instead, she felt his arm come
around her shoulders and his hand slide under her

knees as he lifted her from the chair. She made no protest, but let her head rest against his strong shoulder as he carried her from the scene of unbearable tragedy.

His footfalls echoed on the thinly carpeted floor as he carried her out the door and to the end of the hall, where he began climbing the stairs. A few minutes later, she felt a soft mattress beneath her body as he set her down on a bed.

"Along with everything else that's happened, the dream has taken a hard toll on you this night," he said, sitting next to her. The mattress squeaked under his weight, and the heat from his body seeped into hers. He brushed a stray lock of hair from her forehead. His hand on her skin felt comforting. "When you've rested up a bit, we'll—"

Her brain began to swim again, her senses grow fuzzy as they had in the library before she'd sunk into the dream. Around her, the small bedroom was dark except for a dull yellow wedge of light that sliced from the hallway onto the floor through the slightly open door.

Above her, his face was in shadows. His face . . . *her beloved . . . oh, how she had missed him . . .*

She reached out to touch his arm and the coarse wool of his jacket itched her hand. Easing her palm up to his shoulder, she grabbed a handful of fabric and pulled him toward her. He hesitated only a moment, then let himself be tugged all the way down to place a kiss on her mouth.

"I've missed you so," she murmured against his lips. Behind her closed lids, her eyes stung. *"I've missed you so much . . ."*

"And I, you." He kissed her again, and it was as it had always been between them.

"Make love to me, darlin'," she murmured, tugging at the brass buttons on his uniform. *"Just this once, will you? Just this one last time, Jacob?"*

His hand slid under her chemise to cup her breast. *"I love you,"* he whispered as he moved to cradle his body between her parted thighs. *"I love you, Emma . . . now, and forever . . ."*

When Logan awoke, not only was he naked, so was the woman in his arms.

He shifted position, and she murmured something in her sleep and nestled closer into his embrace.

What in the hell had happened? The last thing he remembered was carrying Andie upstairs and setting her on the bed. They'd talked a bit . . . and after that, things got a little muzzy.

Reaching down, he wrapped his fingers around his dick. Half-mast and sticky. Damn. He'd made love to her, and could remember naught about it. What would he say to her when she awoke? How could he explain? He'd not had a drop to drink and had not had seduction on his mind, so what in the world . . .

Across the room, the single window began to glow behind the lacy curtains. In a moment or two, the room would be illuminated, she'd wake up, and there'd be hell to pay.

He let his gaze settle on her sleeping form. Her cheeks were rosy, her lips slightly parted. So damn beautiful, and naked, and in his arms.

Andie . . .

Smiling to himself, he thought, aye, there'd be hell to pay, but even so, he could *nae* regret the position he found himself in at the moment. She was as desirable as he'd imagined, as soft, alluring. Her breasts were perfect and luscious, and suddenly the need to have her—again, apparently—began to overtake him.

In his arms, she sighed as her eyes slowly inched open. She smiled up at him, into his face. He said nothing, only held her, watching, waiting. Her eyes widened, her lashes fluttered. He saw the moment she realized who he was . . . where they were . . . and what they'd done.

He cleared his throat. "Good morning, lass."

Her jaw dropped a bit, and she simply stared at him.

"Look," he said. "I can explain . . ."

At least, he could make something up, since the explanation for this turn of events was nowhere in his experience.

But as she had done from the moment they'd met, she surprised him. Putting her fingertips to his mouth, she said, "Relax, laddie. It wasn't your fault."

He raised a brow. "So . . . you . . . put me under a spell and had yer way with me, did you?"

She lowered her hand. "No. But I think I know what happened. Emma and Jacob . . ."

With a slow nod, he said, "Aye. 'Tis the only explanation."

Licking her lips, she bent her head so her words were directed at his bare chest. "I'm, um, on the shot, so conception isn't a problem. And I'm healthy, if you know what I mean."

"As am I, lass. If you know what I mean."

"Okay, then. We're good. Do you . . . um, remember any of it?"

His brow furrowed. "Not really. 'Tis more like a dream." With his knuckle, he raised her face to his. Softly, he said, "Or a wish come true."

She nodded, then surprised him yet again by snuggling deeper into his arms. "I don't know how I let it happen, but I have, um, feelings for you, you know?"

"As I do for you, Andie darlin'. As I do for you."

The sun brushed the room in soft shades of amber and rose. She sought his mouth, kissed him.

When the kiss ended, Logan cupped her cheek and eased back a bit so he could look into her eyes. "Darlin', we'd best get up before . . . before—"

"*No,*" she whispered. "No. Please don't. I want

it." Averting her eyes, she murmured, "I want this time for it to be you and me. And this time . . ." She sought his gaze. "I want to remember."

In his arms, her body was warm, inviting. Her eyes quietly beseeched him. Her lips parted as she awaited his kiss.

"Aye, lass," he rasped. "This time . . . it's me, and it's you . . . and it's for us to remember . . ."

He lowered his head and kissed her, slowly teasing her tongue with his own. She responded, moaning in the back of her throat, wrapping her arms around him, tugging him close, closer, pressing her warm body into his.

He reveled in the contact. He'd wanted to make love to her from the first, and he mentally raised a pint to the spirits of Jacob and Emma Harte for giving him a leg up. Andie fitted him perfectly in mind, in body, maybe even in soul for all he knew.

Her back arched, allowing him access to her naked breasts. Trailing kisses down her throat, and down, and down, he cupped one breast, tugging the bit of tender flesh into his mouth, flicking the taut nipple with his tongue. In his arms, she squirmed and let go a long, high sigh.

Parting her thighs with his knee, he settled between them and gazed down at her face. In the sweet light of morning, she looked hot and erotic and more desirable than any woman he'd ever known.

She tossed her head back, raising her hips to rub against his erection, moaning at the contact.

He reached up and tenderly caressed her cheek. For now, for this very moment at least, she was his. His, and only his. The realization made his heart nearly burst with an emotion he'd thought long dead.

It wouldn't last. They'd make love, release their passion, and move on. This was not a prelude to permanence, it could not be. He was not a lucky enough man to win and keep the heart of Andie Darling. Besides, a decade and a half ago, he'd vowed to live in isolation for the rest of his days in payment for his crimes.

But he was still a man, and there were some things that couldn't be put aside altogether. So if a woman such as the likes of this one was willing to welcome him into her arms and her body, he'd take it, and be grateful to her forever for keeping the dark away if only for one night.

In one long, slow, glide, he entered her, so perfect, so right.

"Ah, lass," he whispered into her ear. "God, yer so damn beautiful. You feel so good . . ."

As he began to move within her, she made a soft, mewling sound and lifted her hips to meet his thrusts. He rocked against her again and again, kissing her neck, then lowering his head to suckle her nipple. She liked that, so he did it again.

"Are ye going to come for me, lass?" he murmured.

"Aye," she sighed. "Oh, aye . . . soon. Oh, yes, very very very . . ."

Her muscles tightened, her breathing changed to rapid pants as her hips slammed against his.

"Logan!" she choked. "Logan . . . I . . . oh, God . . ."

As she began bucking under him, a wild woman clinging to her mate, she lifted her head and kissed him, her mouth open, her raw passion affecting him like a shot to the heart of undiluted lust.

Logan came in a heated rush, filling her with himself until he had no more to give.

Collapsing on top of her, his chest heaved as though he'd just scaled the top of Ben Lomond at a dead run, but she slid her arms around him and held him close, murmuring endearing and soothing words. Then she reached up, stroked his damp brow with her fingertips, and smiled into his eyes.

"For us," she whispered. "To remember."

"Aye, lass," he said, then lowered his head and kissed the tip of her nose. "To remember."

By the time Andie showered and finished dressing, Logan had gone downstairs to the kitchen to scrounge up something to eat.

Comb in hand, she sat on the bed and worked the tangles out of her hair. While she did so, she let her idle gaze take in the room from the pretty rose-print wallpaper and mahogany furniture, to the small shelf of books and several Tiffany lamps . . .

This had to have been Emma's room. No wonder then, that she and Logan had been possessed—if that was the right word—by the spirits of Emma and the man she loved.

She lowered her hand to her lap and let her thumb run over the teeth of the comb as she thought about last night's dream . . .

Emma had accidentally killed Jacob, and then she herself had died. What had happened then? Whatever had become of her father? What about Sean, the baby?

For a moment, Andie's thoughts diverted to Logan. How would she feel if she were responsible for *his* death?

She tossed the comb onto the bedspread and let her thoughts go where she'd tried to prevent them going for days now. In spite of her best efforts, she had fallen in love with him and simply couldn't find it within herself to be sorry about it.

Of course, the love she felt for him was the new kind, the kind where there's no baggage between them, nothing but thoughts of anticipation and promise. The fresh, edgy, hot, start-of-something-big kind of love where the future holds only happiness, laughter, shared memories, companionship, and hope.

If she were lucky, when today's heat simmered

down into an easy warmth, he'd still be there to share with her the even richer, forevermore kind of love.

Aye. Smiling to herself, she realized that, in spite of her years-long decision to steer clear of commitment, that she'd actually like that kind of love, if it was with Logan . . .

From her jeans pocket, the strains of Eric Clapton's *Change the World* brought her out of her reverie. Retrieving the cell phone, she flipped it open. "Hey, Ethan. What's up?"

"Hey, brat," he said, his tone more solemn than usual. "Listen, you sitting down?"

Andie's heart squeezed in alarm. "Has something happened to Nate or Mom?"

"No. God, no. They're fine." Ethan cleared his throat and went into his firstborn, older brother, head-of-the-family, deep-voiced, former detective voice. "Hang on to your socks, kiddo. This is going to hit you hard."

Chapter 22

What hangs people . . . is the unfortunate cir-
cumstance of guilt.

Robert Louis Stevenson

She stood by the side of the hospital bed, gazing down
at the comatose form of Dylan Jericho, his handsome
face pale, his cheek too cool to the touch.

Tubes ran everywhere. Bags and bottles hung
from metal rings, feeding him, hydrating him,
medicating him, sustaining him while his body
found a way to heal itself.

ER doctors and nurses had labored for seven
hours to save his life, mend him, repair the damage
the bullets had done to his insides.

Andie shook her head in wonder. He'd taken
three bullets in the chest and had somehow managed not to die.

Way to go, Jericho, she thought to herself. *Way
to go you stubborn bastard.*

But while the slugs had all missed hitting something vital, he'd lost a lot of blood . . . maybe too much. He'd been found on a seldom-used path in Golden Gate Park and rushed to the hospital before he'd bled out, but that didn't mean he'd recover. According to whichever doctor Andie listened to, Dylan's chances of pulling out of the coma were slim . . . to none.

Since *slim* at least didn't write him off completely, as far as Andie was concerned, each day he remained alive was enough to give her hope.

If she knew Dylan, he'd stay alive if only to identify who'd done this to him. He wouldn't like it that somebody had gotten the drop on him. He'd go down fighting, that was for damn sure.

On the other side of the bed, Lieutenant Eagan stood, his stance rigid, his hands clasped in front of him as though he were listening to the national anthem. With his left thumb, he fiddled with his wedding band, absently rolling it around and around his finger.

"A shame," he mumbled. "Real shame. Fine police officer. Good detective. A damn shame."

Andie sucked in a hard breath. "He'll make it, sir. If anybody can make it, he will." If saying the words would make it true, then she'd say them over and over, no matter how deep the doubt she hid inside.

Eagan's weary eyes lifted to meet hers. "I know you two go way back."

"Yes, sir. To the academy."

He nodded, kept nodding as though the motion would punctuate his next words, make his wishes irrefutable. "We'll get who did this. I *want* who did this." Again, he lifted his gaze to meet Andie's. "I want him, you know?"

"Yes, sir." Her voice was a mere whisper, but angry and determined for all that. She swallowed. Framing her next question carefully, she worked to sound interested and yet casual at the same time. "Any leads?"

He shook his head. "The slugs appear to be from a Glock, but without a weapon, no ballistics match. And no witnesses. Nothing."

"What was he doing in the park that night?"

Eagan shrugged. "Who knows. Maybe out for an evening stroll, maybe chasing a lead, maybe meeting somebody. Whoever he ran across caught him off guard, though. He took the slugs in the chest, facing his attacker. No defensive wounds on his arms or hands. His weapon was still secured in its shoulder holster."

Andie peered down at her toes, then slid her hands into her jeans pockets. "What does Commander Bostwick make of all this?"

Again, Eagan shrugged. "I spoke with the commander earlier today. He's made finding Jericho's assailant a top priority. Putting every available detective on it. Everyone's stirred up over this, you know. Everyone's determined to collar the creep who shot a cop."

He adjusted his glasses, then said, "Uh, I have to ask, you know, as routine, your whereabouts two nights ago. You know, the night Jericho was shot."

At first, she felt alarmed that she'd come under suspicion, but almost immediately let it go. People generally were shot by somebody they knew. Eagan was only doing his job.

"I was on the Sinclair case, sir," she said. "I was with him at the time. Besides, I have no motive for killing my partner."

But I know who did . . .

She choked back the words, aching to tell Eagan what was going on. But she didn't dare. For all she knew, Eagan was in Bostwick's pocket, too . . .

The lieutenant nodded again, kept nodding as before. "Had to ask, Inspector. You understand."

"I do, sir. And if I may return the favor, where were you that night?"

Eagan's head came up, and his eyes widened, then he smiled. "Sure. Sure, sure. Not a problem. I was at home with my wife watching a DVD."

She swallowed her trepidation. "And Commander Bostwick?"

Eagan's brows furrowed, and he looked confused. "Are you concerned the commander had something to do with Jericho's attempted murder?"

"No, sir," she lied. "It was a silly question, you know, just a turnabout is fair play kind of thing."

Jamming his hands into his jacket pockets, he stuck out his lower lip. "Well, not that it matters, but I understand he was at one of his wife's fund-raiser dinners that night. Dozens of people around. Can't have a much more solid alibi than that."

She smiled. "Like I said. Silly question."

Returning her attention to Dylan, she reached for his hand and clasped it, giving it a gentle squeeze. His fingers were cold, so she squeezed again to try and infuse him with some of her warmth.

Leaning close, she placed her mouth near his ear. "We're going to get him, Dylan," she rasped harshly. "You just do your part and stay alive, okay?"

As tears burned the back of her throat, she nodded good-bye to Eagan, then turned to the door just as it eased open. Delicate fingers curled around the threshold, and a moment later, a face came into view.

The woman had a thick shock of wavy gray hair, bright blue eyes, a pert nose, and full mouth. She appeared to be around fifty, and was the prettiest lady Andie had ever seen.

She smiled at Andie, and said, "Pardon me, is this . . ." Before she could finish her sentence, her bright gaze darted past Andie's shoulder to land on Dylan. "Oh! There he is!" She turned her head to speak to someone in the hallway. "It's this one. He's in here, girls!"

Andie watched as the woman flung the door all the way open and entered the room, followed by four girls lined up like baby ducks behind their mother, each girl younger and more beautiful than the next.

As a gaggle, they pushed past Lieutenant Eagan, who stepped back to give them more room. Surrounding Dylan's bed, cooing and crying, they patted his hands and lamented his predicament.

The gray-haired lady stood closest, her red-rimmed eyes filled with tears. She placed her fingertips gently on Dylan's brow, then slid her hand down to cup his cheek. Leaning forward, she placed a tender kiss on his forehead, then moved back to let one of her weeping daughters take her place.

Pulling a tissue from the box on the nightstand, Andie handed it to the woman, who took it and gently blew her nose.

"We just flew up from L.A.," she choked. "I'm Mary Jericho, Dylan's mom."

"I figured," Andie said sympathetically. "I'm Andie Darling, your son's partner. And this is Lieutenant Eagan."

Eagan stepped forward, smiled, and took the lady's hand, giving it a single shake. "An honor to meet you, ma'am." Releasing her hand, he said, "My apologies, but I have a prior commitment. I . . . I just want you to know how sorry I am to have to meet you under such disagreeable circumstances."

Mrs. Jericho gave him a watery smile as he turned and pushed through the door. It made a quiet swoosh as it closed behind him.

Returning her attention to Mrs. Jericho, Andie said, "I . . . Look I don't know what to say. I'm so very sorry for—"

"No!" Mrs. Jericho rushed. "He's fine. He's *going* to be fine. Whatever condition he's in right now is only temporary." Her blue eyes pleaded with Andie to accept her desperately optimistic diagnosis.

Andie gave the lady a weak smile and nodded. "I think so, too."

It was then Andie looked around her. Mrs. Jericho and her four girls didn't look as though they'd just stepped off an airplane on a mission to see their critically ill son and brother, they looked like escapees from a New York fashion show.

"You say you flew up from L.A.?" she asked. "Dylan never talks about his personal or family life much. Whereabouts in L.A. do you live?"

Mrs. Jericho's gaze drifted across the room to her son, lying still as death, fighting for his every breath.

"Brentwood," she said absently. "It's near Beverly Hills." Turning back to Andie, she rushed, "They said he lost a lot of blood and that he might not come out of the coma, but he's strong, you know.

Dylan was always a very strong baby. I . . . I'm sure he'll heal quickly." Tears filled her eyes and began spilling down her cheeks. "He's always been so strong. I can't believe . . ."

"Mrs. Jericho," Andie said soothingly. "Please don't do this to yourself. Let's keep a good thought, okay?"

Mary Jericho wiped away her tears, straightened her shoulders, and did her best to smile. "You're right, Andie. You're so right. Girls," she said, and four blond heads turned her way. "This is Andie Darling, Dylan's partner."

"Hello," they all said, and smiled. Andie could only stare in wonder. Macho man Dylan Jericho had a doting mother and four silly sisters? And he was *rich*? In all the years she'd known him, he'd never mentioned any of this, and she had to wonder why.

As soon as he woke up, she'd ask him. Yes, the very minute he came out of this damn coma—and he *would*—that would be the second thing she'd ask him, the first being, could he identify Bradley Bostwick as the man who'd tried to kill him.

It was a moment before Andie realized Mary Jericho was speaking. ". . . father died ten years ago, Dylan refused to take part in the family business. Insisted he wanted to be a police officer. A detective." She gave Andie another sad look. "How did your mother feel about you becoming a police officer, Andie?"

"My family and law enforcement go way back," she said. "With a grandfather, a father, two brothers, and various other relatives all police officers, I don't think it was a surprise when I—"

"But they were all *male*," she said, concern glowing in her eyes. "Your mother must be very proud of you for choosing such a noble path, even though it puts her only daughter at risk. It's hard enough to watch a son put himself in harm's way, but a daughter . . ."

Her voice trailed off as she looked over at her four budding beauty queens, still cooing over their brother's prone and silent form.

"Dylan's the eldest," she volunteered, staring at him wistfully. "When Janine, Josie, Erin, and Terri came along, he was such a good big brother to them. They adore him."

It was plain to see that Mary Jericho and her four daughters all adored Dylan. For a moment, Andie wanted to laugh out loud. This must be where the smoother-than-smooth Jericho had learned how to deal with—and conquer—the fairer sex. She imagined he was a fierce protector of his sisters, and any guy dumb enough to mess with a Jericho daughter would have big brother Dylan to answer to.

"Well, I'll leave you to your privacy," Andie said. "It was nice meeting you, and if you need anything . . ." She handed Mrs. Jericho her card. "Please contact me, any day, any hour. I *mean* that."

As Mrs. Jericho slipped the card into her purse, she said, "Dylan talked about you, you know."

"He *did*?"

"He always had something nice to say. He said if there was anybody he'd ever trust to watch his back, it would be you."

Inside Andie's chest, her heart crimped. He hadn't talked about her looks, or the fact he'd wanted to date her, and she'd spurned him. Instead, he'd told his mother he *trusted* her.

And she'd let him down. She'd been too wrapped up in her own troubles, she hadn't watched Dylan's back, and look what had happened. She'd known Bostwick was going to pull something but had no idea whether he was serious, or if he was, what he would do. His targeting Dylan had never even crossed her mind.

And if her partner died as a result, the burden of his death would be on her. How could she ever make something like that up to Dylan's obviously sweet mother and four adoring sisters?

"Thank you," she choked. She had to get out of there before she broke down completely. "Please call me if there's any change."

Wishing a hasty good-bye to the Jericho family, she left the room and headed down the brightly lit hall. Just past the nurses' station, she stopped to grab a tissue from her purse. With her head down, her mind preoccupied, and a damp wad of Kleenex to her nose, she didn't notice his approach until it was too late.

"And how's our patient doing today, Inspector?"

For a moment, she froze. Slowly raising her head, she let her eyes meet his. "Commander."

His face held a satisfied expression, like a cat who'd cornered a mouse and was moving in for the kill. Gesturing to Dylan's closed door, he said, "I hear the prognosis is poor. A sad day for the department."

"I can see how broken up about it you are."

"Inside," he whispered in a serious tone. "I'm weeping on the *inside*. I've sworn to my superiors that I will personally oversee the apprehension and prosecution of the perpetrator of this heinous crime."

"Cut the crap, Commander," she snapped. "If you're running for office, you'll never get my vote." Crossing her arms over her stomach, she took a half step back from him. "My only question is, did you do it, or did you hire it done?"

He gave her a hurt look. "Inspector, are you implying I had anything to do with the attack on your partner?"

"I'm not wearing a wire, you dickhead. I just want to know if you had the guts to do it yourself."

He said nothing for a few moments, then pursed his lips. Rocking back on his heels, he seemed lost in thought, then tilted his head. "Not that it has anything to do with your question, Inspector, but I've always been someone who takes a particular pride in being a man of action."

"Bully for you."

"I understand Jericho's family is here. I must go in and offer my condolences. If you'll excuse me."

He began walking down the hall toward Dylan's room, then stopped a few paces away and turned to face her. Under his breath, so only she could hear, he said, "Knock yourself out, Andrea. You'll never be able to prove anything. I'm smarter and more clever than any of you. You don't know who you can trust, do you? You're all by yourself out there."

She took a step toward him, but he put up his hand, halting her before she got too close.

"I no longer care about convicting Sinclair. He has the necklace. Get it from him by midnight tomorrow night. Contact me when you have it." Without making a sound, he mouthed, "Or someone else you care about will suffer."

Through her fury, she arched a brow, and said dryly, "Midnight, Commander? Isn't that a little trite?"

Leaning toward her a fraction, he hissed, "Ask me if I care, sweetheart. Do. It." With one last menacing glare, he left her standing in the hallway, staring at his retreating back.

As soon as he disappeared through Dylan's hospital room door, she retrieved her cell phone from her purse. Flipping the phone open, she pressed the button and put the phone to her ear. When Logan answered, she said quietly, "Did you get it?"

"Aye, lass," came the reply. "The wire picked up the entire conversation. But it will do us no good without an admission of guilt, confession of some sort, or a demand. He was careful. His wording could be construed any number of ways."

"Then there's only one thing we can do," she said, pressing the button for the elevator. "We're going to have to give him the necklace."

Chapter 23

When it comes to my own turn to lay my weapons down, I shall do so with thankfulness and fatigue . . .

Robert Louis Stevenson

Awaiting Andie's return, Logan wandered the mansion, being sure to avoid the library, the essential heart and soul of the place.

Though he fought off impressions from the entire house, it was the library where they were strongest, so he shunned the room and its tangled mass of emotions. Doing so was the only way to maintain his hard-won detachment.

Aye, he entered the room for Andie's sake, but now that he knew the perils waiting there, he avoided it as much as possible.

Meandering into the kitchen, he poured himself a mug of coffee from the carafe on the counter, took a sip, looked around.

While the exterior of the house had not been

changed in the last two centuries, except for the odd bit of maintenance here and there, the kitchen and plumbing had been duly upgraded. And a good thing it was. There were houses in the UK hundreds of years older than those in America which, though picturesque, were the worse for want of a few modern touches.

He checked his watch. Even using evasive maneuvers to keep from being followed, it shouldn't take Andie more than half an hour to return from her trip to the hospital. He hoped she would not be delayed; they had a lot to discuss.

Setting his coffee on the white-tile counter, he turned toward the window over the sink and stared out into the bright day. Either by the man's own hand, or hired out, Bostwick had put Andie's partner in hospital; who would he go after next? Since he seemed to act with impunity, it would take a clever and subtle plan to catch him at his game. For all intents and purposes, a sting operation where he would not suspect he was being set up.

From what Andie had said, Bostwick never discussed anything self-incriminating over the phone, never put anything condemning in writing, and in conversation, any pointed innuendo could be innocently interpreted. The man had obviously been fine-tuning his ability to steer clear of entrapment for years.

Turning away from the window, Logan rested his backside against the tile counter, crossed his arms over his chest, and bowed his head in concentration.

There must be a way, had to be. Bostwick had killed Tolley and Drew Mochrie, and nearly succeeded in taking Dylan Jericho's life. And there was no guarantee even yet that Jericho would pull through. The commander used coercion, blackmail, and who knew what other means to get what he wanted.

And right now, what he wanted was that necklace. Andie had suggested they give it over to the bastard, and maybe she was right. However, giving it over might be done in such a way that doing so would snare Bostwick in his own trap.

When Logan was a little boy, his father had often taken him fishing for salmon in one of the lochs strewn about the Scottish countryside.

"To catch a grand fish," his father would say as he tackled up his line, "you have to use the right bait, lad. Generally, a man catches what he goes fishing for." He'd winked at Logan. "Same holds true in life."

Logan tried to ignore the tug at his heart the cherished memory stirred. His father had been a wonderful man, as kind and generous as any man could claim. As kind and generous a man as Logan had once wished himself to be.

Angrily, he swiped up the mug and drained it in one gulp, choking down his emotions along with the cold, bitter coffee. Blowing out a harsh breath, he forced his mind back to the matter at hand.

Bradley Bostwick was a very big fish, and Logan happened to be in possession of the tastiest, shiniest lure there ever was. All he had to do was dangle it in such a way that the commander couldna snap the line and take off with the bait.

Or hurt Andie.

As soon as he thought of her, the humming inside his head began again. It had been that way since the moment he'd come with her to this house. Over the last few days, he'd begun to realize that letting himself fall in love with her meant weakening the barriers he'd erected against his own powers. He was only strong when his feelings were not engaged.

In spite of his best efforts to thwart them, thoughts of his father drifted through his mind again. He'd loved his family and let his powers run roughshod o'er him, to his everlasting regret. But he'd been a much younger man then, a mere lad. He was grown now, and come into his own. Maybe he could relax his guard a wee bit and make use of his gifts without seeing anyone come the worse for it.

Falling in love with Andie had changed him more than she would ever realize, maybe more than he realized himself. At first, he'd wanted to curse his deficiency in being unable to sustain his years-long emotional shield, but the more he saw of her, spoke to her, the more he let himself become attached to her, the more he realized he was tired of standing sentry over his God-given proficiencies out of fear of hurting anyone the way he'd hurt his family.

Then he'd made love to her, and that had shattered any reservations he'd had once and for all. He'd wanted to tell her then how he felt, but the timing was piss poor at best, what with one thing and another. And now with her partner in hospital and Bostwick making more threats . . .

Maybe it would help if he talked to someone about all this. It had been years since he'd let himself feel this way about a woman, and his nerves were a wreck.

Sentiments and sensations he'd suppressed for so long were surfacing, confusing him, making him doubt himself. What if he told Andie he loved her, and she tossed it back in his face? She could. He knew she liked him well enough, but how would she accept a confession of love? After all, they'd started out by lying to each other. Not exactly a rock-solid foundation for a relationship, no matter how the circumstances had warranted it.

He thought of his grandmother, and suddenly realized he wanted very much to talk to her. She'd always been a kind woman, kind of heart, kind of soul, two things he needed at the moment, though he'd bloody the nose of any man who accused him of it to his face.

Edging his cell phone out of his pocket, he pressed

her number. He sucked in a deep breath, feeling ridiculous, bewildered by his own nerves.

After four rings, he was ready to end the call when she answered. "Hello?"

He cleared his throat. "Uh, Gran? It's, uh, me. It's Logan."

"Logan?" she repeated, her voice high-pitched and small. "I was so hoping you'd call again. Is all well with you?"

Running his fingers through his hair, he said, "Aye. I'm good, Gran. Uh, listen. I . . . I lied to you the other day when I called."

"Lied?" Her gentle voice sounded worried, even a bit frantic. "Lied about what?"

"I'm in San Francisco, Gran," he rushed. "I'm here."

There was silence for a moment, then he heard what sounded like soft crying. She sniffed, cleared her throat. "Can I see you, dear? I would so love to see you."

"Well, I . . . I'm on a case, Gran. It's a wee bit of a tangle. But when it's over . . . aye, I'd like to maybe pay a visit. I . . . well, there's some things we probably need to talk about."

"Yes," she said on a breath. "So many things. So many years to catch up on. Are you married, Logan? Do you have children? Please . . . I need to . . . to apologize. You must believe me. All those years ago. I was wrong to say the things I did. I—"

"Let's not talk about that now, Gran. I, well, it's like, I've met this woman, and—"

"And you're in love? Oh, Logan! I want to hear all about her. I want to hear all about *every*thing!"

He smiled to himself, happy to hear his grandmother's voice, her enthusiasm, and he realized he was glad he'd decided to contact her. It felt good and right, and for the first time in a long, long while, he didn't feel so far away from everyone who had once been the whole world to him.

He heard Andie's car pull around to the back of the house.

"Look, Gran, I have to go now. But I'll call you again. Soon. I promise. And we'll get together, okay?"

Andie closed the back door behind her just as Logan was sliding his cell phone into his jeans pocket. For a moment, they just looked at each other without speaking. She smiled at him, gazing into his aquamarine eyes. He smiled back.

It felt to Andie as though they'd done it just this way a thousand times before. Their quiet greeting was comfortable, familiar, and filled with something she was almost afraid to name.

"Hi," he said.

"Hi, yourself."

He moved away from the sink to walk toward her. Putting his arms around her waist, he tugged her into a welcoming hug. She slid her hands around his shoulders, setting her head against his chest. A moment later, she felt him kiss her hair, then lay his cheek on the top of her head.

"You certain you weren't followed?" he asked.

"I'm certain."

"I'm worried, lass. So many things could go wrong."

"Nothing will go wrong," she said with more confidence than she felt. "Once I tell him I have the necklace, it should all fall into place."

"But what if he pulls something unexpected? I won't be near enough to—"

"I'll be fine. Look, I met Dylan's family at the hospital. They're so nice, and they love him so much. We have to do this, not only because it's the right thing, but we owe it to the Jerichos, and your friend, Tolley."

She felt her hair stir as he breathed, "Aye."

They stood that way for what seemed like forever while he caressed her back, running his palms in slow circles, warming her, making her feel incredibly cherished. Through the soft fabric of his dark T-shirt, she listened to the steady beating of his heart, felt the movement of his muscles and bones as he inhaled, exhaled, shifted his weight on his feet. Closing her eyes, she took in his scent, clean and a bit musky. A good smell.

Though she hadn't originally intended it, she raised her head and kissed him, eager to connect with him on every possible level. The kiss he returned was both tender and urgent, and seemed to go on and on, and by the time it was over, she found herself naked, every stitch of her clothing in a heap on the floor at her feet.

He braced his body by backing up against the sink, then lifted her, wrapping her bare legs around his hips.

"Logan, Logan, Logan," she whispered, running her hands up under his shirt, enjoying the feel of the hard muscles of his abs and chest. "I want you so much." He responded by easing open the fly of his jeans. She felt his warm, moist tip against her thigh, and became frantic to impale herself on him.

She reached between them, wrapping her fingers around his rigid thickness. She rubbed the blunt, hot head against herself until the pleasure of it made her arch her neck back and feel . . . just mindlessly *feel* . . .

Logan curved his strong hand around hers, helping her drive her pleasure, and his own, higher and higher until they both moaned.

Edging her fingers away, he positioned himself and thrust into her. Then he halted and stood motionless while they both adjusted to his presence in her body. His breathing was harsh, labored. He looked into her eyes for a moment, then lowered his head to nuzzle her neck, murmuring softly to her in Gaelic.

While she didn't understand the words, she grasped their underlying passion and felt her heart swell with joy.

When he rolled his hips, she caught her breath, unable to do anything but let the tension mount. Each thrust was stronger than the next, sending her pulse racing, pitching her desire for Logan into emotional overdrive.

"Logan," she breathed. "Logan . . . I . . ."

The orgasm hit her before she could finish her thought. Her body tensed from the impending pleasure, then released as she came, her hips jerking against him again and again until she could barely breathe.

She was still panting when he found his own release. In a hot rush, he filled her, his fingers on her hips grinding her hard into him as he groaned in pleasure over and over.

Exhausted, she let her body slump against him while he lowered his head to her shoulder. They were both sweating, panting, smiling. When he lifted his head to look deeply into her eyes, he mumbled, "You're somethin', lass." Then he kissed her, softly, slowly. Pulling back, he repeated, "Really somethin'."

Andie unwrapped her legs from around Logan's waist, and eased herself down until her bare feet touched the floor. She raised herself on her tiptoes and kissed him on the mouth, then settled into his embrace.

"What was it you said?" she asked.

He raised his hand and stroked her hair. "When?"

She nestled closer. "You said something in Gaelic, I guess it was. What did you say?"

Lifting her face, she looked up at him and waited.

"It . . . eh, what I said was . . ."

She blinked, then backed up a little. "Well, was it something gross or mindless or dirty?"

He shook his head. "*Nae*, lass. None of those."

"Then why can't you translate it for me? I'd like to learn a *wee bit* o' Gaelic, lad."

"It's not that I can't, it's that . . . I've never, I mean . . ." His cheeks flushed and he looked suddenly like he'd been caught stealing money from his mother's dresser drawer. "Well, you see, it loses a wee bit in the translation."

Her brows furrowed. "It seemed to me you said something like *tagrammaert* . . ."

"It's actually *Tha gràdh agam ort*."

She raised her brows. "It's not one of the much sought-after, missing verses to that Ode To A Haggis thing, is it? Because that would *so* put me out of the mood, if you know what I mean—"

"Andie." His eyes softened and so did his voice. "It means *I love you*." Placing his knuckle under her chin, he raised her face to look deeply into her eyes. "To state it another way, I love you."

Her lashes fluttered as she gazed up at him, trying to process what he'd just said.

"Gaelic," he continued, "doesn't have a verb for

to love, so what I actually said was *There is love at me on you.*" He smiled and waggled his dark brows. "Dead sexy, eh, lass?"

Her heart crimped, and her eyes burned. She swallowed, then moved back into his embrace.

"Oh, Logan," she whispered, tightening her arms around his waist. "Then we have something in common. There is love at me on you, too."

Chapter 24

If your morals make you dreary . . . they are wrong.

Robert Louis Stevenson

This was it. Time to set a trap for a rat.

Andie had agreed with Logan that Bostwick was too slippery for any kind of conventional sting. They knew the commander had to be nervous after what Logan had said to him during the interrogation. The fact they hadn't seen Bostwick or any sign of a tail since then meant he was probably worried going after Logan would raise questions he didn't want to answer.

Or he didn't know where Logan was hiding out, which was probably closer to the truth than anything.

Bostwick apparently hadn't put a tail on Andie, or she'd successfully evaded any followers. Either way, Logan couldn't hide out in the mansion forever. Who knew which police officers Bostwick had in his pocket, or what their orders were if they spotted Logan.

Turning the corner onto the Embarcadero, Andie pulled over into a minimart parking lot. After a deep and fortifying breath, she pressed the speed dial on her cell. Bostwick answered on the first ring.

"Sir. I need to talk to you. Can I meet you somewhere?"

"Inspector," he said jovially. She could almost see him leaning back in his chair, putting his feet up on his desk, pleased with himself that he still had her on a short leash. The jerk. "I was wondering when you were going to come groveling. I had intended to contact you today vis-à-vis your status, but now, here you are. Great minds do think alike."

"Whatever. Sir."

"Ah, it's nice to hear the deference in your voice," he said smoothly. "It reminds me of our very divergent positions. Speaking of which, are you still riding Sinclair's ass?"

"With great enthusiasm, sir." Snort. If he only knew.

"Good," he said sharply. "But he hasn't been back to his hotel. Do you . . . happen to know where he's gone?"

"Negative, sir. He contacts me by phone, and we meet in public places. After your conversation with him at the station the other day, he seemed to feel it best to take up residence elsewhere. I'm not sure I understand what went on that day, but—"

"Enough!" he snapped. "Status report, Inspector."

"Okay," she said calmly. "I've uncovered some new information."

"Such as?"

"Sinclair's not his real name," she said flatly. "And he's not a con man. He's a cop."

Let him sweat that one out, she thought.

A little time ticked by, then a little more. She could almost hear the wheels turning frantically in Bostwick's head as he tried to decide if he should just cut his losses and run, track Logan down and kill him, or stay the course and go for the necklace.

Forcing the issue, she said, "We need to meet, Commander. I am in possession of . . . the item."

"You have . . ." He halted midsentence. She could almost hear him salivating. "You have it?"

"Yes, sir. I'm sure you can see now why we need to meet personally."

The noise she heard must have been his chair falling over as he jumped to his greedy little feet. "Well, why in the fuck didn't you say so in the first place!"

And the hook is set . . .

Ignoring his question, she said, "How about we meet in thirty minutes in Golden Gate Park? It's very public, and yet we can find a quiet place to . . . talk."

"Sure." Then he laughed and lowered his voice. "If you think to set me up, Andie, I warned you before about that. Just so you'll know, don't bother wearing a wire because I'm going to search you."

"Knock yourself out, Commander. Where in the park—"

"Tell you what, sweetheart," he said. "You just go to the park. I'll find you." The line went dead.

Glancing up the street, she pulled back out into traffic and pressed the speed dial for Logan's number. When he answered, she said, "The meet's in thirty minutes. Golden Gate Park. I'm on my way now. I'll stall him as long as possible."

"Be on your guard, lass."

She snorted a laugh. "What would he try? When I told him you were a cop, he was quiet so long, I thought he'd fainted."

"Blacked out."

"Oh, right. I forgot the men-don't-faint thing."

Turning left at the next corner, she headed north toward the park.

How Bostwick would find her in a place that size, she had no idea, and didn't really care. As long as he stayed away from his house for about an hour, whether she actually ran into him or not didn't matter.

In her ear, Logan said, "I want you to be careful, lass. He's killed twice that I know of. He's a rapacious bastard who covers his tracks well. You may be too much of a liability to him at this point, and he may decide to—"

"Don't worry about me, laddie. He knows I don't have any evidence that can be used to prosecute him, only accusations, which he can refute. He doesn't know you and I are working together. He'll want the necklace too badly to pull anything. But I'm not stupid, I'll be on guard, just in case. You just do your part so we can hang this guy by his balls, okay?"

"As retribution goes, that's a start."

Ahead of her, the park's entrance came into view. "That reminds me, Logan. I've been wondering about something."

"Okay."

"Well, you're pursuing this case on your own time, right?"

"Aye."

"Can you tell me why?"

Logan was quiet for a moment, then said, "I was at university when my family died in a car accident. My father, mother, and sisters."

"Oh, Logan. I'm so sorry . . ."

"It all but destroyed me, especially since . . . especially since it was my fault."

"Logan, no. Oh, God, I'm so—"

"I was near suicidal with grief and guilt, but my university roommate kept me sane. He saved my life, not that I wanted it saved at the time. He was a good friend, a good man. Even when he came to the US, we never lost touch. Not until a year ago, when he was murdered."

Andie heard him swallow, take in a deep breath.

"Tolley Mochrie was the best friend a man could ever have, and that's a fact. Loved him like a brother, I did. When I found out what happened, what Bostwick did, I swore . . . I . . . I . . ."

Everything Logan said confirmed what Ethan had discovered about Logan Macmillan, but she hadn't wanted Logan to know she'd had her brother do a background on him, not with their history of trust issues.

Though she knew what had happened, she hadn't been prepared for the profound grief she heard in Logan's voice. The accident had happened fifteen years ago, but he was still punishing himself; perhaps he always would.

And because she loved him, she had to know . . .

"Logan?"

Silence. Then a quiet, "Aye?"

"Tell me the truth now."

"Aye."

She licked her lips. "Tell me, is it your intention to capture Bradley Bostwick," she said, "or kill him?"

Andie parked her car in the small lot near the pagoda. According to her information, Dylan had been shot somewhere near here, which was why she'd chosen it. Maybe the location would make

Bostwick nervous, and if anyone deserved to be nervous, it was that son of a bitch.

One of the perils of setting up the commander was that she had to do it alone. *Had* to. She hadn't even told her brothers what she was up to. They either would have tried to stop her, or butted in. Bostwick was *her* commander. He'd tried to take down *her* partner. He'd bullied her, blackmailed her, and basically treated her like shit, and now it was payback time.

She didn't want anybody else horning in on taking the bastard down. Anybody except Logan, of course. But then, she couldn't begrudge Logan; he had his own axe to grind with Bostwick.

The afternoon was waning; it would be evening soon. The spring air felt cool but not cold against her face as she walked down the empty pathway that led to a rose garden.

It would go like this: Bostwick would approach. She'd tell him about Sinclair and what the Scotland Yard detective had in mind. A frantic Bostwick would then race back to his home only to find Logan and the San Francisco PD waiting for him, evidence in hand linking him to his crimes. The commander would be arrested and indicted on two counts of homicide . . . and one count of theft. The DA's office would prosecute, they'd go to trial where Andie—and others, hopefully—would describe in detail the skanky defendant's proclivity for manipulation and blackmail. Good old Bradley

would be professionally disgraced, publicly humili-
ated, and ultimately convicted.

Sure, the case would drag on and on; she was
prepared for lawyers' tricks. Favors would be
called in. There'd be appeals, but in the end, justice
would prevail.

It had to, or all this was for nothing.

The only hitch in the plan was Logan. He wouldn't
throw away everything for a chance to kill Bostwick, would he? Dammit, *would* he? Not that she
cared one way or the other about Bostwick's sorry
hide. She didn't want Logan ruining his life—or
their life together—to avenge his friend.

When he came face-to-face with the commander,
Logan would do the right thing, wouldn't he?

Of course, if Dylan died, maybe her feelings
about all that would change. If the situation were
different, and Bostwick had killed somebody she
loved . . . Ethan or Nate . . . would she be able
to stay her hand, keep her weapon holstered, or
would the taste of revenge be too sweet, too seductive?

If she was brutally honest with herself, she'd have
to say she just didn't know . . . and that fact alone
was terrifying.

She glanced around. No more cars on the road
behind her, the path ahead was empty, too. How
Bostwick would find her, given the size and com-
plexity of Golden Gate Park, she wasn't sure, so
she stayed within view of the pagoda. In the dis-

tance, a car drove slowly by; not the commander's, at least, not one she recognized.

Wandering up and down the path, she tried to stay calm, relaxed. Everything would work out. If Bostwick showed up and gave her any trouble, she felt confident she could handle him. After all, he'd been sitting behind a desk for twenty years and hired his dirty work done.

Even so, it wouldn't be prudent to underestimate him. A caged animal had a certain motivation for prevailing, and Bostwick might not be as lame as he appeared.

Her stomach began to feel queasy as her instincts kicked into gear. It wouldn't be good to get too confident, or cocky. The guy was no dummy; he could probably pull a fast one on her, so she'd best be on guard. Her .38 was in easy reach under her jacket, and she was in a public place. It would be okay.

Of course, Dylan had been in the same public place, and look what had happened to him. But no, she thought. This was different; it would play out differently. She was out to get Bostwick, not the other way around.

She rubbed the bridge of her nose. God, she was way overthinking this whole thing. What she needed was to relax a little . . .

Blowing out a breath, she wandered back toward the rose garden. This early in April, the buds were just beginning to open, and the honeyed scent of a

Peace rose met her nose. She stopped and bent to touch one of the fragile petals.

Someone moved up quickly behind her and she whirled to face him, her hand automatically darting under her jacket. "Commander." She slowly lowered her arm.

Bradley Bostwick looked awful. His skin seemed too tight for his face, his eyes were bloodshot, and his mouth turned down at an ugly angle.

"Do you have it?" Though he all but snarled the words, his voice held a weary note. Thrusting his hand toward her, he quietly ordered, "Give it to me."

"I, well, I didn't exactly bring it with me—"

His eyes widened, and he lunged toward her, grabbing at her purse. He tore it open and tossed the contents onto the path. When he didn't find the necklace, he stalked toward Andie. "You stupid bitch! If you set me up—"

His arm snaked out and before she could move back out of reach, he took hold of her wrist. With his free hand, he curled his fingers over the collar of her shirt and jerked at the fabric. Buttons popped as the blouse gave way, ripping open, revealing bare skin and nothing more.

Bostwick let go of her arm as he simply stared at her chest.

"I told you I wasn't going to wear a wire," she drawled, then reached up to tug the edges of her shirt together. "Did you really think I was dumb enough to drive around with a necklace worth ten million dollars in my handbag?"

He stood a couple of feet from her, his back bent, shoulders hunched, his arms out, and fingers splayed like a gymnast preparing to do a handstand. "I hate to sound like a broken record, Andie," he choked, "but where is the goddamned necklace!"

"You answer one of my questions," she said, "and I'll answer one of yours."

"What in the hell are you—"

"Did you personally shoot Dylan Jericho?"

His head came up, and his eyes narrowed. He gave a little shrug as though he didn't care one way or the other what she did with the information. "Yeah, I shot him. He was doing some valuable favors for me in return for me keeping what I know about him to myself."

"You blackmailed him," she said flatly. "The way you did me."

"Yeah. What of it?"

"If he was so valuable, as you say, why'd you shoot him?"

Bostwick eyed her for a moment, then calmly, he said, "Because I promised to punish you if you didn't get me the necklace, and I am, after all, a man of my word. So if anyone's to blame, it's you, Inspector Darling. Not me. You. I was simply fulfilling my obligation." He grinned a little then and offered up another casual shrug.

"But Dylan didn't die," she said evenly. "He

might even recover." In the fading light, she glared at him. "And if he does, what you have on him will be *nothing* compared to what he has on you."

Bostwick ran splayed fingers through his hair. His eyes gleamed with malice and fear. Judging by his jerky motions, his nerves were getting to him. He was disasssembling before her very eyes, making him more unpredictable and dangerous than ever.

He nodded a few times, absently, as though checking off a grocery list inside his head. Then, "Where is the necklace?"

Andie waited a moment until she had his full attention. When his eyes met hers, she said, "It's at your house, Commander." When Bostwick's brows raised, she said, "Sinclair's on his way there right now, planting it for the police to find. *He who has the necklace did the Mochrie murder*, isn't that what you said, Commander, or words to that effect? You *did* kill your girlfriend to get it, didn't you?" She began backing away from him. "If you hurry, you might be able to find it and get to the airport before the good guys close in."

"You set me up." His voice was hoarse, the words barely audible.

She didn't so much as bat an eye. "Abso-fuckin'-lutely, you bastard."

He took a step toward her, so she jabbed her hand under her jacket, reaching for her weapon.

But Bostwick was a lot faster than she ever would

have given him credit for. His hand darted behind his back, and the next thing she knew, a blade flashed in his hand.

The butt of her gun was in her palm . . .

The long blade in Bostwick's fingers flashed in the dying sunlight . . .

She threw the safety on her weapon, raised her arms, aimed . . .

Bostwick lurched forward, his arm down, the knife pointed up to gut her . . .

She fired point-blank just as the blade sliced into her ribs like a white-hot lance. She choked, and buckled under the pain. Her weapon fell from her paralyzed fingers.

Bostwick's free hand clamped down hard over her open mouth while his knife hand encircled her waist. He tried to jab her again, but she kicked at him and let her body go limp, trying to use her deadweight against him, but he dragged her backwards into a thick copse of trees.

She struggled, tried to claw at his hands and face, keep the knife away, but the pain from her wound made her dizzy and weak. Nausea threatened to overtake her, but she fought on, slamming into his shins with her heel as hard as she could.

In the shadows under the trees, she caught a glimpse of his face. Bostwick, his features contorted into a grim and hideous mask. He said nothing, but shoved her to an arm's length and grabbed her throat, choking her as he raised the blood-slicked knife over her head.

With the last ounce of strength she possessed, she gripped his wrists and brought her knee up directly into his crotch, sending him backwards, doubled over in pain.

She was free of him, but the effort cost her control of her balance. She fell, landing on her wounded side, agony turning her muscles to useless jelly. Helpless to stand, her body began rolling down the steep slope that led to a dark and secluded pond. Twigs, rocks, broken leaves bit her face and hands as she tried to slow her downward motion, but nothing worked. She slammed into the trunk of a small tree, her feet resting in the shallow water at the edge of the pond.

Dazed, she opened her eyes to see the silhouette of a man standing at the top of the hill, the knife gripped in his hand. Slowly, she dragged her body into the shadows where she was sure he couldn't see her. He seemed to be trying to decide whether to come after her or not, but to do so might cost him the necklace.

In the end, greed won out, and the commander disappeared from view.

Andie tried to reach for her phone, but the muscles in her arms seemed dead, and would not respond. It felt as though hours passed before she edged her hand near enough her waistband to grab the phone, but when her fingers finally found the cell's holster, it was empty.

Gasping for breath, she let her head fall back onto the stiff grass. She narrowed her eyes and looked to the top of the hill to see if Bostwick had returned, but the night shrouded the entire woods, leaving her essentially blind.

God, her lids weighed a ton, too heavy to keep open. Closing her eyes, she silently moved her lips.

"Logan, can you hear me? He's on his way . . . careful, careful now . . . stay safe . . . stay safe . . . love you . . ."

Too dark . . . too much pain . . . going to faint . . . no, not faint, goddammit . . . black out . . .

Chapter 25

... if we are loved we are indispensable.

Robert Louis Stevenson

Logan sat in his car on the darkest part of the street across from Bostwick's house, waiting. He hadn't heard from Andie, which made him a bit nervous. She was, after all, a trained police officer, he rationalized. More than capable of taking care of herself.

Still . . . Bostwick had a lot to lose, and that might make him more lethal than either of them had anticipated. Logan had wanted to alert her brothers, but she'd been adamant that she could keep Bostwick busy and not fall for any trick he might pull.

Against his better judgment, Logan had agreed, and now regretted that decision.

To divert his attention from his anxieties, he glanced around. Everything was in place. Sev-

eral unmarked cars had arrived and taken positions. Though Logan had promised Andie not to
involve her brothers in what *she* was doing, there
was nothing stopping him from involving Nate in
what *he* was doing. Nate was, after all, the only
SFPD police officer Logan knew he could trust at
the moment.

Of course, none of them knew, including Nate,
that Logan had arrived an hour earlier to have a
private word with Mrs. Bostwick, who soon there-
after departed with a sudden urge to do a little
"last-minute" shopping.

Logan's original plan had been to come to the
US, hunt Bostwick down, and simply kill him.
Quick, and of relatively little cost to anyone. Tolley's merciless murder deserved to be avenged in
kind, after all.

Tolley Mochrie. Now there was a good lad.

"You've many a reason to live," Tolley'd urged,
two weeks after Logan's family had been buried.
"'Twas not yer fault, Logan."

"Aye, it was," Logan protested. "They'd all be
alive now if not for me."

Tolley's arm had encircled Logan's shoulders; his
free hand gently taking the loaded pistol from Logan's bloodless fingers.

"Listen to me," Tolley said somberly. "Taking
yer own life will do no one any good, least of all
you." He'd smiled a bit at his own quiet humor,
but Logan had remained silent. The grin fading,

Tolley said, "It's true, they're dead, and no bringin' them back, but taking yer life is *nae* the answer, my friend."

Logan reacted with fury. "So what exactly is the answer, eh?" he shouted. "I've killed my *family*. What does a man do after such a thing as that?"

Tolley's brows knit together, and he nodded slowly. "Then make their lives have had some meanin'. Do something in their name, something good, something true and right and honorable. Dedicate yer life to it so their deaths won't be a side note in some forgotten book." He shrugged. "You think your family would want you to end your life like this, do ya? I can't imagine they would! Live on, live a good life, for *them*."

He extended his palm, the gun black and shiny in his hand. "I might not come back from class early to stay yer hand next time, lad. 'Tis somethin' you have to decide for yourself, and soon, and forever."

Logan wiped the moisture from his eyes. He'd taken his friend's advice. He'd become a police officer—one who was good and true and right and honorable. What he'd done to his family couldna be undone, but dedicating his life to their memory was something, after all.

And now the man who'd saved Logan's life was dead, murdered by a greedy bastard for nothing more than a handful of glittering glass. Was that what a man's life was worth, then? Was that what

Bostwick's life was worth? When he came again face-to-face with the commander, would Logan be able to stay his hand, or avenge his friend without a second thought?

A car rounded the far corner and barreled into Bostwick's driveway. The door swung wide, and the commander stepped out, glanced around, then seemed to relax a little.

Just what in the hell had Andie told him, anyway? She was only supposed to keep him away from home so Logan could plant the necklace . . .

Jesus . . . *Andie* . . . why hadn't she called to tell him Bostwick was on his way? She was supposed to call . . . something had gone wrong . . .

Then he saw the blood on the bastard's hands, jacket, pants.

That being the case, all bets were off.

As Bostwick lurched up the front porch steps, Logan shoved open his car door and started across the street, signaling to Nate, parked farther down. Immediately, he and Matthews were out of their car and running toward the house, weapons drawn.

His own weapon in his hands, Logan leveled the barrel on Bostwick's back.

"Halt!" he yelled. The commander froze, his left foot in midair. "Now turn around! Keep your hands where I can see them!"

"Don't shoot! You're making a mistake! I haven't done anything!" Slowly, Bostwick turned. His eyes widened, then narrowed as his gaze landed on

Logan. As Nate moved to stand next to him, Inspector Matthews and a uniformed officer hurried up the steps.

"We have a warrant," Matthews said to Bostwick, then held up a key chain for him to see. "From your car. I trust your house key is on it?"

He nodded. "Go on in. Don't know what you think you're going to find."

"So what's all the blood from?" Nate said. "You cut yourself shaving?"

Bostwick shrugged, but kept his hands up. "Look, there's a reasonable explanation for this. If you'd just calm down, and come on inside, let me get cleaned up, I can explain everything."

"Where's Andie?" Logan shouted, shoving forward, his weapon still trained on Bostwick's heart. "You were supposed to meet her in Golden Gate Park."

Bostwick didn't react, but instead stuck out his lower lip and shook his head. "You must be mistaken, and just who are you, Mr. Sinclair, to draw a weapon on me?"

"The name's Macmillan," he growled. "Scotland Yard."

Bostwick's jaw tightened. There was fear in his eyes, but when he spoke, he was smooth as polished glass.

"I did talk to her earlier," he admitted, "and we did plan on getting together to go over her performance eval, but as for Golden Gate Park?" He laughed. "It would hardly be appropriate for conducting a business meeting, now would it?"

His teeth clenched so tightly he could barely speak, Logan bit out, "Cut the crap, bastard. Tell me where she is!"

Before Bostwick could make up another lie, Inspector Matthews appeared in the doorway, holding an evidence bag. "Found it," she said to Nate.

Advancing up the steps, Nate grabbed Bostwick's bloody left wrist and wrenched it behind the man's back. Cuffing him, he said, "Bradley Bostwick, you're under arrest for the murders of Bartholomew Mochrie, Drew Mochrie, and for the theft of the Star of Avril. You have the—"

"What!" Bostwick screamed. "What's in that bag? Is that the necklace? *Is it?*"

Matthews nodded.

"Goddammit! God*dammit*! I didn't take that necklace! You're nuts! You're all nuts! This is a fucking *conspiracy*. I'll have your badges for this, all of you, all—"

Grabbing Bostwick by the throat, Logan leaned in close. "Shut. Up."

The commander complied. Sweat beaded his forehead, and he smelled of blood and grime.

"Where is Andie?" Logan ground out from between clenched teeth. "Tell me now, or I'll castrate you where you stand, and not one officer here will do a thing to stop me."

*   *   *

"Somewhere in Golden Gate Park isn't much to go on!" Nate shouted as he jumped into the passenger side of the Lexus. "I'd stay and beat the information out of the son of a bitch myself, but my sister could already be . . ."

"Never say it." Logan's tone was even, his voice calm. She wasn't dead; if she were, he'd know it.

Bostwick had hurt her and left her to die . . . but she was still hanging on. She wasn't one to give up, and as long as she had breath in her body, she'd fight.

If they only knew where she was . . . if they could get to her fast enough . . .

Next to him, Nate was on his cell. "Officer down! Officer down! Golden Gate Park, exact location, unknown. Inspector Andrea Darling. Caucasian, female, blond hair . . ."

As Nate went on with the physical description, Logan drove like hell toward the park. He gripped the wheel, while inside his head, he blasted away the barriers he'd erected fifteen years ago, hoping his so-called gift hadn't atrophied from lack of use.

Where is she? Guide me. For the love of God, guide me . . .

In front of him, the light turned red, but he tore through the intersection without so much as slowing down. He kept his eyes on the road while he opened his mind, searching for, begging for guidance.

As he hit the entrance to the park, the murmuring began.

At first, he couldn't make it out, then the voices grew louder, stronger, as though they were trying to reach him from some distant galaxy.

But he heard, and he understood.

To Nate, he said, "What's the quickest way to the pagoda?"

Nate's head whipped around. "How do you . . . never mind. Go left at the next corner. I'll guide you from there."

A few minutes later, the pagoda came into view.

"There's her car!" Nate shouted.

Logan slammed on the brakes and squealed to a halt in the near-empty parking lot. As the two men leaped out of the Lexus, Logan slowed for a moment.

Over here . . . over here . . . find me . . . find me . . .

Without a word, Logan turned on his heel and ran across the narrow street toward the rose garden. "Where?" he shouted to the air. "Which way?"

His heart felt as though it would burst, but he kept running. He heard Nate behind him, but didn't dare take any precious seconds to stop and explain.

The night was dark. A cold fog had crept in, oozing between the trees like a gray snake, transforming the landscape into something surreal.

Logan stopped. The voices were getting weaker. She was dying.

"No!" Putting his fists to his temples, he cried, "Show me where! I'll do anything you want, but show me where!"

A murmur, a mere whisper of sound thrummed against his eardrum, and he turned his attention toward a dense copse of trees.

Grabbing Nate's arm, he shouted, "Get an aid car here. Now!" With that, he took off at a dead run through the trees. He reached a small hill, and looked down. A muted glow emanated from the bottom. Water, a pond of some kind, but the light was too dim . . .

He blinked, then blinked again, unsure what he was seeing.

The figure of a woman appeared to float in the air a few yards in front of him. Her gown was luminescent, her face radiant. She was lovely, and for a moment, he was mesmerized.

She raised her arms as if to welcome him, then slowly retreated. He followed. Down the hill and down toward the water. Her long blond hair shimmered in the scant light, and at the edge of the calm, flat pond, she began to fade like a warm mist into the night.

In a moment, she was gone. Vanished.

He wanted to shout after her, beg her for her help, but then he heard a sound to his left near his feet, and he turned.

Relief flooded his system like a straight shot of adrenaline to the heart.

Quickly kneeling beside Andie, he put his fingers to her wrist. Her heartbeat was weak, but it was there.

On the hill above him, sirens screamed to the edge of the woods. Lights shone crazily in all directions, flooding the area as Nate led the paramedics down toward the pond.

Gently, Logan lifted Andie's shoulders, cradling her in his lap. Tearing at her clothing, he found the wound in her side, and pressed his bare hand to it, trying to stanch the slow but steady flow of blood.

She made a small sound of pain as she lifted one hand and wrapped her fingers around his wrist. "I knew you'd come," she whispered. "I called for you. I knew you'd hear . . ."

"Live," he begged. "Don't give it up. That's all I ask, Andie darlin'. Don't give it up . . ."

I'm in that house again, the—what did I call it? The mansion? But why am I here?

Last thing I remember, I was lying in Logan's arms, looking up into his eyes. So sad. Like he was losing his best friend. Such pain in those beautiful eyes, such regret. Oh, Logan . . . we had so little time . . .

I understand now. Somehow, I know everything about him—and always have and forever will.

How could I not have seen it before? It's all so very clear.

Sweet Logan. Do not mourn me. We'll be together again . . . my once and forever love . . .

How did I not recognize you when I was . . .

But I don't want to leave you, not like this. I feel as though I'm losing my best friend, too.

Maybe I can get back . . . maybe I can find a way . . . I want to go back . . . Logan . . . Logan!

What's that? I'm distracted from my thoughts. There's a light coming from somewhere down the hall, and I move toward it. But am I walking, or floating? How odd . . . there is no pain, no fear, no worry . . . it's all good now, all good.

The double doors are open to the library, and I go in, look around. Such a nice room. All these books. I love books. And now I'll have time to settle back and relax, maybe read a few. Catch up on the classics, maybe work a Sudoku or a crossword. No problems, no deadlines, no bad guys to catch. Just time . . . an eternity, really.

I feel so good, so happy . . . wrong word . . . not happy exactly. Content. That's it. I feel content. At peace. Like a small child snuggled under the covers in a warm bed . . . full tummy . . . stuffed bunny to hug . . . Mommy and Daddy who love me. Content. Perfect. I have never known such peace.

I'm smiling. Every breath I take comes and goes with ease. My muscles are no longer bound by gravity, and I feel lighter than the air around me.

As I look on, a mist forms in the center of the room, snaring my interest. The glistening fog takes a shape . . . three shapes . . . a woman and two men. One is her husband, the other, her father.

Anger and fear permeate the room. I can feel it, see it as it swirls about the father like a dark and menacing shroud.

But my focus stays on the woman; she's so pretty. Blond, with pale skin and full lips. She turns her face to me and smiles, and I know her for who she is.

Ah. Yes. Of course . . . of course . . . I should have realized . . . so silly, so blind . . .

She turns away again, moving to her husband. Their bond is strong. The translucent silver ribbon connecting them to each other gleams in the muted light of the library.

As I watch, the husband raises his arm and aims a pistol at the father, but the woman intervenes, thrusting her body against her husband's. The gun disappears from view.

Across the room, the father levels his own weapon, aiming it at the couple. He shouts something, and though I'm only a few feet away, I cannot hear it.

He is furious, and gestures for his daughter to get out of the way.

I watch, helpless, as the husband grabs her by the arm and pulls her behind him . . . just as the father's weapon discharges.

My hands rush to my face, and I try to scream, but there is no sound. I want to move forward, to stop that bullet, but am helpless to do so. I cannot intervene, I can only witness . . .

The world stands still. I can see the bullet as it leaves the gun, round and blunt and drifting, it seems, through time and space, moving in a straight line across the room to find its mark.

I know what will happen now. I want to stop it, stop that evil thing in midair, put a halt to the destruction of three lives.

Then, in a burst of light, the bullet pierces the husband's heart . . . but does not stop there.

The couple collapses to the floor, while the father cries out. The pistol falls from his fingers and drops to the floor, but makes not a sound.

As her husband's life ebbs away, the woman cradles the man she loves in her arms. She rocks him, speaks to him, but I cannot hear her vows of love, her testament to sorrow . . .

Slowly, she lifts her tear-stained face and looks straight at me. Her lips move as she tries to speak. And though the words never reach my ears, I hear them in my heart . . .

I stare into her anguished eyes, and understand.

Epilogue

To become what we are capable of becoming
is the only end in life.

Robert Louis Stevenson

One month later . . .

"This is insane," Logan groused as he escorted
Andie up the front steps of the mansion. "I never
should have agreed to this nonsense."

Andie tightened her arm around his waist. "It's
not nonsense, and you know it. It's something I
have to do. She saved my life, and now I'm going
to save hers."

"But you're just out of hospital, lass. You're still
too weak to—"

"I'm far stronger than you can imagine," she said,
and it was true. Right after she'd been wounded—
and far closer to death than she'd ever care to be
again—she'd been too weak to whisper her own

name. But in the ensuing weeks, what with good care, the loving support of her family, and about a ton of hot soup, she was beginning to feel her old self again.

"For the last month," she said as they reached the porch, "I've thought of almost nothing but getting back to this place and helping Emma on her way. Her poor spirit won't be at peace until she knows what happened that night. Since I can't hear her, or speak to her, you'll have to do it."

Behind her, the rest of the Darlings were on their way up the steps, including two very pregnant Darling wives.

As Nate helped Tabitha up the last step, Ethan was waiting about halfway down with Georgie, huffing and puffing, trying to catch her breath before attempting to reach the summit.

"This place has a bathroom, right?" she panted.

"It has one for each of you," Andie laughed, noting the desperate look in Tabitha's eyes.

"Aye," Logan said, pushing open the front door. "We'll wait while you ladies all attend to Nature's call."

Andie pointed out the two downstairs bathrooms to her sisters-in-law, then looped arms with her brothers and, together, followed Logan down the hall to the library.

As she crossed over the threshold, Andie felt the room greet her. She'd told her family about what she'd gone through that night. Psychic dream interpreter Tabitha, New Age feng shui devotee Georgie, and even reluctant-paranormal-by-association Nate got it; somber and irascible Ethan was the single holdout.

Logan helped Andie into a chair. Gazing around the room, she said, "The night I nearly died, I came here. Well, my spirit or soul or whatever you want to call it came here."

Ethan snorted. "Uh-huh."

She scowled at him. "I wouldn't expect you to understand, but at least show some respect for those who do."

"Hey," he said, lifting his broad shoulders in a halfhearted shrug. "You're alive. That's all I care about. You can talk to the spirit of Mickey Mouse for all I care, as long as you stay alive. Say, how's Jericho's recovery coming along?"

"Super," she said. "He'll be well enough to testify against Bostwick next month."

"Mickey Mouse," Nate snorted, then crossed his arms over his chest and scowled at Ethan. "You are such a dick."

Glaring at Nate, Ethan said, "Prick."

"Boys!" Tabitha and Georgie waddled through the library door, arm in arm, both shaking their heads at their respective husbands' childish behavior.

As they stood, Ethan and Nate grinned at each other. "They'll never get it, will they, big brother?" Nate said.

Ethan settled into his chair. "Nope."

As Tabby and Georgie took the chairs their husbands held for them, Andie crossed her hands in her lap.

"I knew the moment I saw her in this room that night, the moment she looked at me, that Emma Harte was my great-grandmother. It was just . . . there."

Logan pulled up a chair next to Andie. "Who could have known that Emma Harte's best friend, Mary *Darling*, would come looking for Emma, find the *bairn*, and take him to raise as her own. With so many records burned or lost that night, if Sean was ever officially adopted, there is no way to know."

Andie nodded. "It's what Emma was trying to tell me from the minute I entered this house. I had no idea that my Grandpa Jack Darling was really Sean Harte."

"Yeah," said Nate. "The baby's name was Sean, which is the Irish equivalent of John. And somehow, Jack is a common nickname for John." He pushed his glasses up on his nose. "Pretty convoluted."

"Yes." Georgie sighed. "You'd think with all these freaking *detectives* in the family, *some*body would have figured it out." She set her palm on her swollen tummy. "Say, is there anything to eat in this place?"

Ethan set his own hand atop his wife's and smiled into her eyes. "We'll stop on the way home and get some pickles and ice cream, okay?"

She smiled back. "Okay."

Tabitha made a choking sound and covered her mouth.

"You all right?" Nate asked.

Her eyes narrowed on him. "I weigh seventeen thousand pounds, have a belly the size of a PT Cruiser and a bladder with the liquid capacity of a dime. My ankles look like tree stumps, and I'm tired all the time, but I can't sleep because *your child* keeps slamming me in the ribs with his fists!" She smiled over at Nate. Sweetly, she purred, "I'm good."

Logan pursed his lips and looked at Andie. "Odd, don't you think, that the surnames are both so . . . so . . ."

"Romantic?" she provided. "Instead of Darling, our name is really Harte? I don't know. Maybe it was meant to be. I don't know how all this stuff works. I only know that Emma needs to know the truth so she can go on to . . . to wherever she needs to go."

Logan turned his chair to face her. "All right then, lass. Let's help Emma on her way."

Andie settled back in the chair and relaxed her shoulders and arms. When Logan began to speak, she closed her eyes and concentrated on his words.

"Emma Harte. If you can hear me, make yourself known . . ."

Andie felt a rush of energy fill her. Images began to take shape behind her lids. In the distance, a soft voice whispered . . .

Have you seen my babe? I set him in the corner to be safe, but he's not there now. I need to find him—

I've seen him, Emma. He's fine. He's fine.

Oh, thank the Lord! I search the house top to bottom all the night and day, but every corner is empty, and I wonder what's become of him. I miss him so, his sweet baby kisses, his bright eyes, so like his da's . . .

He's fine, Emma. He's grown up and lived a full life, then moved on, as you must move on now.

But I can not! I've sinned and must be punished. Heaven is not for me, nor I for it.

What have you done, Emma?

Why, I've gone and kilt me husband, me Jacob! Shot him, I did, and he died just so in me arms. Dear Lord, and I loved him so! And miss him to the marrow of me bones!

Emma . . . you didn't kill Jacob.

But I did! The pistol in his hand . . . I grab fer it to keep him and me own da from havin' it out, but something makes it discharge, and I kill—

No. Your father shot Jacob, and the bullet passed through him and into you. You died only moments after Jacob did, but while his spirit went on, you stayed behind, filled with grief and remorse at what you thought you'd done.

I . . . I did not kill me Jacob?

Nae, Emma. It was your father what done it. You need to go on now. Jacob waits for you . . .

*and Seanie, too. And yer father who never forgave
himself. He moved Jacob's body to a shop where it
would be found, then took his own life that night,
Emma. In grief and guilt over what he'd done . . .*

*They're . . . they're waitin' for me? I can see
them? Me darlin' Jacob and wee small son, and
me da, too?*

*Aye, Emma. Release this life, let yourself drift
away now. Let the burden you've carried all these
years dissolve. Go to them . . .*

*Oh! I see it! There's a cloud off in the distance,
and it's brilliant with light. And there are people
there, walkin' toward me. And I know them! Oh,
Sweet Jesus . . . Jacob! He sees me, he's coming
toward me, so handsome in his uniform. He's a
smile on his face, and his hand is outstretched. And
I take it! I can touch him, and . . . Oh! It's Seanie
there, too, all grown-up . . . and me da . . . and
what do you think? There's Mrs. Bernstein, bless
her heart, smilin' at me and wavin' for me to come
along. And look, there's me darlin' Mary, who I've
missed so all these years!*

Go Emma. Go now . . . and be at peace . . .

*Jacob . . . Jacob, me own sweet love. Together now,
together, just like you promised me on our weddin'
day. Together now . . . now and forever . . .*

"So now and forever is it, lass?" Logan said through
a soft smile. He took Andie's hand, patted it. "Is
that what you'll be wanting from me?"

Across the room, Georgie and Tabitha were crying into handkerchiefs as their husbands tried to console them.

"So sad . . ." Tabby sobbed against Nate's chest.

"How terrible . . ." Georgie choked in Ethan's arms.

Nate and Ethan looked at each other over the tops of their wives' heads, their own eyes rimmed with red. They both swallowed, then bent to murmur comforting words to the women they loved.

Andie watched them. *I want that*, she thought to herself. *That's what I want.*

"Aye," she said, turning to Logan. "Now and forever."

Leaning forward, she placed her palm on his chest, and kissed him. He cupped the nape of her neck with his hand, and returned the kiss with more love and tenderness than she could have imagined possible.

When he broke the kiss, he gazed into her eyes. "You've helped me in more ways than I can possibly repay," he said. "You've not only changed me, you've released me."

She kissed him again. Together, they rose to their feet. Logan's arms came around Andie, and she let herself melt into him. Placing her head on his shoulder, she whispered, "Say them, Logan. Say those seven magic words every girls longs to hear."

"You want me to say, *We're having haggis for dinner tonight?*"

She slapped at his chest. "Those aren't magic words, laddie. Those are fighting words!"

Pulling back a bit, she smiled into his eyes. "Logan Macmillan," she whispered. "There is love at me on you."

His aquamarine eyes sparkled as he gazed down at her. A moment later, the sparkle turned to smoke as he tugged her closer.

"Aye, lass. There is love at me on you, too. And there always will be. Now . . . and forever."